INSPECTOR HOBBES

and the

COMMON PEOPLE

unhuman

I
Inspector Hobbes and the Blood

II
Inspector Hobbes and the Curse

III
Inspector Hobbes and the Gold Diggers

IV
Inspector Hobbes and the Bones

V
Inspector Hobbes and the Common People

Also by Wilkie Martin
Razor
Relative Disasters

As A. C. Caplet
Hobbes's Choice Recipes

Children's books as Wilkie J. Martin
All in the Same Boat
The Lazy Rabbit

INSPECTOR HOBBES

and the

COMMON PEOPLE

unhuman V

Wilkie Martin

The Witcherley Book Company
United Kingdom

Published in the United Kingdom
by The Witcherley Book Company.

Copyright © 2021 Martin J. Wilkinson and Julia How.

The right of Martin J. Wilkinson (Wilkie Martin) to be
identified as the author of this work has been asserted by him in
accordance with the Copyright, Designs and Patents Act 1988.

British Library Cataloguing in Publication Data.
A catalogue record for this book is available from the British Library.

ISBN 9781912348565 (paperback)
ISBN 9781912348558 (ebook)
ISBN 9781912348572 (hardback)
ISBN 9781912348589 (large print paperback)
ISBN 9781912348596 (audiobook)

A frisbee came skimming over the gorse bush. As I reached out to grab it, a thump in the solar plexus flattened me. I curled up on the frosty ground amid gorse thorns, fighting for breath, with a big, black, hairy dog standing over me, his tail beating as if he'd done something clever. Unmoved by my whimpering, he dropped the frisbee onto my face and tried to bully me into throwing it again.

A vast figure in well-polished black boots, baggy brown trousers and flapping gabardine raincoat loomed over us like a baron's castle above a peasant's hovel. 'Are you alright, Andy?'

I nodded, trying to show Hobbes how brave I was, and managed to draw a breath.

He helped me to my feet. 'I've warned him to watch where he's going, but he gets carried away.'

Taking the frisbee from the dog's jaws, he launched it. Dregs set off in excited pursuit and, within a few seconds, his normal rumbling bark took on the higher pitch of canine frustration—his toy was stuck up a birch tree, well out of reach, no matter how high he bounced. Hobbes went to the rescue, leaving me to recover.

As breathing returned to normal, I took a moment to enjoy the scenery. Although we were barely a mile outside Sorenchester, the small Cotswold town where I lived, it was my first visit to this place of rough grass, scrub and woodland. In fact, I hadn't even known Sorenchester Common existed until Hobbes mentioned taking Dregs for walks on it. My ignorance was not surprising, since no roads or good paths led here, and it was surrounded by the walls of Colonel Squire's estates to the east, and by a mix of marshland, dense, scrubby woodland and almost impenetrable blackthorn thickets on the other sides.

I could understand why Hobbes came here—he sometimes needed time out of the modern world to relax and be himself. In truth, I'd been a little surprised when he'd invited me along, but he knew I needed fresh air and exercise as I recovered from a virus that had kept me indoors for two weeks. His one proviso was that I promised not to tell anyone how to get there.

He retrieved the frisbee and hurled it again. Dregs set off with dogged determination to bring it to earth, his paws pounding the rough turf, his pink tongue lolling.

A hint of a rustle made me glance at a leggy gorse bush by my side. A pair of dark eyes was looking at me through slits in a weird sort of mask.

I blinked and the eyes and mask had vanished.

'Hello? Who's there?' I asked.

The bush said nothing.

'What's up?' asked Hobbes as he approached.

'I thought I saw something in there.'

'What sort of something?'

'A face,' I said, trying to think, 'but I'm not sure how to describe it.'

'Have a go,' he urged.

' ... umm ... it had eyes.'

'As do many faces.'

Dregs trotted back with the prize.

'The thing is,' I continued, 'I didn't actually see a face—it was behind a mask of some sort.'

'A mask of leaves?' asked Hobbes with a slight smile.

I nodded. 'That's right! It was all interwoven and layered. Mostly ivy, I think, but there were other bits and pieces too. The eyes were dark, like an animal's, but animals don't wear masks.'

Hobbes accepted the frisbee from Dregs and spun it away above the grass tussocks. The excited dog took off in pursuit, barking like a pup.

'What sort of person lurks in gorse bushes wearing a mask?' I asked.

Hobbes shrugged. 'I don't know, but I meet them from time to time. We nod and go about our business.'

'Them?'

'A group lives here, and since they prefer to keep themselves to themselves and since none has broken any laws as far as I know, l respect their privacy. It is perfectly legal to conceal one's identity behind a mask, unless one is intending to commit a crime.'

'I suppose so, but aren't they ... umm ... trespassing or something?'

'Possibly,' said Hobbes, 'but trespass is not of itself a criminal offence. Besides, I don't actually know who this land belongs to. It's been common land for centuries, but someone probably still has legal ownership of it. I'd hazard a guess that it might be Colonel Squire, since it runs on from his estates.'

I shook my head. 'I doubt it. It doesn't look as if it's being used for anything, and the Colonel would surely have tried to make money from it—that's what he does.'

'True,' said Hobbes, 'but I've recently heard of plans to build a large housing estate here, which is bad news for the current inhabitants.'

I thought for a moment. 'Who are these inhabitants? Would they make a good article in the *Bugle*?'

He shook his head. 'Curiosity is commendable in a reporter, Andy, but sometimes it's better to respect people's right to privacy. I ask you not to pry or to tell anyone about them. Let them avoid us if that's their wish. Just think of them as the Common People and leave them be. With luck, the housing development may not come to anything, and they won't be disturbed.'

Dregs, having performed a spectacular and totally show-off forward roll to catch the flying disc, trotted over. With his sharp ears and sensitive nose, I would have been surprised he hadn't responded to my bush lurker, had frisbees not been his most recent obsession—he tended to forget everything else in the thrill of the chase.

Hobbes sniffed the air. 'It's time we headed back for lunch.'

A glance at my watch proved him correct—and we'd have to set a pretty hot pace if we weren't to be late. However, I was confident we'd make it because Mrs Goodfellow, his housekeeper, had been cooking up a cauldron of pea and ham soup when we'd left, and no one who'd been lucky enough to sample the old girl's cooking was late for meals if they could help it—Hobbes had invited Daphne, my wife, and me to join him for lunch.

'Come on, Dregs,' said Hobbes. 'Home.'

The dog greeted the end of playtime with a slight droop of the tail before accepting the situation and trotting ahead of us, holding the disc in his jaws like a trophy.

On the walk back, I contemplated my future—there were worrying rumours that the *Sorenchester and*

District Bugle, the SAD B as it was affectionately known, was up for sale. I'd heard that 'Editorsaurus' Rex Witcherley, the owner, needed cash to pay for an experimental treatment for his insane wife, who'd once tried to kill Hobbes and me. As a result, an air of uncertainty was blowing through the office and, although I was officially only the paper's part-time food critic, I'd felt its chill. It was a concern, not least because I was enjoying my job, and Phil Waring, the editor, was trusting me with all sorts of reporting.

Yet, though the thought of change was unsettling, there was nothing I could do about it, so worrying would be pointless. Instead, I concentrated on keeping up with Hobbes's long strides, my mouth already moist with anticipation of the feast to come. I was in a cheerful frame of mind by the time we reached Number 13 Blackdog Street where he lived, and when he opened the door, the scent of soup and freshly baked bread rolled out on a mouth-watering wave.

I completely forgot about the Common People until the Christmas Day service in Sorenchester's stately old church, a few weeks later. Although not a regular churchgoer, I rather enjoyed belting out a few Christmas carols. Daphne and I took seats in the pew next to Mrs Goodfellow and Hobbes and joined in. The singing was lusty and mostly in tune, the organist only fluffed the occasional note, and there was the enticing prospect of Christmas lunch at Blackdog Street a little later. However, there was a bit I was dreading—the Reverend Timothy Monkton's address. He was the new vicar, and, although it wasn't his fault, he had one of those pompous voices that droned on interminably, but, in the spirit of goodwill to all men, even to Reverend

5

Tim, I tried to concentrate on his Christmas message. After what felt like an age, I glanced at my watch, assuming he must be approaching the end, to discover that he'd only been going for three minutes!

My head and eyelids drooped. I swallowed a yawn and jerked upright. With a great effort of will, I tried to distract my mind by examining the carvings on the intricate wooden screen to my right. They were worth a look: weird, fantastic creatures, oddly shaped people in quaint costumes, and what appeared to be angels on unicycles, among others. I was wondering what sort of mind had conceived such things when my gaze settled on a carving that made me sit up and gasp. The old pew creaked.

'Shh!' said a lady in the row behind. Daphne gave me a nudge and a smile.

There, right in front of me, was surely a depiction of the masked face I'd seen on the common.

I pointed it out to Daphne, after Reverend Monkton had droned to a standstill, we'd sung the last carol, and were free to go.

'That's a Green Man,' she said. 'There are depictions of him or her in many English churches. They're a bit of a puzzle—no one knows what they are or why they exist. Some think they have pagan roots.'

'Come along, dears,' said the quavering voice of Mrs Goodfellow. 'It's time to get ready for lunch.'

We filed out into the grey, drizzly street. After greeting friends and neighbours, all topped up with Christmas spirit and the relief that Reverend Tim was no longer talking, we headed for Hobbes's house and Mrs Goodfellow's Christmas lunch.

2

The rumours about the *Bugle* proved correct and the new owner, a mysterious, faceless corporation, took control of the paper in late January. Its first act was to sack Phil Waring and bring in a new editor, an Italian-suited, chubby, but otherwise nondescript individual who introduced himself as Ralph Pildown. During his first month, Ralph smiled a lot, talked to all the staff, complimented my food reviews, and changed nothing other than bringing in a new kettle to replace our leaky old one. At the start of his second month, he suggested a small tweak to editorial policy; he wanted the paper to be a little more upbeat and to make readers feel good about themselves and the region.

I was happy to go along with him—I'd always preferred to stress the positive aspects of my eating experiences, assuming there were any. Overly harsh reviews were not my style, though I believed I owed it to my readers and to the restaurant owners themselves to point out possible improvements. As a result, my post bag bulged with appreciative letters from chefs and managers, thanking me for my efforts and explaining how they intended to make things even better. Well, I didn't really have a post bag, but I did receive the occasional email.

Phil invited his former colleagues for leaving drinks

at the Bear with a Sore Head. He was in good spirits and had already secured a new position as editor-in-chief of a major London magazine. Still, he claimed he was sad to leave.

'Yeah, right,' muttered cynical Basil Dean, the *Bugle's* veteran reporter, who was standing at my shoulder, waiting for me to buy him a beer. 'The lucky bastard will be delighted to see the back of this place. Still, I reckon we're going to miss him.'

I nodded. 'So do I. Still, Ralph doesn't seem so bad, does he?'

'I don't trust that sconner as far as I could spit,' said Basil, shaking his head, his Liverpudlian accent still raging despite decades of living in the Cotswolds. 'I looked him up—he's a hitman.'

'What can I get you?' asked the trendy young barman. His name was Tarquin, according to his badge.

'Umm ... ' I stared at the pumps.

'Come on lad, get the ales in,' said Basil, one eye gazing lustfully at the beer pumps, while the strange one fixed me with a glassy stare. 'I'm dying of thirst here. Mine's a pint of Sorenchester Gold.'

'Right ... and I'll have a pint of lager,' I said.

'You've got it,' said Tarquin, and set to work.

I turned back to Basil. 'What do you mean he's a hitman?'

'I mean, mate, that wherever he goes, he cuts costs, sacks staff and emasculates the reporting. All that nonsense about making our reports more upbeat—he'll have us writing fairy tales and fluff before too long.'

I paid for the drinks, handed the Sorenchester Gold to Basil, and took a sip of my lager. 'I'm sure it won't be as bad as that,' I said, uncertain that I believed myself.

'Mark my words,' said Basil. 'That's what he did at the

Threadington Times and the *Maudlin Mirror*. Right, I'm off outside for a ciggy.' He gulped his beer in one glug and headed for the exit, pouring tobacco onto a cigarette paper.

I hoped he was wrong, but only time would tell.

A couple of days and a hangover later, Sorenchester enjoyed a long-hoped-for spell of early spring sunshine. I sauntered along Rampart Street in my capacity as food critic, enjoying and resisting the siren aromas of hot food wafting from lunchtime restaurants and pubs because I was aiming for Papa's Piri-Piri Palace. It was a week-old restaurant, on the site of the unlamented Jaipur Johnny's, where I'd once caught a nasty case of the Jaipur trots that had confined me to the bathroom for an extremely long and revolting night. My review had been one of my rare stinkers and may have contributed to the restaurant's demise. I felt no guilt.

When I reached Papa's, the door was open, but the restaurant looked deserted. Guessing I was its first customer of the day, I took the opportunity to look around. It was airy and clean, with bench seats, stretched trestle tables, and wooden chairs fitted with soft-looking cushions. Industrial chic steel beams and pillars supported the ceiling, while lush vegetation dangled from hanging baskets. Combined with grass green paint, it gave the place a tropical feel—a distinct improvement on its grim, tired and grubby predecessor.

'Hello,' I called to the room. 'Anybody home?'

It took a couple of minutes before a diminutive waiter in a brilliant white jacket appeared from the kitchen and greeted me. 'Good afternoon, sir. Have you booked?'

'Afternoon.' I checked my watch—ten minutes past twelve. 'No, is that a problem?'

He pursed his lips, furrowed his brow in deep thought, and looked around the empty restaurant before answering, 'No, sir, not at all. Please, sit wherever you like.'

I chose a corner table by the window from where I could watch the world pass by.

'Would you care for a drink while you're waiting?' the waiter asked as he handed me a menu.

'A large glass of house red, please.'

The menu wasn't extensive: a small selection of starters, with chicken piri-piri and various sides as the main course. I selected cod and chickpea fritters as an appetiser and chicken piri-piri with batatas fritas to follow. The waiter reappeared with my wine, took my order, and scuttled back to the kitchen.

I reached for my mobile, took a few snaps to jog my memory, and sniffed the wine. Its bouquet reminded me of thin vinegar. Undaunted, I took a sip and grimaced— it tasted of sour blackberry with a hint of mould; it might have been even nastier had it not been served at near-freezing point. Sharp slivers of ice pierced the surface, making drinking perilous. I would have spat the nasty stuff straight out into a napkin had there been one. Instead, I swallowed, shuddered, grimaced and pushed the glass away. Still, although it was disappointing, the critic in me was happy—acid remarks about acid wine would give a bit of oomph to my review.

I sat twiddling my thumbs for twenty minutes, my hunger aroused, though my expectations were low since I'd often noted a link between poor house wines and below-average food. Another ten minutes passed, and I was wondering whether they'd forgotten me, though I remained the only customer. I was considering giving up and moving on when the waiter finally returned, plonked my starter on the table and hurried away without a word.

I called him back with the suggestion that cutlery might be useful. He apologised, fetched a set and left me to eat. To my surprise, the fritters were amazing— golden-brown, crispy and deliciously, but not overwhelmingly, fishy. I savoured every mouthful, made an appreciative note in my book and sat back to await the main course.

It took another half an hour to arrive and, though my professional eye suggested a little more finesse in the layout would not have gone amiss, I'd seen worse, and a mouth-watering, spicy aroma rose from the plate.

I cut a chunk of chicken and impaled it on my fork as a sudden hubbub in the street outside drew my attention. People were marching with banners, shouting slogans against the proposed housing development on Sorenchester Common, and handing out flyers.

Distracted, I poked the chicken into my mouth and bit. The texture was slimy, and it was ice cold in the middle. Far worse was the nauseating taste that overwhelmed my taste buds as soon as my teeth were through the chilli coating. I gagged. Desperate, I was on the point of spitting the gunk into my hand when an attractive young woman glanced through the window. For reasons I never could fathom, I gulped and swallowed, which, at least, removed the foul flavour from my mouth. I dissected the chicken portion— beneath the spice it was quite raw. Worse, it looked greenish.

'Is everything satisfactory with your meal, sir?' asked the waiter, appearing at my shoulder.

I very nearly nodded, a childhood of being told not to make a fuss asserting its malign influence.

But I was no longer that child, and this was too much. Besides, there was no one to judge me if I wanted to make a fuss.

'No, it is not satisfactory.'

'Perhaps it's a little too spicy for you?' suggested the waiter with a complacent smile.

'The spice is fine, but,' I pointed at my plate, 'the chicken is raw.'

He peered down and shrugged. 'Perhaps it is a little on the rare side, sir. I'll ask the chef to put it back on the grill.'

'Thank you,' I said before coming to my senses. 'Actually, no, that's not good at all—it's rotten.'

'I can assure you we only use fresh chicken.'

I thrust the plate toward his nose. 'Take a sniff.'

'Smells all right to me,' he said.

He gulped.

His face paled.

He turned and rushed for the door, his hand clamped to his mouth.

I gargled with the rest of the horrible vinegary wine in a futile attempt to dilute the disgusting taste that was rising up my throat and settling in my mouth.

Without wasting another moment, I walked out, appalled by the restaurant's reckless incompetence, though at least I'd got a zinger of a review to sink my teeth into. Papa's Piri-Piri Palace was a health hazard, and would fully deserve the salvos of righteous fury I intended to launch at it.

I checked my watch—twenty-five past one already!

And Ralph had asked me to report on a council meeting at two. The meeting was about the proposed new housing development, and since it was open to the public, would take place at Redvers Hall instead of the tiny Council Offices. It would take about twenty-minutes to walk there, which gave me only fifteen minutes to cleanse the putrid taste from my mouth and grab a bite of lunch. Having decided on fish and chips, I headed towards The Fat Frier near the bottom of The Shambles, only to be repelled by the length of the queue. With time running out, I resorted to the old routine that I'd followed until acquaintance with Mrs Goodfellow's cookery had turned me into a gourmet—I picked up a pack of sandwiches and a can of ginger beer from the convenience store. Trying to make the most of the sunlight, I took my meal to the bench at Pansy Corner, sat down, popped the can, and took a huge swig to wash away the foulness. A gingery froth erupted in my mouth, shot up my nose and poured out all over me. I choked, spluttered and burped.

Mrs Nutter, a blue-haired, older lady who'd taken a dislike to me following a misunderstanding over a church leaflet she, rightly, thought I'd stolen, happened to be coming out of the flower shop carrying a potted peace lily. 'You disgusting pig!' she said.

I was in no state to argue until the volcanic disturbances had settled, by which time she'd walked away, still muttering. At least the ginger beer had diluted the appalling taste in my mouth and I felt able to eat. Opening my sandwiches, I took one, raised it to my mouth, and cursed as a glob of tuna mayo plopped into my lap. Still, waste not, want not, I picked up the mess, poked it into my mouth and licked my fingers clean.

I finished lunch without further mishap, relaxing in

the spring sun and observing my fellow citizens as they went about their business. Although Sorenchester was a small market town, it struck me how few people I recognised. It was different for Hobbes, who seemed to know many of the town folk by name, as well as their family histories. Most of them knew him, too, though I didn't think they were all criminals.

The church clock struck the quarter hour—I was going to be late!

I jumped to my feet, brushed the crumbs from my lap and used the inadequate napkin that came with the sandwiches to mop up the fishy mayonnaise stains on my groin. If anything, it spread the mess and made it worse. Plus, it was typical that I was wearing new, pale grey trousers that showed every greasy mark as a stain of shame. Though, normally, I stuck to darker colours, Daphne had said they looked sexy on me and I'd succumbed to flattery.

I broke into a run. Sweat soon rolled down my face, my stomach gurgled, and the foulness of putrid chicken bubbled back into my mouth. Knowing I had no chance of keeping up the pace, I slowed to a jog and then to a walk. In truth, I felt rotten and wanted to go home, but the intrepid reporter in me kept heading in the right direction and I was just a few minutes late on reaching Redvers Hall. Anti-development protesters milled around outside, holding up placards and looking determined. I wound my way through them and slipped into the building.

The meeting had not yet started but, to my surprise, the hall was full—very different to the last one I'd attended while deputising for Basil who'd been on holiday. On that occasion, the meeting had taken place in the council chamber, with six unsmiling councillors around a table to discuss the annual budget, and me perched on a hard chair in the corner with a notebook. One after another, they'd rambled on about matters unrelated to finance, and my eyelids had become increasingly heavy as the interminable afternoon continued. Only the arrival of a bewildered young man who wandered in thinking it was a job interview alleviated my boredom. After they'd pointed the poor sap in the right direction, the meeting had come to a decision: it would not make any budgetary decisions until the next session.

Since it was standing room only for latecomers like me, I made my way to the back and propped myself against the wall. The chair of the meeting, Councillor Ethel Fishlock, a bony, grey-haired, bespectacled woman in a smart business suit, called us to order. Taking out my reporter's notebook and pencil, ignoring the subterranean rumblings of my guts, I prepared for action. The move proved premature, for the next half-hour was taken up with procedural matters, bureaucratic nonsense, apologies for absences, and pointless points of order, while the hall grew hotter and stuffier. My head swam and my stomach gurgled so much that people kept turning to stare at me.

When all hope and energy had drained from the attendees, Councillor Fishlock got round to the principal topic—the proposed development. She introduced the protagonists. Speaking for the scheme was Colonel Toby Squire, the owner of Sorenchester Common, and Mr Valentine Grubbe, a property developer. A local engineer called Trevor Baker, leader-elect of Sorenchester Opposes the Development, the SODs as they were known, was to speak against it.

At the chair's invitation, Valentine Grubbe, a tall,

slim, distinguished-looking man in his late-forties, took the microphone. He spoke with passion and used a PowerPoint presentation, showing marvellous artist's impressions of the development and all the happy, healthy people who would soon be privileged to live there. It impressed me, and I could imagine moving with Daphne from our rather rundown old house into one of the palatial new residences, where we could enjoy all the great new facilities and amenities, only a gentle walk from the centre of Sorenchester.

Mr Grubbe had moved on to extolling the amazing benefits the development would bring to local businesses, to the public, and to the environment when my stomach cramped. My mouth filled with saliva.

I had to get out of there.

Fast!

I ran towards the gents' toilets.

I got there just in time.

As soon as I was in the cubicle, I assumed the position, and threw up my lunch. In the aftermath, drained and exhausted, I sprawled on the cold white tiles and sweated, cursing Papa's Piri-Piri Palace with every spare breath. A bout of shivers set me shuddering and groaning.

Someone knocked on the door. 'Are you all right?'

'No.'

'Are you going to be long?'

'Yes,' I said, and returned my attention to the great white bowl before me.

I may have passed out. I certainly missed the rest of the meeting, and came close to being locked in the hall. Fortunately, the caretaker, a conscientious woman, found me and helped me upright. I turned down her offer to call an ambulance, and tottered homewards. It was gone seven o'clock when I reached it, and I spent the next few hours alternating between bed and bathroom. Daphne made sympathetic noises, stroked my forehead and supplied fresh water whenever I felt I might hold it down.

It was a long night.

But, by morning, I was feeling much better, though a pale shadow of my usual self. Daphne brought me tea and a slice of dry toast for breakfast. The tea soothed and revitalised, but the toast was a problem—my poor throat felt as if someone had sandpapered it. Still, I forced it down and kept it down. When Daphne left for work, I slept and did not wake until well after lunchtime. I got up, made myself more tea and toast, and felt living might be an option.

No one should suffer like that. So, burning with indignation, I opened my laptop and banged out an excoriating review of Papa's Piri-Piri Palace. I was particularly proud of 'Salmonella City', 'purveyors of putrid poultry', and 'abandon hope all ye who enter there', though, admittedly, I could not claim the last as original. I emailed my piece to Ralph with an explanation of why I'd failed to report the council meeting.

The rest of the afternoon, I slumped in front of the television, too lethargic to do anything else. Eventually, I got to watching a black-and-white film from the nineteen-thirties, going by the name of 'Cotswold Capers'. Although billed as a comedy, it made me wonder if anyone had ever found it amusing, though it was fascinating to see how much or, sometimes, how little had changed in the region over the intervening years. One scene in particular caught my attention—a laughable attempt at a comic car chase through Sorenchester. I was almost certain a police constable standing in the background of a crowd scene was Hobbes.

As the film came to its inane and obvious conclusion, Daphne returned. 'How are you?' she asked.

'Much better,' I said. 'I think I could eat properly again, and my tummy muscles don't hurt so much. I was able to do a bit of work—I think I wrote my worst ever restaurant review.'

'That's because of how you were feeling. You can make it better when you're a bit more yourself. What was wrong with it? Your spelling or your grammar?'

'I mean it was a damning review of the piri-piri restaurant.'

'Good,' she said.

I continued. 'The only thing that worries me is that Ralph has a down on negative articles. He feels we should keep the public happy.'

'You'll just keep them ignorant unless you also report bad things—or is that his point?' She shrugged. 'You're right to give that place a bad review. It shouldn't be allowed to poison people, not even you.' She smiled and kissed me.

'You're right. I guess it's okay to look for the positives, but when there are none, I have a duty to write the truth. After all, I have principles.'

'And if you don't like them ... well, I have others,' said Daphne with a smile. She paused. 'Who said that?'

'Umm ... you just did, didn't you?'

She laughed. 'I mean, who said it first?'

I shrugged. 'Oscar Wilde? Shakespeare? It's usually one or the other.'

Daphne went over to my laptop and tapped in a

query. 'Groucho Marx.'

'Good for him.' I said and asked about her day.

'Well, to start with, it was much the same as usual—I was trying to discover the provenance of a collection of bronze-age artifacts that had fallen behind a cupboard in the stores. Eventually, I unearthed the relevant documents—they came from a nineteenth century dig in Hedbury. I was just sorting them out when Mr Hobbes came round to ask a few questions.'

That surprised me—he rarely showed much interest in the past unless it had a bearing on something he was working on. 'What sort of questions?'

'You know I studied that module on cryptids last year?'

'How could I forget?' I said, trying to remember.

'Well,' she continued, 'he asked about that and wanted to know if the museum had records of any living around here.'

'Cryptids being?' I asked, giving up on memory.

'Creatures whose existence is doubted or disputed.'

'Yes, of course,' I said. 'Like the Loch Ness Monster.'

She nodded. 'I'd always assumed they were creatures from people's imaginations, but I've not been so sure since I moved here. This place is a little weird, isn't it?'

'More than a little, but does Hobbes really think there's something like the Loch Ness Monster around here? It would have to be miniscule to live in the River Soren, or in Church Lake.' I laughed.

'It wasn't that,' she said. 'He was especially interested in the Sorenchester Common area, though he was a little vague about why.'

'Did you find anything?'

'Nothing much yet, but I did uncover an old filing box

from the nineteenth century that looks promising. I'd have liked to go through it tonight, but the thought of my poor sick husband wasting away for lack of food made me come home. The box can wait—Mr Hobbes said he was in no great hurry.'

'You are so kind to an invalid,' I said.

'You're welcome. What do you fancy tonight?'

'Nothing with chicken,' I said with a grimace.

'I could order a pizza.'

'That,' I said, 'would be perfect.'

Had it been an option, I would have preferred to go round to Hobbes's for one of Mrs G's meals, but as it wasn't, a pizza was acceptable and, though I would never have told her, better than anything Daphne might have conjured up.

When it came, our hot and spicy pizza lived up to its promise and slipped down well enough, assisted by a glass or two of some of the excellent red wine that Hobbes had given us for Christmas. We'd just finished when something came through the letterbox. Daphne went to see what it was.

'It's for you,' she said, coming back and handing me a gold-edged envelope.

3

I opened the envelope, pulled out a card, and grunted in surprise as I read it. 'It's from Colonel Squire. He's invited me to a reception at Sorenchester Manor tomorrow evening. It looks like I'm moving into higher circles of society! You too, if you'd like to come—it says Mr Andrew Caplet plus one.'

The Colonel was the wealthiest man in the region, and I was astonished he even knew of my existence, though Daphne and I had once, at great personal risk, thwarted one of his dodgy business schemes.

Daphne shrugged. 'Don't get too excited—it's all part of his effort to butter up local people so they accept his development without too much fuss. He's inviting anyone with local influence.'

'Why do you say that?' I asked, peeved by her lack of enthusiasm.

'Because I got one last week, as did all the museum staff.'

'Why didn't you tell me?'

'I wasn't interested, and didn't think you would be either. Don't forget, Squire nearly got us killed.'

'I haven't forgotten,' I said with a shudder. 'I'll reply that we can't make it ... umm ... but if he's inviting those with influence, why me?'

'Because, my love, you write for the local newspaper.'

'But Ralph is hardly likely to ask me to report on the development—that would be Basil's job.'

She smiled. 'Squire probably doesn't know that. Admit it, you were flattered to receive an invitation.'

'Maybe a little. Besides, I have sometimes wondered what the manor looks like inside.'

I put the card to one side as Daphne turned on the television to watch a documentary about Viking culture. Once upon a time, I wouldn't have been interested, but she'd almost convinced me that the past was a universe of infinite amazement, and I looked forward to watching. Anyway, I'd once overheard Pinky, her astonishingly beautiful friend, telling Sid Sharples, her vampire lover and our bank manager, that she thought I had a touch of the Norseman about me. She might have been right—a couple of red hairs had sprouted in the ill-advised and short-lived moustache I'd cultivated the previous November. I could picture myself as Andy the Red, standing proud in the prow of a Viking longship— providing I ignored my tendency to seasickness.

On waking the following morning, I'd changed my mind and decided to accept the invitation. After all, where was the harm? I held firm to the principles of honest journalism when I could get away with it, and I was not the sort to be bought off with a few drinks and nibbles. I would go, satisfy my curiosity, gather facts and write an article in any case. Although unconvinced, Daphne agreed to accompany me, if only to keep me out of trouble. I emailed our acceptance and spent the rest of the day mooching about the house, watching daytime telly, and still not back to my sparkling best. By early evening when Daphne returned, I'd revived enough to be looking forward to the evening.

The invitation stipulated smart casual dress, which I

made into a problem since my wardrobe comprised three categories: smart, casual, or ancient relics. There was no overlap. In the end, tired of my dithering, Daphne told me to shut up and put on a suit, explaining that it was better to go a little over-dressed than to feel scruffy. And, if that did not feel sufficiently casual, I could always not wear a tie. I took her advice—I owned several good suits that rarely saw the light of day, though it still freaked me out that they'd once belonged to Mrs Goodfellow's husband, Robin, who we'd last heard of working as a deckhand on a Mombasa ferry. All his cast-off clothes fitted me as if they'd been made-to-measure, and I suspected Milord Schmidt, Hobbes's hard-pressed tailor, had been responsible, though he had never measured me—at least not to my knowledge.

Daphne never had a problem with dressing for the occasion and always looked fabulous whatever she wore, though I may have been biased. So, while I faffed about, taking forever to decide which socks went with my suit, she picked out a simple pale blue dress that complemented her soft-brown hair and was ready within ten minutes.

When I was finally satisfied with my appearance, it was time to go. I suggested a taxi but, since the evening was pleasantly warm for early April, Daphne suggested a walk. We set off for Sorenchester Manor.

A minute later, I ran home to pick up a notebook and pen.

'Are you sure you've got everything now?' she asked when I rejoined her.

I nodded.

'What about your invitation? It said to bring it.'

'Damn!'

A few minutes later than anticipated, we arrived at the tall, solid gates of Sorenchester Manor where a burly doorman, bursting out of a fashionable grey suit, checked our invitation and let us into the grounds. The evening sun was peeking over the garden hedge, bathing the smooth, Cotswold stone walls of the manor in a warm, pinkish glow.

'It looks splendid,' I said, impressed more than I'd wanted to be as we strolled along a gravelled path that bisected a broad, neat lawn.

Daphne shrugged. 'It's alright, I suppose, but there are many far better examples of Palladian architecture all over the Cotswolds—there's even one or two in town. This looks neglected, and even from here I can see problems—there are loose slates on the roof, there's a small tree growing from the gutter, and other than this lawn, the garden looks overgrown and tired.'

I could see what she meant. The place reminded me of our little house, which we'd bought after our flat exploded, and which was in need of repairs we couldn't yet afford.

'It might mean the Colonel's short of cash,' I suggested. 'Perhaps that's why he wants the development?'

She shrugged. 'Maybe, but he can't really be poor— he owns a good chunk of the town and has all the rents coming in, not to mention the income from his farms.'

'Maybe he's a spendthrift or a gambler,' I said. 'Or has an expensive drug habit?'

'Who knows? But he owns a roomful of paintings by old masters—he could raise a fortune by selling just one of them.'

As we approached the manor, a young woman in a maid's uniform opened the door. She curtsied before ushering us into a long hall with an ornate, painted ceiling and walls plastered with portraits. I guessed they were of long-dead members of the Squire family: knights in shining armour, cavaliers in flamboyant costumes, dark, buttoned-up Victorians, bewhiskered military men in scarlet tunics festooned with medals, and a handful that looked almost modern. I estimated that well over one hundred guests were already there— my invitation had hardly been exclusive. The hall felt warm and stuffy, but along the far wall was a long, white-clothed table where another pretty maid was serving drinks. Thinking a glass of something might help the evening along, I guided Daphne that way.

'Red or white, sir?' asked the maid as we approached.

'Umm ...' I said, caught out by a choice I should have anticipated. 'One moment ... '

'May I have an orange juice, please?' said Daphne when the maid turned to her.

'Of course.' The maid picked up a jug and smiled. 'I would have offered, only I'd asked everyone else and you're the first to want a soft drink.' She poured out a glass, handed it to Daphne, and turned to me with a smile. 'Have you come to a decision yet, sir?'

'Yes ... maybe ... do you have a lager, by any chance?'

'I'm afraid we only have red or white wine, orange juice or cola, sir. Or there is water if you'd prefer.'

'No, no,' I said, determined not to appear indecisive, 'I'll have a glass of white ... no, make that a glass of red ... no, I'll have the white after all ... please.'

She glanced at Daphne, who shrugged with a 'seen it all before' expression and poured me out a glass. I took it, sipped and grimaced, for although not a connoisseur, I could tell it was not great. It took me back to the stuff I'd buy before I'd met Hobbes—cheap and bad for the head. Still, it wasn't nearly as nasty and vinegary as the stuff from Papa's Piri-Piri Palace.

Armed with our drinks, we mingled with the horde, and although I recognised some, I was taken aback by how many knew Daphne—most of them through attending her lectures at the museum. I'd gone to a few myself, when I could take time out from my busy schedule, and was proud of the way she could engage her audience and make the past come alive. If I'd had a history teacher like her, I would probably not have failed my exams.

A bald, brawny man with a broken nose, a face criss-crossed with scars, and fewer than the standard complement of teeth introduced himself as Bruce Wainright. Despite his fearsome appearance, he had a soft voice and came across as an affable sort of chap.

'What do you do?' I asked after depleting my store of inane small talk about the unseasonal warm weather.

'I'm in the ladies' hairdressing game—I've recently opened a salon down Vermin Street.' He reached into his jacket pocket, pulled out a business card, and offered it to Daphne. I was impressed by the size and solidity of his hand—not that it compared to Hobbes's.

'Thank you,' she said, taking the card, 'but don't I know you from somewhere?'

'Perhaps you remember me from my previous life.'

She frowned and then broke into a smile. 'Of course, you're "Bruiser" Wainright—I used to enjoy watching the boxing. Weren't you a contender?'

A tall, good-looking man, older in close-up, edged out Bruiser and me and introduced himself to Daphne.

It was Valentine Grubbe. 'Good evening,' he said, the epitome of social ease.

'You're the developer,' I said, jockeying to maintain

my position.

He nodded graciously. 'Indeed. I hope the wine is to your taste?'

'Delicious,' I lied.

'Good. I was afraid Toby's choice might be a little rough for most people—it certainly is for me, which is why I'm sticking to orange juice.' He glanced at Daphne's glass and smiled. 'I see you are a lady of taste.'

She smiled. 'I'm Daphne Caplet and this is my husband, Andy.'

'Of course, the lady from the museum. I was hoping to meet you—I've heard so much about you.'

'Good things, I hope,' said Daphne.

'Indeed, yes. Your expertise is well regarded.' He flashed a gold Rolex and looked down at me. 'I wonder if you'd mind if I had a word with your wife ... in private? It's about business.'

'Umm ... no ... not at all,' I said, too startled to object.

'Good man.' He directed Daphne to an alcove away from the milling crowd, leaving me with Bruiser.

'Is she really your wife?' asked Bruiser.

'She is.'

'But she's lovely.'

'I know,' I said, wondering if he was hinting that she was too good for me, which was astute of him.

'Well, if I were you, I wouldn't trust that guy,' said Bruiser, shaking his battle-scarred head.

'Why not?'

He shrugged. 'I knew plenty like him in the old days—flashy, entitled types with too much money and too little conscience. They'd shag anything in a skirt.'

'She's wearing a dress,' I pointed out.

'Just take care,' said Bruiser. He finished his drink and set off in search of a refill.

I turned to keep an eye on the alcove. Daphne was laughing—evidently, Valentine Grubbe was not only tall, good-looking and rich, but had a sense of humour too. I wondered if I should feel threatened and despite being sure that I shouldn't, I was.

A sweet, earthy scent alerted me that someone was approaching.

'Good evening,' said a slightly breathless, tall, thin woman. Her hair was grey-blonde and in long dreadlocks, or braids, with little sparkly bits. I'd noticed her among the SODs at the council meeting—her long orange dress and knitted tank top had stood out. She'd apparently not bothered to change since then.

'Evening,' I responded.

'I noticed you talking to Mr Grubbe,' she said. 'What do you think of his plans?'

'Well ...' I said, 'they are interesting. I ... suppose they might benefit the town.'

She frowned. 'So, you're in favour?'

'Not necessarily. There are ... certain things I'm not sure about. What's your opinion?'

She sipped from her glass of water. 'I'm totally opposed. Nearly all the supposed benefits to the public are nebulous while the harm to the local environment and the town will be tremendous and irreversible. The only winners will be Squire and Grubbe.'

I nodded. 'But there will be jobs though, so it's good news for builders and ... umm ... quantity surveyors and the like.'

'For a short while, but I ask you, at what cost? Read this.' She thrust a flyer into my hand and merged into the crowd.

The flyer was from the SODs, but before I could read it, Colonel Squire sauntered over, beaming as if at an old friend.

'Ah, Mr Caplet, Andrew, so glad you could make it. I always make a point of reading your marvellous reviews in the *Bugle*—they're refreshingly honest and so witty.'

'Thank you,' I said, flattered.

'I do hope that crazy woman wasn't bothering you?'

'No, not at all—she was just explaining her point of view. Who is she?'

'You've just encountered Rosemary Crackers. She shouldn't really be here. I didn't invite her, but she came as Trevor Baker's plus one. Do you know Trevor?'

'I know of him—he's head of Baker Engineering and leader of the SODs. I saw him at the meeting.'

'On the ball, as always,' said Colonel Squire. 'I've spoken several times with him and discovered that he, at least, has an open mind and can be won over by well-reasoned arguments.' Squire looked around as if to make sure we weren't being overheard, and whispered, 'Our development team is hoping to bring him on board in the near future, though he is undecided as yet. Seeing that woman with him is a bit of a blow, though.'

'Why?' I asked.

'Because she's an environmental extremist, and totally opposed to all forms of development. I doubt she's ever seen Sorenchester Common, which is just useless, wasteland with little value to man or nature. People like her make a hobby of getting in the way of progress to pass the time—she claims to be an artist, but in reality, has independent means. She doesn't know what it's like having to strive for a living in a hard world, like you and I.'

I nodded sympathetically.

Colonel Squire shook my hand again. 'Splendid to

meet you, Andrew, and I'd love to stay and chat for longer, but I really must circulate—a host's duty, you know?' He smiled and joined a group of local shop owners.

I gulped down the remains of my wine and set off to find some more. This time, I opted for the red, though a sip confirmed my expectation that it was as bad as the white. I also picked up another orange juice for Daphne. But she was nowhere to be seen. Nor was Valentine Grubbe, for that matter. Had she already been seduced by his dastardly charm and money? Had I already lost her to the big bully?

In truth, I didn't really believe this—it was just my insecurity speaking. I refused to listen anymore.

And I was right not to believe it—she was making her way toward me through the crowd, exchanging nods and smiles, and looking thoughtful.

A hearty slap on my back made me spill the orange juice down my shirt and the front of my trousers.

'Careful!' I said, and forced my angry scowl into a friendly grin when I turned and identified the culprit.

'I see you've miraculously risen from your sickbed,' said Ralph.

'Oh, hi.' I felt guilty, as if he'd caught me with my fingers in the petty cash. 'Yes, I'm … umm … feeling so much better now. Thank you for asking.'

'Good.' He smiled. 'Back at the *Bugle* tomorrow?'

It was more a command than a question.

'Yes, of course,' I said, hoping to come across as keen and raring to go.

'Excellent,' said Ralph. 'By the way, your piece on Papa's Piri-Piri Palace was good.'

'It was?' I said, surprised.

'Of course, to get the tone right, I had to edit it a little here and there, but a fine piece of writing. It made me wonder if your talents might have been underused and under-appreciated by my predecessor.'

'Thanks,' I mumbled. 'Umm ... are you enjoying the evening?' I gestured at the room.

'It's delightful, like all of Valentine's bashes.' Ralph glanced at his glass and grimaced. 'Apart from the wine though—Colonel Squire's responsibility, I understand. It reminds me of paint stripper.'

Daphne joined us.

'I got you another drink,' I said, holding out the near-empty glass, 'but I ... umm ... spilled most of it. By the way, this is Ralph. Ralph, this is my wife, Daphne.'

'Delighted to meet you,' said Ralph, lifting her right hand to his lips.

Daphne smiled. 'You, too.'

Ralph continued. 'I was just telling Andy that his reporting skills should be more widely appreciated.'

'Good,' she said while I cringed, expecting a punchline that never came.

'So, I intend to give him more opportunities to shine.'

'A promotion?' she asked.

Ralph nodded. 'In a way. Obviously, I can't offer a salary increase—that's the responsibility of the new owner, but I might be suggesting one next time I meet him.'

'Thank you.' I said, half flattered, half annoyed—hard money would have been better than a nugget of praise.

'When might that be?' asked Daphne.

'Very soon, I'm sure,' said Ralph with a vague shrug. 'Oh well, must circulate. I'll see you at the office tomorrow, Andy. Bright and early. A pleasure to meet you, Daphne.'

Ralph slipped into the throng and the evening

dragged on until Grubbe's presentation about the fabulous new development. After about half an hour of this, Daphne took me to one side and whispered that she was bored.

'Let's go home,' I said.

I, too, was tired of the whole tedious affair. Perhaps, if the wine had been better ...

On the walk back, I planned a short, balanced article about the development—after all, Basil had not been present. It was, I felt, the proper, proactive response from a reporter whose skills should be more widely appreciated.

4

The following morning, I went into the *Bugle* thirty minutes earlier than usual, and drafted a thought-provoking article about the proposed development. Impressed by my even-handed and insightful writing, I emailed it to Ralph.

He called me to his office five minutes later. 'Thank you for your piece,' he said.

I nodded and smiled—smugly confident that it was a good one.

He frowned. 'However, it won't do at all. I will not allow this newspaper to blatantly take sides on such an issue. Our advertisers and customers must see us as fair and balanced in all things.'

'I thought it was fair and balan ... '

Ralph held up his hand and halted my protestation. 'It was not. Your bias against the development showed right through it.'

'But ... but I ... '

'If you'd allow me to have my say, Mr Caplet! I was shocked by your stick-in-the-mud agenda—are you working for those cranky opponents of the scheme? It certainly looks like it—I noticed you waving a piece of their seditious propaganda at the party last night.'

'I'd only just been given it!'

'Be quiet, please. Your article is full of prejudice and

ective against the development.'

'I was trying to be fair—I haven't even made up my own mind yet.'

'Stop interrupting! I will not have such blatant insubordination and negativity at my paper. It seems the previous regime was lax in this regard, but I run a tight ship. Anyone who can't take the discipline will be ... '

'Keel-hauled?' I muttered.

' ... fired! Do you understand me?'

I nodded. 'Umm ... yes but ... '

'But me no buts,' said Ralph, looking severe.

Out of the blue, he smiled. 'It wasn't that the article was all bad. After I'd expunged the negative stuff and added a few observations of my own, it now strikes the right note. Honestly, Andy, you have potential and a promising future—just don't allow your prejudices to show when you write for the *Bugle*. Always aim for truth and balance.'

'Yes, but ... '

'Enough. Let's move on. This was just a friendly warning. Now, go into the world and report. Remember to be fair and positive.' He dismissed me with a wave.

I was shaking with rage as I walked away. Or was it fear of losing my job?

Basil Dean, the *Bugle*'s senior reporter, gave me a sympathetic look. At least, I assumed the look was meant for me but, with his strange eye, it might have been intended for the pigeon on the window ledge. I sat down at my computer and looked at what Ralph had done to my article. Balanced? Like hell it was! He'd removed all mention of potential problems and downsides, every hint of nuance, and had turned it into a gushing adulation of the development and the developers. Even worse, he'd left my name on the by-line.

If not for the mortgage and the repairs our house needed, I might have resigned on the spot. As it was, I had to walk away from the office and breathe fresh air. I stamped up The Shambles, weaving through the shoppers and tourists, and tried to come to terms with everything that had just happened. My brain was seething, but my feet found their own way to Blackdog Street. I paused a moment before climbing the steps of Number 13 and ringing the bell.

The scrawny figure of Mrs Goodfellow, wrapped in a floury apron, opened the door. 'Hello, dear.'

Before I could reply, Dregs expressed his delight at seeing me for the first time in a week by bullying me to the ground and trying to lick my face. Although I made a show of disgust and fought to keep his tongue out of range, I wasn't displeased—the welcome was sincere.

'Are you coming in?' asked Mrs G in her high-pitched, quavering voice as she pulled Dregs off. 'I was about to put the kettle on.'

I smiled. 'That would be lovely.' Her mugs of tea made all kinds of problems a little better.

I got up and followed her inside. Something, no doubt delicious, was being baked and the mere scent was soothing to frayed nerves, though stimulating to the salivary glands. I was reassured by how little had changed in the small, plain sitting room since I'd lived there as Hobbes's unpaying guest. Although I'd barely known him at the time, he'd taken me in after my flat burned down. I was forever grateful to him and the old girl, and although my developing friendship with them had exposed me to terror, pain and discomfort, it had transformed my humdrum life. Back then, I'd been a drunken, resentful, envious, lonely man, failing at being a reporter, and failing in life. Thinking about it, apart from the current business with Ralph, everything was so much better now.

'The old fellow's out in the back,' she said as she led me into the red-bricked kitchen. 'He's preparing the soil before planting his delphiniums. I'll call him in when the tea's ready.'

I sat down at the scrubbed wooden table in the middle of the room. Dregs rested his muzzle in my lap, hoping for, and receiving, a head massage.

'How are you and Daphne?' asked Mrs G as she lit the gas under the kettle.

'Very well,' I said. 'Umm ... that is to say she's doing well, but I'm not sure I am. You know the *Bugle* has new owners?'

'So, I'd heard, dear.'

'It's also got a new editor. I thought I was doing a good job—Ralph was giving me interesting stories to write as well as the food stuff, and last night, he hinted at promotion. Now I think he might want to get rid of me and it's not fair!'

I told her all about Colonel Squire's party, my article, and Ralph's response.

She listened, made sympathetic noises and nodded when I'd finished. The kettle boiled, and she filled the old brown teapot. 'People are bound to have different opinions on a project like this. There is always some good comes out of a development, if only for the developers, but there's a downside for whoever or whatever lives in the area. I know the old fellow has concerns about the Common People, though he hasn't said much yet.'

'But no one actually really lives on the common, do

they?' The memory of the masked face in the gorse bush came back to my mind. 'Well, there are no houses there. At least, I didn't see any.'

'Well, dear, you wouldn't see them if you were looking in the wrong places.'

She stirred the teapot and called for Hobbes, who entered, mud-spattered and grinning. 'Good morning, Andy,' he said, took off his heavy boots and turned to wash his hands in the big, white sink. He was up to his elbows in suds when the doorbell rang.

Dregs sprang into life, barking and quivering as if he intended tearing the visitors to shreds. It was all bluff though—he'd become a civilised dog since the day I'd first bumped into him and had feared for my life.

Mrs G was bending to open the oven door. 'Would you mind answering that, dear?'

'Not at all.' I got up, walked to the kitchen door and, after a brief struggle, confined Dregs behind it.

After a quick adjustment to my dog-afflicted trousers, I hurried to the front door and opened it. Two ordinary-looking men in grey suits stood there, and a large, grey car with mirrored windows was blocking the traffic on Blackdog Street.

'Good morning,' I said.

'Inspector Hobbes?' asked the taller of the men, looking disappointed.

'No, I'm Andy ... Andy Caplet ... '

'But this is the correct address for Inspector Hobbes?'

'It is.' Hobbes voice rumbled in my ears, making me jump—I could never work out how such a massive policeman could be so light on his feet.

Both men flinched—they were only human, after all. They showed him ID.

'Simon and Tom. I was expecting you. Come in.'

The grey car drove away.

I stepped aside as the men entered, and closed the door behind them.

'Take a seat,' said Hobbes, gesturing at the worn but comfortable red velour sofa in the sitting room. 'What brings you two lads all the way from London?'

Tom, the taller of the two, spoke as they sat. 'There is a problem overseas which our department hopes you can help resolve.'

Simon, an inch or two shorter, nodded. 'Your ... unique abilities might prove vital.'

'Andy,' said Hobbes, as I hovered in the background, 'I'm afraid this is government business and not for your ears. Would you mind leaving us? Sorry about the tea.'

'No problem ... I ... umm ... really ought to get back to work, anyway. Shall I ask Mrs Goodfellow to give you some privacy?'

Simon shook his head. 'No need—she's fully cleared.'

When I returned to the kitchen, Dregs had been exiled to the back garden, but his hairy black head kept appearing in the window as he bounced. I grabbed my jacket, took a sip of tea, which tasted as fragrant and delicious as it always did there, and said goodbye to Mrs G who was making up a tray to take into the guests. On the side, an aromatic tray of lemon biscuits was still shimmering with heat—they'd be far too hot to handle yet. I gave them a longing look as I walked away.

My curiosity about the visitors fired up as I headed for the front door, but although I walked as slowly as possible, hoping to hear something of interest, all I picked up was Tom and Simon talking about the motorway traffic.

'Bye,' I said as I passed them.

Hobbes raised his huge, hairy hand.

I went out into Blackdog Street, pulled the door behind me and lingered on the steps. Ralph had encouraged us to use any means possible to get a story, short of breaking the law and getting caught. What golden nuggets might I hear if I pressed my ear to the door? Yet I didn't do it—eavesdropping on a secret conversation seemed too sneaky, and I feared Hobbes's anger if he ever found out. Although I'd never been the target of his explosive rage, I had been close enough to feel terrified by the fallout. Feeling virtuous, I drew myself up and marched away. I doubted I'd have heard much anyway.

I made a point of never reporting anything connected with Hobbes unless he'd given it the all-clear first. This wasn't because I feared his wrath, though I did, it was because he was a friend and he had a secret. Not a guilty one. As far as I was aware, he'd done nothing too terrible, it was just that he wasn't exactly human, though he could do a passable impression of one of them—or one of us I should say. Hardly anyone else had worked this out though, since it is a truth universally acknowledged that few can see what lies beneath the facade of a police officer.

For a moment, I wished I could be a fly on the wall of his sitting room, but further reflection suggested the stupidity of that wish—flies, I was almost certain, lacked ears. Even if they had them, I doubted they'd understand English. Even more to the point, Mrs G couldn't abide bugs indoors and would assassinate invaders with a pea-shooter, with which she was astonishingly accurate. I shrugged—I'd probably never know why two secretive officials would come all the way from London to talk to him.

I speculated that it might be connected to his occasional disappearances. Without explanation, he sometimes just wouldn't be around, and though usually he was only away for a few days, on occasions he'd been gone for weeks and had returned with a deep tan on his already swarthy face. He'd never say where he'd been, or what he'd been doing, and I'd soon learned to avoid questioning him. However, on occasions, he'd mentioned weird stuff like policing a rogue anubis, or misbehaving chupacabras. At the time, I'd half assumed he'd been joking, but having seen so much oddness surrounding him, I now tended to believe him.

When I got back to the office, Ralph grinned and joked, made no mention of my supposed bias, and was encouraging about my career. I decided to give him the benefit of the doubt for the time being. Perhaps he'd just done what he'd done to impose his authority. Perhaps everything would be fine and dandy when we'd all got to know each other better. When he went out at lunchtime, I mentioned my hypothesis to Basil, who was eating a limp cheese sandwich at his desk.

'Don't be such a muppet, lad,' Basil replied. 'He's messing with us, trying to make us insecure so he can turn this fine old newspaper into a fluffy, happy rag without opposition. Tell you what, mate, I'm a *Bugle* man through and through—I've worked here for more than thirty years, but I'm no longer sure I want to stay. To tell you the truth, if I thought anyone would give me a similar job with similar pay at my age, I'd go now. Not that it matters—if he does here what he's done at the other papers he's edited, he'll give me the boot soon and bring in some kid on a fraction of the pay who'll do what he's told without question. Even worse, he could start using AI and that'll be the end of us and of real news.'

I had much to think about when I got home that night, but Hobbes turned up a few moments after Daphne had returned. I let him in, and he took a seat.

'What's up?' I asked.

'I could do with your help,' he said.

To Daphne.

'With what?' she asked.

'I'll come to that in a moment, but firstly, do you have a current passport?'

She nodded. 'Yes.'

'That's good. If you agree to my proposal, you'll need it.'

'I'm intrigued,' she said, looking excited.

'Me too,' I said. 'What's going on?'

He drew a breath. 'The government has asked me to resolve a slight problem that has arisen in a distant country, and I have indicated my willingness to be of service. However, when I discussed the problem with the department, it made me believe that someone with archaeological skills will be required ... and your knowledge of cryptids will also be helpful.'

'Billy Shawcroft knows about archaeology,' I said, butting in because I feared he was going to drag my poor wife off to dangerous foreign parts.

Hobbes nodded. 'True, and he has helped me in the past. However, in this case there is likely to be some deep snow, which is tricky for him.'

Billy, though a man of massive abilities, was also a man of diminutive stature.

'I hoped you might be interested,' Hobbes continued, looking towards Daphne. 'The task should take a few weeks ... maybe a month.'

'Where is it?' she asked.

'In Asia, but I regret that I can't reveal any more until

you agree. If you do, you will have to sign the Official Secrets Act. You will require a medical and if all is well, the department will brief you on the details of the mission.'

'Asia is big,' I said with my usual perspicacity. 'You can't ask her to head off to some mysterious place—it might be dangerous!'

'Since the mission will take us into wild and lonely places,' said Hobbes, 'I cannot guarantee there'll be no danger.'

'She can't leave her job at the drop of a hat,' I said. Our domestic finances were already parlous without losing her salary.

'It's my job and I can speak for myself,' Daphne pointed out. 'But it's a good point.'

'Don't worry about that. The department will sort out any issues with your employers,' said Hobbes. 'Furthermore, you will be compensated for your time.'

I wanted her to say no and to end this conversation, but she'd already made her point—I kept quiet. After all, her career had already taken her to foreign parts more than once, and though I worried, I accepted that it was her choice. She'd always come back. So far.

'How many people will be on the mission?' she asked, as if she'd already decided.

'Just the two of us and a local guide who will also supply tents, food and transport.'

'Tents?' asked Daphne.

My heart sank and my stomach lurched with fear, seeing how eager she looked.

He nodded. 'We will camp for most of the time. If you come, and I hope you do, you will need a suitable sleeping bag and mountain gear.'

'Mountain?' The word came out of my mouth as a

squeak.

'I have stuff I used in the Blacker Mountains,' she said. 'Would that be suitable?'

'Probably not,' he admitted. 'The conditions we are likely to encounter will be far more extreme. You must be prepared.'

Her eyes were bright with excitement. 'If I agree, when will it all happen?'

'Very soon,' said Hobbes. 'If you have no security or health issues, you will receive your briefing in London before the end of next week. Then we'll go as soon as the department sorts out our travel arrangements.'

Daphne sat quietly for a few moments. 'I agree. It sounds most mysterious.'

His big yellow teeth set into a wide grin. 'Thank you—I hoped you would. I will inform the department.'

'Isn't this exciting?' she said, turning to me with a smile and giving me a hug.

I grimaced. 'I suppose it is for those of us who are off to exotic places.'

'I know, but I won't be away for long—a month, didn't you say?' She glanced at Hobbes, who nodded.

'Thereabouts.'

I had an idea. 'You'll need someone to help with the baggage and around camp—I could do that.'

Hobbes shook his head. 'I don't think that would be a good idea.'

5

The turbulence and vibration had stopped, and I could no longer hear the engine's drone. We were at a crazy angle. I jerked awake in a mad panic—we were crashing!

Of course, we weren't—we'd already landed. Snow-draped mountains surrounded the battered little Cessna, and a breeze chilled around my ankles.

'Nice sleep?' asked Daphne, smiling. Like me, she was wearing the colourful high-tech mountain gear the department had provided. Unlike me, she was on her feet and ready to go.

'Umm ... I slept?'

'Most of the way.' She bent to kiss me. 'You'd better get your things.'

'And quickly!' said Hobbes, who was leaning in through the door. He was dressed in a battered tweed coat and baggy trousers.

'Yes, of course.' I stood up and cracked my head on the low ceiling.

'Mind your brain, sir,' said Dilip, our pilot, grinning despite his lack of front teeth. 'And put on your hat and sunglasses.'

Though yawning and muzzy-headed, I shook myself and did as he asked before shuffling toward the fresh air. I stepped down onto short grass and looked around.

The deep blue of the sky reminded me of tropical oceans, but the chill soon dispelled that thought. The previous day, when we'd looked down on the mountains from the jet, it had been impossible to appreciate their scale. Now, as I looked up from ground level and saw just how massive they were, and how they appeared to extend forever, they took my breath away. At least, I assumed that was why I was gasping for air. Ground level was wrong, too—ground sloping made more sense—our little plane was pointing uphill on the edge of the football pitch-sized meadow where it had landed.

Hobbes noticed me struggling. 'Try to relax, Andy. It's the altitude—we're over ten thousand feet above sea level. Take it easy until your body adjusts.'

I nodded, and regained some control of my breathing, wondering why the others didn't appear affected.

Dilip started unloading our bags. Hobbes stacked them on a pile of rocks that would have made mincemeat of the Cessna's undercarriage had the landing gone just a little off course.

Daphne went to help. 'You'd better rest for a moment,' she told me as she struggled under an orange rucksack.

'I'm fine,' I said, taking it off her, but when I reached the rocks, I had to sit down. 'What on earth's in this thing? Dumbbells?'

She laughed. 'You should know—it's yours.'

Hobbes chuckled. 'Don't worry, you'll get used to it soon enough ... I hope.'

I took deep breaths. 'Remind me why I agreed to come here.'

'If I recall correctly, you did not agree to come, you

begged,' said Daphne. 'That's right, isn't it, Mr Hobbes?'

He nodded. 'You insisted that it would be foolish to leave you behind because your skills would be indispensable.'

'Yeah, alright,' I admitted.

In fact, I had few camping skills, and my real reason for getting onto the expedition was to look after Daphne and keep her safe from the perils of the mountains, whatever they might be. Besides Hobbes, I was aware of a few: wolves, leopards, avalanches. What I'd actually do if we encountered any remained to be seen. A deeper reason for coming that I didn't care to acknowledge was my need not to feel left out.

Dilip was ready to leave within fifteen minutes. After a quick round of 'Goodbyes', he climbed back into the cockpit and ran through a few checks. When all was well and the engine was running, he signalled to Hobbes who put his shoulder to the tail, turned the plane around and stepped aside. The engine's roar rose in pitch, the prop blurred, and the little plane shot downhill. It was airborne within seconds and we watched as it made a sharp turn to avoid a rocky outcrop before setting course for the remote airfield in the hazy, green valley far below. Then, other than the muted chitter of unseen birds and the buzz of insects, the world fell silent. In that moment, despite Daphne and Hobbes being within touching distance, I felt crushed by the isolation and the sense of being so far from civilisation. If there were problems, no one would know, no one would come to help and, according to Hobbes's rather vague map, the nearest hill village was at least a week's hard trek away. Although I'd experienced something similar when Hobbes, Dregs and I made an excursion into the bleak and lonely

Blacker Mountains, I'd known then that if things got too bad, I might walk to a small town only a few hours away. Up here, I was insignificant, helpless, cowed and useless and almost wished I'd stayed home, though I knew I'd be fretting if I had. I checked my mobile—no signal, as I'd expected.

Hobbes sat cross-legged on top of the rock pile with his eyes closed. Daphne lounged beside him, making notes in her journal. I stared at the patch of sky where I'd last seen the plane. Dilip wouldn't return for days.

'So, what now?' I asked.

'We wait for Akar,' said Hobbes, opening one eye.

'A car? Up here?'

'You didn't read the briefing notes, did you?' said Daphne, putting down her pencil.

'I did ... sort of ... why?'

'Because if you had, you'd know that Akar is our guide.'

'Oh, that Akar. When's he getting here?'

'When he can,' said Hobbes. 'Terrain and climate control the pace of travel in these parts. However, I expect him soon. He's always proved reliable before.'

'You know him?'

He nodded.

'Have you been here before?'

'A few times.'

'Why?' I asked, hoping to learn more of his exploits.

'On secret government business.'

I didn't push any further. Only a few days earlier, and much to my surprise, he'd taken Daphne and me to a small office in London where we'd signed the Official Secrets Act. As soon as our signatures were on the form, an official informed me that I'd volunteered for a secret mission and would only be given information on a

47

strictly need-to-know basis. Apparently, I didn't need to know nearly as much as Daphne, who they took to another room for over an hour, leaving me to coffee and biscuits. Still, I would probably have known a bit more had I read the briefing notes rather than skimmed through them as I stared out the window at the busy London streets. Despite this, I had taken away the vital knowledge that I was forbidden from revealing the country I was visiting, and which foreign government had requested Hobbes's assistance. Failure to comply would result in dire consequences. Still, it was frustrating that the department hadn't let me know what Hobbes was doing or why he needed my wife's help.

While the other two relaxed, I wandered about, doing my best not to pant or to fall into panic. The little meadow, despite a sprinkling of the most lovely, sweet-scented spring flowers I'd ever seen, struck me as an inhospitable and exposed place and the prospect of spending a night there was terrifying.

I'd reached the topmost edge and was throwing pebbles at an innocent thorny shrub when a huge shaggy face appeared over the ridge.

Worse than the face were the long, sharp, curved horns, the hump of massive shoulders and the sturdy legs.

I yelped, though the dark brown eyes were not fierce. They stared at me with mild bemusement.

'Akar's here,' said Hobbes, getting to his feet.

'This cow thing is our guide?' It was insane, even for Hobbes!

'No, you idiot,' said Daphne with a grin. 'That, I believe, is Akar's yak, Flossy.'

I stepped back nervously as the great beast passed

by. As she lowered her head to munch on the foliage, a short, stocky man in a long hide coat, his ruddy face half-concealed by an oversized fur hat, approached in her tracks. He raised his hand and stuck out his tongue—an act of unprovoked rudeness that left me speechless.

'Greetings,' he said with a BBC English accent. 'I assume you are with Inspector Hobbes.'

I nodded as the man reached the top of the rise.

'Greetings, my friend and well met!' said Hobbes, running up. 'I trust all is well?' He stuck out his tongue and shook Akar's gloved hand.

'Everything is indeed well,' said Akar. 'Apart from the business we're here for, of course.'

'Of course,' said Hobbes.

Daphne joined us. When she, too, stuck out her tongue, I began to suspect I'd missed something.

'You must be our archaeologist,' said Akar.

'Yes, I'm Daphne. Pleased to meet you.' She held out her hand. Akar bowed and raised it to his lips.

I, for one, wasn't impressed.

Hobbes patted Flossy, who was happily chewing meadow flowers and herbs.

'And who are you, sir?' asked Akar, smiling at me.

'I'm her husband,' I said, moving beside her.

'He is Andy,' said Hobbes. 'He's here to help around the camp and to keep a photographic record of our expedition, though I have yet to see him with a camera.'

'It's still in my rucksack,' I said. 'I'll get it soon.'

'And I believe soon would be a good time to eat,' said Hobbes as Akar laid down his pack. 'The days are still short and we need to get moving before the afternoon gets too old.'

'Okay, Chief, I'll start cooking the tsampa,' said Akar,

taking a battered leather pouch from his pack.

Hobbes started a fire, using a stash of dry wood and what looked like animal droppings he'd found among the rocks, while Akar tipped a complicated mass of rusty ironwork from his pack, twisted it like a balloon wrangler, and turned it into a tripod. He set it over the fire and hung a blackened kettle of water from it. As I watched, I began to feel ravenous, despite the colossal breakfast I'd enjoyed at the Imperial Hotel in the small market town whose name and location the law forbade me from ever disclosing.

To take my mind off the interminable wait for lunch, I rummaged through my pack. The camera was right at the bottom, but appeared to have survived the journey intact. I took a few snaps of our party, including rather too many close-ups of Flossy who kept blundering into shot. Then I focussed on the scenery: white-tipped mountains glinted all around, lush valleys lurked far below, a distant ribbon of river glinted, and a vast purple-blue lake appeared to be iced over along one edge. Although my rudimentary photographic skills could never do justice to the magnificence of nature in the wild, I was satisfied with the results.

Akar crouched over the fire, a sorcerer in the midst of billowing steam and smoke. He poured a pan of boiling water into a pot, chucked in handfuls of a greyish powder and a hefty lump of what appeared to be soft cheese and stirred the concoction with a long wooden spoon. 'Lunch is served, lady and gentlemen,' he said, filling four plain wooden bowls with the gunk and handing them out.

Hobbes said grace, which was his way except when possessed by one of his wild, dangerous moods.

'What the hell is it? Gruel?' I whispered to Daphne

and stared at the greyish-brown sludge in front of me.

'It's tsampa—roasted barley flour boiled with salted yak butter—a staple food for peasants and travellers up here. I'm sure it tastes better than it looks.'

'God, I hope so! But what if it … umm … looks better than it tastes?'

'Then smile and get used to it, darling—unless you want to starve.'

It was possible that as food writer for the *Sorenchester and District Bugle* and as a keen admirer of the culinary skills of Mrs Goodfellow, I'd become a little spoiled. I was used to well-presented food with varied colours and textures, but this gloop was lacking in all three departments. Yet, hunger is a fine relish, so I dipped my spoon and took a tentative taste. The consistency was somewhere between porridge and dough, and it felt gritty on the teeth, though the nutty flavour wasn't bad. I tried a little more and concluded that it was edible, though it hit my stomach like a lump of lead, and I was unable to finish the whole bowl.

Hobbes went back for seconds. 'I've missed this,' he said. 'The old girl has tried making it at home, but it's not the same without yak butter and mountain air.'

When we'd finished eating and had drunk a little water, Akar took our bowls and spoons to the edge of the meadow and washed them in snow. 'Ready to go?' he asked as he stowed the stuff back into his pack.

'Yes, we'd better get a move on if we're to reach the tasam before dark,' said Hobbes, getting to his feet.

'It's a nomadic caravan house,' said Daphne in response to my baffled expression. 'A sheltered place to camp.'

'Flossy! It's time for work,' said Akar.

The shaggy beast who'd been relaxing and chewing cud at the far side of the meadow, stood up and sauntered towards us. Akar loaded her.

'What about the rest of our baggage?' I asked, eyeing the pile that was left.

'That's for us to carry,' said Hobbes.

Although my rucksack was heavier than I'd have wished and my knees sagged, I made light of it as Hobbes hoisted it onto my back. The truth was that Daphne had helped me pack, ensuring I only put in essentials, but I'd sneaked in a few other items I'd thought might prove useful, including paperbacks to read in the evenings. Perhaps that had been foolish. I looked at Daphne's light pack with envy.

'Could Flossy carry my stuff?' I asked. 'She seems to be managing her load without any problem.'

'No,' said Hobbes. 'She's already taking more than her share, and we don't want to wear her out.'

'Oh, well … just a thought.'

Leaving the landing meadow, we set off along a stony path that snaked between massive boulders and patches of snow. Akar took the lead, followed by Hobbes. I was sandwiched towards the rear between Daphne and Flossy, who ensured I kept moving—I wasn't sure she'd stop if I did, and the path was too narrow to stand aside. At first, the going was reasonably smooth and level, but before long we'd reached rugged terrain and were climbing hard. I was soon staggering and gasping. Sweat dripped into my eyes and as I slowed to wipe a handkerchief over my face, Flossy nudged me gently in the back. I nearly fell, and had I done so, I doubted I would have had the strength to get up again.

How long was this trek? Would I make it or would my

racing heart explode first? Why on earth had I asked to come to this godforsaken place? Why was no one helping me? Why weren't they struggling for air? And why was Daphne not making sure her poor, toiling husband was keeping up?

Flossy nudged me again, and I groaned.

'Are you alright?' asked Daphne.

I shook my head. 'I can't keep this pace up. Are we nearly there yet?'

'I doubt it—we've only been going for twenty minutes.'

'What's the matter?' asked Hobbes, turning to see why we'd fallen behind.

'Andy's struggling,' said Daphne.

'But we've only just started! And the path grows steep soon.'

My legs and lungs argued that it was too steep already.

'I guess it's the altitude,' said Daphne, 'though his rucksack is really heavy.'

'I'll take it,' said Hobbes, and slung it over his shoulder, alongside his own small bag.

Akar offered me water from a leather flask that was hairy on the outside, like Hobbes's horrid wallet. After a few gulps, I felt a little better. They allowed me five minutes to get my breath back, and we were off again.

'We need to shift ourselves if we are going to reach shelter before dusk,' said Hobbes. 'Are you up for it, Andy?'

I nodded, unwilling to waste breath on words, though nothing felt right and I wanted nothing more than to lie down and let nature take its course. Although it took all my willpower to place one foot in front of the other, I trudged on, assisted by occasional reminders from Flossy.

Darkness closed in.

My nose was cold, though a shell of sublime warmth encased my body. I assumed I was tucked up in bed, waking on a frosty morning, though I couldn't understand why the bed was swaying and lurching. My befuddled mind jumped to the only conclusion.

'Earthquake!' I yelled, and opened my eyes.

I blinked in confusion. It was not yet dark, and what were massive grey rocks and icy mountains doing in our bedroom? As my brain regained some function, I raised my head and saw I was wrapped in blankets and perched on Flossy's back. Her yak scent was all around—it was sweet and not unpleasant. The peaks to my left shone fiery red in the sunset.

'What's happening?' I asked of the world in general.

'We had to put you up there when you fainted,' said Daphne, coming into view. 'How are you feeling?'

'Sick. Tired. And I've got a headache.'

'Well, never mind,' said Hobbes. 'Akar says we'll be there in ten minutes.'

'Good. It'll be nice to reach somewhere comfortable.'

'It won't be as comfortable as all that—the place was abandoned decades ago,' said Hobbes.

'What's the point of going there?'

'Because there's a spring of good water and the walls are still standing—they'll provide shelter from the weather and other things.'

'What other things?'

'You know—leopards, wolves, brigands?'

'Why did I come here?' I asked, as my spirits cowered in my boots.

'To protect us from harm,' said Hobbes, his face

expressionless.

'Me? What can I do?'

'You might come in handy as bait,' he said and chuckled.

I hoped he was joking.

At last, Flossy stopped by what looked like a derelict sheep pen. Hobbes plucked me from her back.

'Welcome to tonight's palatial residence,' said Akar with a grin. 'Alfresco dining, sleeping, and ablutions and no mod cons whatsoever. Make yourself comfortable. I'll see to Flossy.'

'Thank her for carrying me,' I said. 'I thought you didn't want to overload her?'

'We didn't,' said Daphne, wrapping a supportive arm around my waist. 'Mr Hobbes carried some of her load. Come on, let's find you somewhere out of the wind.'

She helped me into the flat, grassy space inside the walls and I leaned against a pile of rocks, stretching my legs and trying to appear stronger than I felt. Hobbes unpacked our brand-new igloo tents and winter sleeping bags from the baggage that Flossy would have been carrying had I not been so afflicted. He started setting up camp, pulling the tents into shape and pounding tent pegs into the rocky ground with his fist. I'd camped with him before, so this came as no surprise, but Daphne gasped—she'd rarely seen him in the wild and I was sure she thought I'd exaggerated his weirdness. Within a couple of minutes, he'd got both of them up, ready for occupation. One was for Daphne and me; the other was for him and Akar.

Akar gave Flossy water and a few handfuls of hay from her load and ensured a ramshackle wall would shelter her from the bitter wind. When satisfied, he joined us and started to build a fire with wood from a pile in a corner.

'We'd better make a good one,' he said. 'There's snow coming.'

Hobbes, who'd been sniffing out the area, came back between the walls and nodded. 'And there are wolves upwind.'

'Wolves!' I cried. 'Will they bother us? Do we have a gun?'

'Possibly, and no,' said Akar.

'What do we ... umm ... do if they attack us?'

'Reason with them,' said Hobbes. 'They'll be alright ... probably. If all else fails, grab a stick.'

'To fight them off?'

'To throw so they can go fetch,' he said with an evil grin.

At this point, I fell into a trembling fit—I'd never felt quite so helpless before, and I was well used to feeling helpless.

'Calm down,' said Daphne, hugging me. 'I'm sure Mr Hobbes and Akar know what they're doing.'

I wasn't.

My head felt as if it were spinning like a plate in a juggler's set. I tried to control myself but headache, fatigue and nausea overwhelmed me.

And then, for some reason, I was slumped on the cold, hard ground with Daphne stroking my forehead and Hobbes, Akar and Flossy staring down at me.

'His altitude sickness is not improving,' said Akar, frowning.

'What can we do to make it better?' asked Daphne, giving my hand a squeeze.

'I don't know,' said Hobbes. 'I've never seen anyone suffer so badly at such a low altitude. He may have done too much too soon.'

'Susceptible people can be afflicted above four thousand feet,' said Akar, 'but even then, it rarely happens so quickly. The usual treatment is to give paracetamol for the headache, an anti-sickness drug for his stomach, and to descend for a few days' rest before a slow climb back up. Unfortunately, we are travelling light and have no anti-sickness medication.'

I groaned as my stomach churned.

'At least we have paracetamol,' said Daphne.

Hobbes looked grave. 'We can give him some of those, but we can't descend. We're on a tight schedule—lives are at stake.'

'What will happen if we don't go down?' asked Daphne, biting her lip.

'Bad things,' said Akar gravely. 'Possibly very bad.'

'I'm sure I'll feel better in the morning,' I said bravely, panting and feeling as if I'd just sprinted the last mile of a marathon.

Daphne pushed two paracetamol tablets into my mouth and I washed them down with water from my bottle.

The wind howled. I hoped it was the wind. I shivered and my comrades' talk turned into the distant buzz of insects.

My eyes closed.

6

When I woke up, I was inside the tent with Daphne sleeping at my side. Every breath was a struggle and my head felt that it might burst, but at least the nausea had reduced—possibly because I had eaten nothing. My body craved further sleep, but my bladder insisted it was time to get up or to wet myself. I suppressed a groan, sat up, and wriggled from the warm cocoon of the sleeping bag. After a struggle to put on a fleece jacket, I slipped on my boots, not bothering to lace them, and unzipped the tent's door.

The world had turned white. It glistened in the pre-dawn half-light. Snowflakes swirled in a nasty wind that threatened to blow away what little breath I had left. I was gasping even before I was on my feet. My balance was all over the place—I felt as if I were on the rolling deck of a storm-tossed ship. Fighting the wind and the dizziness, I lurched away until I deemed I was far enough from the tents for hygiene, and released the pent-up pressure in a cloud of steam. On the way back, I had time to notice the prints patterning the snow all around.

'Wolves!' I yelled with the last of my breath, and fell face first into soft snow—my flapping bootlaces had tangled.

Hobbes, dressed only in woollen long johns, burst

from his tent. 'Where?'

I sat up and pointed at the prints.

He laughed. 'Calm down—they're only kyangs.'

'What?'

'Wild asses,' said Akar, running over. 'Quite harmless if left alone.'

'Why are you sitting in the snow?' asked Daphne, emerging from our tent.

'I fell.'

'How are you feeling?'

'My head's thumping like a ten-pint hangover, and I can't catch my breath. I'm cold.'

Hobbes hauled me to my feet and was helping me back to the tent when he stopped and pointed up the rock face opposite. 'Somebody's up there.'

I followed the direction of his finger to where the rising sun lit up a rectangular stone building with rows of dark, square holes. The place was massive and looked almost as if it was a natural part of the landscape.

'It's an old monastery,' said Akar. 'It was abandoned a century ago.'

Daphne squinted into the brightening light. 'He's waving.'

A man-shaped figure wearing a robe belted at the waist and with long sleeves, was sitting cross-legged by one of the holes. He rose to his feet, bounded down the steep mountain side and stuck out his tongue as he drew near—I'd worked out that it must be a form of greeting in these parts. He doffed his fur cap.

The excitement was too much. Breathing was too much. The shutters came down again.

A bitter liquid ran into my mouth. I gagged and fought the strong hands clamping my jaw and pinching my nose. All I could do was swallow the vile stuff. When they let me go, I retched.

They'd propped me up on a hard bed in a bleak stone cell. Daphne, Hobbes and Akar were at my side. The stranger, his face looking as old as time and twice as hairy, grinned. It took a moment to work out that he was wearing a mask of twigs and fur. He was holding a wooden bowl and spoon—I blamed him for the disgusting concoction.

'Drink this,' said Akar, handing me a steaming cup. 'It'll take the taste away.'

I took a swig. It lived up to his promise, though I wasn't convinced it was much of an improvement. 'What devilish drink is that?'

'Buttered tea,' said Hobbes. 'An acquired taste.'

'How are you feeling?' asked Akar.

I stopped making disgusted noises and grimaces to consider the question. 'Actually, I'm feeling better … a whole lot better. What did he give me?'

Hobbes smiled. 'A mixture of mysterious herbs. Our friend gathers them in a valley beyond the big peak, mixes them with holy water from the Tsangpo river, and brews them up into a cordial. He says it works wonders for altitude sickness.'

'It does,' I agreed, and turned to thank him.

He'd already gone.

'He's not used to people,' said Akar.

'I'll thank him later,' I said. 'By the way, is there any breakfast? I'm starving.'

Following a huge bowlful of tsampa, I felt almost miraculously well. In fact, I'd never before had so much energy and clarity of mind. I was delighted the stranger had left me a small leather flask of the stuff.

After I'd breakfasted, Akar took me down a dusty

corridor, opened a creaking wooden door and ushered me into a small walled garden where the overnight snow was already melting beneath a warm sun. Huge bees hummed in blossoming fruit trees and a rivulet tinkled like bells, making music as it meandered through the garden and plunged down the mountainside in a haze of rainbows.

Daphne was sitting on an ancient wooden bench, a blissful smile on her face. 'You should take some pictures of this,' she said and handed me my camera. I did as she asked, for it was a special place. Then we sat together in this earthly paradise, holding hands, lost in thought. Was our masked friend the gardener of this Eden? I could have stayed there forever.

The garden's door thumped open again and like a great, ugly ape, Hobbes gatecrashed the bliss. 'We're packed, Flossy is loaded, it's time to shift yourselves ... and quickly!'

Within ten minutes, we'd resumed the trek. My rucksack felt as light as a cloud, and I strode along, keeping up with ease, full of gratitude for the mysterious stranger. I wondered at my newfound vigour, and only later discovered that Hobbes had taken out my books and left them in the monastery. Although our route was rough and steep, I caught myself singing for sheer joy, revelling in the exercise, the meal breaks, and the magnificence of the mountains. I was still going strong when we made camp for the evening.

The next three days were much the same: waking, eating, walking, sleeping. After a drop of the potion, a few moments of gagging, and a hearty breakfast, I was ready for anything. We climbed steadily higher, the scenery ever more spectacular as the temperature dropped, despite a fierce sun that glared down—

Daphne and I were grateful the department had given us tubes of sunblock.

Late afternoon on the third day, we crested a ridge. A steep cliff glittered and dazzled in the distance.

'What's that?' I asked.

Hobbes, who was in shirt sleeves, his heavy tweed jacket slung over his pack, grinned. 'That's Khyags-Klung—mountaineers call it "The Unclimbable Glacier". We'll reach it tomorrow.'

'And then what?' I asked.

'We'll climb it. Our destination is a valley on the far side.'

'Even Flossy?'

'As the briefing said, she will remain at the base with Akar to await our return. Hopefully, that won't be too long—three or four days at the most.'

'But she's carrying all our food and a lot of our stuff.'

'Which is why we'll only take what we need,' said Daphne.

I put it down to the potion that I accepted the situation with equanimity. After all, why should I worry when climbing unclimbable ice walls was all in a day's work for the likes of me? I just hoped Hobbes and Daphne could keep up. Sauntering to what looked like the edge of the world, I gazed out over a torrent roaring through a rocky valley hundreds of feet below, and took a few photos.

As I turned back, a slight movement caught my eye. A face was staring down from the sheer, grey rock face.

A spotted face.

A leopard.

'Look!' I said, and pointed, as it sprang.

The beast landed at my side and reared up. Great, shaggy paws thumped against my chest, knocking me

62

onto my back, and before I knew what was happening, the leopard's face was pressed against mine.

Daphne screamed.

The leopard ignored her, and the last thing I was expecting happened—it licked my face and purred. Its tongue was rough, its breath foul.

'Go away at once!' said Hobbes in his best police voice.

The leopard rolled across my body, stretching out as if on a sofa.

Hobbes grabbed it by the scruff of the neck and dragged it off. It snarled and took a raking swipe at him.

'There's no need for that, my girl,' said Hobbes, swatting the paw aside. ' ... and spitting is a filthy habit! Be off with you ... and quickly.' He slapped the puzzled big cat on its backside, growled, and sent it on its way.

Daphne rushed to me as it slunk down the path. 'Are you hurt?'

'No,' I said, amazed, and sat up. 'It didn't hurt me. It might have brushed its teeth though—god knows what it had eaten.'

Flossy came up and nuzzled my neck, which would have been fine had she not sneezed—I could have done without the splat of yak snot down my jacket, but it didn't take away my euphoria. I stood up, brushed myself down, and thanked Hobbes.

'You're welcome,' he said.

Akar stroked his chin. 'That was most peculiar behaviour for a leopard—they're usually rather shy.'

Hobbes nodded. 'It wasn't hunting, so why do that to Andy? And why now?'

'The potion?' Akar suggested.

'Perhaps, though he has been known to attract cats before. Could I see it?' asked Hobbes.

I took the flask from my rucksack and handed it over.

He pulled the plug, sniffed, and tasted a drop. 'Ugh! That's nasty—I understand why you struggled.' He took another sniff. 'It's a strange mixture. There are hints of ginkgo and poppy and goldenroot ... and something else ... ' He laughed. 'Catnip!'

'Is that why it attacked?' asked Daphne, squeezing my hand so hard I yelped.

'It wasn't exactly an attack,' said Hobbes, 'but, catnip does strange things to felines ... and to Andy, too—I've never seen him so cheerful.'

'We'd better get a move on,' Akar said. 'We must reach Arun Da Valley before dark and there's still some way to go.'

'Why there?' asked Daphne.

'Because it offers some shelter. There will be a great wind later.'

'Blame that on the tsampa,' I quipped.

Akar ignored me. 'I like your modern tents,' he said. 'They are light and convenient, but I hope they're up to the mountain weather—they look flimsy.'

'They're tough enough,' said Hobbes, 'but we don't want them blowing away.' He sniffed the air and looked around. 'I reckon the storm will be upon us in two hours.'

Akar nodded. 'Perhaps a little less.'

'Then let's get going,' I said, shouldering my pack and striding ahead, determined to show my leadership qualities.

'Good idea, but wrong direction,' said Hobbes, grabbing my arm and directing me onto a narrow path I'd missed.

Our new route was smoother and less steep for the most part, and we made excellent progress. Even so, the huge red sun was barely glancing over the top of peaks when we reached Arun Da Valley. It was not, as I'd imagined, a verdant paradise, but a bleak corrugation in a rare bit of flatness. A ferocious cascade plummeted from a cliff above, tumbled down the slope and disappeared into a narrow gorge at the bottom.

'We'll pitch the tents under there,' said Akar, pointing to a rocky overhang.

'That's too steep,' I said. 'We'll slide out! What's wrong with there?' I pointed to a smooth, level area near the water.

'The overhang offers some protection from the storm,' said Akar. 'There is none down there, and it's prone to flash floods, especially in the spring.'

Daphne nodded. 'I understand, but Andy has a point—it really is steep under the overhang.'

'It isn't ideal,' said Hobbes, 'but we must endure.' He sniffed the air and frowned.

The sky had turned the colour of a livid bruise, and the gentle breeze that had cooled our march was getting fractious and cold.

'The wind's building and I can smell rain,' said Hobbes.

'It will be snow,' said Akar.

Hobbes shrugged. 'Sleet?'

'Maybe,' said Akar. 'We'd better get the tents up—night falls swiftly in this valley.'

We scrambled down the slope and Flossy led the way to the campsite.

'Looks like she's been here before,' I said.

Akar nodded. 'She's a sensible beast.'

We unloaded Flossy, pitched our tents and carried our gear inside as the sun slipped behind a tall peak, leaving us in a world of shadow. Akar produced a pair of ancient hurricane lamps and lit them.

'What's for supper?' I asked.

'Nothing until the worst of the storm has passed,' said Hobbes. 'There's no chance of cooking—the fire would blow away.'

Though I was inclined to argue, I kept quiet, except for my stomach, which grumbled even as my legs relaxed.

'Dehydration is a real danger at these altitudes,' said Akar, and insisted that we drank from the cascade and filled our flasks.

The icy water was clean and sparkling with bubbles. I slurped it down, though it made me shiver. Refreshed, we carried our flasks back to the tents as a vicious, roaring wind struck the valley. It would have blown Daphne off her feet had I not grabbed her. A bitter gust of sleet stung our eyes, snuffing out the last lingering traces of daylight and, like desperate moths, we aimed for Akar's lamps. Hand in hand, we struggled towards the overhang and shelter. Behind us, the valley turned as dark as a midnight coal mine.

'It's going to get rough,' said Akar. 'I advise taking to our tents.'

No one argued. Flossy retreated to the back of the overhang and munched on the scant grass between the rocks. Daphne and I removed our boots and dived into the tent, which, despite the relative shelter, flapped and jumped in the bellowing wind. Rain or sleet pounded down outside.

'What a storm!' I yelled.

Daphne shouted something back but I couldn't make it out. I retreated into my sleeping bag. She joined me, snuggling for warmth.

I must have dozed off. When I awoke, Daphne lay

asleep with her head on my chest. We'd slid down the slope, and our feet pressed up against the bottom of the tent. The wind had died away and I could hear Hobbes and Akar talking.

'They were checking us out earlier,' said Hobbes, 'I could smell them.'

'Let's hope they make contact,' said Akar. 'If they don't, you'll have to attempt the glacier without their help, and I don't fancy the others' chances—particularly his.'

'Andy is surprisingly resilient,' said Hobbes, 'though, I agree, it might be perilous with so much melt water coming down so early in the year. It's far worse than London led me to believe.'

'It's been happening for the last few years,' said Akar. 'However, let's not worry too much about something that may never happen. If our friends are aware of us, they might recognise you and come to talk.'

'I hope so,' Hobbes replied. 'But first things first—we should be able to get a fire going now. I could do with some grub and a cup of tea.'

I saw the silhouette of Hobbes leave the tent and wondered who the friends they'd mentioned were.

Warm and cosy, I dozed again, until Daphne looked into the tent to wake me. 'Supper's ready, if you'd care to join us.'

I did care, and joined the others as soon as I'd flung on my jacket and tied my boots. Supper, eaten while squatting in the glow of the hurricane lamps, was tsampa again. However, I was ravenous and in no mood to be fussy. I wolfed it down, a very different approach to my normal savouring of every mouthful. The tea, of course, was the local type, with a scummy layer of grease on top. Still, it slipped down easily enough and warmed me from the inside out, though, like the tsampa, it wasn't as hot as I'd expected. I'd finally worked out why—the thin atmosphere up here meant water boiled at a lower temperature.

As we finished our meal, the sleet returned, so we slipped back into the tents and bedded down for the night.

Despite worrying that Daphne and Hobbes would struggle to keep up with my newfound energy, if we had to climb the glacier, I soon dropped off to sleep.

A surprisingly hot sun melted the overnight sleet and snow before we'd finished our breakfast tea and tsampa. We set off and the day's journey proved uneventful.

By early afternoon, we were approaching the great ice cliff of the glacier. Melt water gushed from a tunnel at its base, forming a small river before flinging itself over the edge of an abyss, filling the air with noise and colour. Although a ribbon of smooth, flat ground along its side looked suitable for our camp, Akar shook his head and said it was quicksand. We pitched the tents in a rocky hollow well above the water.

Whoever 'the friends' were, they did not make contact.

After our evening tea and tsampa, we sat around the fire, talking. Hobbes came to a decision—we would climb the glacier in the morning. Akar briefed us on what to expect and what to do and, despite my previous exhilaration, I didn't like the sound of it—Daphne and I lacked climbing experience. I even wondered about Hobbes. Were his hob-nailed boots and wooden alpenstock up to the task?

With these concerns and the eerie creaking and grinding of the glacier, I was sure I'd never sleep that night, until Hobbes woke us. I pointed out that it was still dark.

'We need to get going before the sun's up,' he said, his breath steaming in the lamplight. 'Climbing on ice can be tricky, but it's far better than climbing on melting ice. Get a move on, get dressed, do what you have to do and your breakfast will be ready in five minutes. Can you guess what it is?'

'Tsampa?'

He grinned and nodded.

We ate on our feet, picked up our packs and equipment, said quick farewells to Akar and Flossy, and started the ascent. Although Daphne and I were well equipped in our mountain gear, wore crampons and carried ice-axes, it felt like a daunting task. The thin, grey, pre-dawn light showed boulder-strewn ice ramparts looming above, awaiting their opportunity to crash down. Hobbes took the lead as we scrambled upwards, warning us of crevasses and thin ice. For me, the worst horrors were the appalling vertical shafts we passed, and the roar of torrential water rising from their black depths.

And this looked like the easy bit of the climb. In truth, I'm not sure we would have made it to the top had someone not anchored lines of yak-hair rope to guide us. Seeing Hobbes's smile, I guessed the mysterious 'friends' had made contact after all.

The rest of the climb, though exhausting, turned out to be more of a scramble. The ropes led us through relatively safe places, though we still had to keep our wits about us. When, at last, we reached a precipitous bit, I was delighted by the sight of solid wooden ladders that were fixed to the ice by leather straps. Filled with new confidence and energy, I leapt onto the first rung and stuck fast—a sensible man would have removed his crampons first.

Hobbes released me, and we reached the top of the glacier just as the sun topped the mountains. We continued following the ropes until we were on solid rock and there was a clear path forward. After a rest, a drink and a bite of cold tsampa, we marched until we reached a suitable place to camp. Hobbes pitched our tents. He'd brought a small one for himself—I was surprised he could fit into it.

We rested, and I made supper. It wasn't that bad, though I was already bored of the tsampa diet. Still, it kept us going—no doubt because it was full of fibre.

7

As soon as the light faded, we turned in and I enjoyed a deep sleep. Next morning, we had the usual tsampa—what wouldn't I have given for a full English breakfast?

After I'd washed the bowls and spoons in the stream, Hobbes fixed me with a stern gaze. 'Thank you for that, but this is where we say goodbye. Daphne and I have to visit our friends.'

'And me?'

'You will stay here.'

'But why can't I come with you? I've got a security clearance—I had to sign the Official Secrets Act!'

He shook his head. 'As you well know, this entire mission is on a need-to-know basis, and you've been told only what you needed to come this far. Daphne received further clearances. Her knowledge and skills will be invaluable in resolving the issue.'

'Sorry, Andy,' said Daphne, giving me a consolation hug, 'but I couldn't say anything.'

I had no choice—there was no point in arguing with Hobbes. 'What am I here for? And what do I do when you're away?'

'Your task,' said Hobbes, 'is to protect the tents.'

'From what?' I asked, feeling like a pet dog left 'on guard', by callous owners intent on enjoying a night out.

'From bandits. We'll need the tents and the baggage

when we return.'

I scoffed. 'Bandits? Really?'

He nodded. 'Yes, really, though they haven't bothered us so far.'

I'd skimmed over something about them in the briefing notes, but hadn't incorporated them into my list of potential dangers. Perhaps I'd become complacent, assuming the mountains were peaceful havens, beautiful in their stark way, and that the only dangers came from wild animals ... and falling from high places ... and raging torrents ... and bad weather ... and avalanches.

'What if they attack?' I asked, fear fluttering my innards.

'They won't try anything in daylight if they see the camp is occupied,' said Hobbes. 'So, don't worry, we should be back before dusk—assuming all goes to plan. Just make sure you don't go wandering off anywhere and getting lost.'

Unable to think of a suitably biting retort, I forced a brave little smile.

'See you later,' said Daphne, her eyes bright with excitement. She kissed me, swung her pack onto her back, and smiled. 'Take care.'

'You too,' I said.

Hobbes picked up a light bag and his alpenstock, and I watched them march away, winding upward between boulders. When they reached the top of a rise, Daphne turned to wave. I waved back, and they were gone.

I was all alone in bandit country, without protection—unless you counted my ice axe, which I didn't. Despite Hobbes's confident assertion that bandits wouldn't bother me in daylight, I twitched and started at any noise: snatches of bird song, the wind whistling between rocks, a furry bee the size of my thumb buzzing by. Once, I leapt to my feet, hearing furtive movement, but it was just the scurrying of a small rodent. Although there was nothing that should have alarmed me, I took a sip from the monk's flask and felt up to anything. Should any bandits turn up looking for trouble, they'd get it and regret it! No one stole tents from Andy Caplet.

As time passed and nothing happened, I relaxed. I was still amazed Ralph had allowed me to come, though I suspected the department could be very persuasive. Ralph's only request was that I drafted an epic account of the expedition for the *Bugle* and the department had agreed, providing I avoided any mention of why I was there. I'd already got plenty of suitable material, especially if I embellished the leopard incident, and my bravery in guarding the camp from marauding bandits. I grabbed the camera and headed uphill to get a few suitable illustrations.

I followed what appeared to be a narrow track, and although I had to scramble on all fours like a beast on the steeper bits, the monk's potion made it seem easy. After a few minutes, I paused to take a few shots of the tents, miniscule against the backdrop of towering mountains. Eventually, I reached a ridge that dropped away into a ravine. A few stunted, twisted conifers scraped a living in the thin soil, and a small stream rippled and trilled. In the far distance, I could make out a green valley where smoke suggested the presence of people.

The hairs on the back of my neck prickled as if I was being watched.

I turned.

A leopard was making eyes at me.

I recoiled. My foot skidded on a sliver of loose rock. Losing my balance, I tumbled into the ravine, crashing down, bouncing, out of control, until the stream's icy water took away my breath. Gasping, I tried to pull myself out, but pain overwhelmed me.

A piteous groan woke me. It took a moment to realise it had come from me. When I moved, my left leg throbbed and twinged as if the devil's own pitchfork had skewered it. I was in a chamber, lit only by the feeble flickering of a small lamp. The silence, the stillness of the air, the rancid, greasy odour and the almost-sweet reek of wood-smoke suggested I was indoors. I could smell unwashed bodies and a weird background taint, reminiscent of Hobbes's feral scent. A fur blanket covered my body, and I was lying on something I could only describe as a hairy hammock. My clothes were gone.

Where on earth was I?

Memories returned: a leopard, a fall, water, cold, and pain.

Though my guts lurched with fear of what I might see, I hauled myself up onto my elbows and lifted the fur. Someone had bound leather straps around my lower leg, but my calf had swollen up like a rugby ball. A multitude of bruises and grazes adorned the rest of my body, all of them daubed with a stinking yellowish ointment. It was reassuring in a way, for if somebody had done this for me, then they meant me no harm. Probably not, anyway.

I wondered what time it was, but my watch was smashed.

'Hello!' I shouted into the smoke that was stinging my eyes. 'Is anybody there? Daphne? Hobbes?'

Had their meeting gone to plan? Had they returned, found me in the stream, and brought me here? Where was here? There were no clues. I made a tentative attempt to stand, but the resulting eruption of agony ensured I didn't try that again.

A slight movement in the air warned me I was no longer alone. A pair of deep-set, dark eyes were watching from the gloom. As they drew nearer, I saw, as I'd expected, that they were in a face. However, it was not a human face—it was too big, almost ape-like, as were its long, hairy arms. Thick, reddish brown fur, almost as shaggy as Flossy's pelt, covered its stocky body.

'Hello,' I said, forcing a smile.

It appeared to hear, but did not reply.

'Me—Andy,' I said, tapping my chest.

It came within touching range, though I kept my hands to myself. Still, something in its expression reassured me—it looked like compassion.

I stuck out my tongue like a local.

It responded in like manner.

'It's jolly good of you to look after me,' I babbled. 'A leopard surprised me and I had a fall, you know?'

It grunted, and I had a flash of inspiration—I knew what it was.

It was a Yeti.

And I was cool with that—my experiences with Hobbes had made me accept that such unhuman beings existed. Most were no worse than regular people. Many were better. It occurred to me that Hobbes might have brought Daphne and me all this way to resolve a Yeti problem—he'd mentioned dealings with them in the past, but back then, I'd assumed he was joking.

'Do you speak English?' I asked in a loud, clear voice.

It grunted again and, although the deep rumbling tones sounded more like an extended burp than a call, a group of Yetis materialised from the darkness. They gathered around, staring and making guttural noises. Once I'd got over the indignity of being an exhibit, I noticed them as individuals. Some were as tall and broad as Hobbes, while others were about my height and much slimmer. I guessed they were a mixed group of males and females. One, far smaller than the rest, ran from the gloom, making a sound like laughter. It was wearing my underpants on its head. A big Yeti grunted and gave it a playful cuff around the head.

One of the shorter ones lifted my fur coverlet and stared at my nakedness—I would have squirmed with embarrassment had I been capable. Much grunting arose from the onlookers. The shorter one bent forward and began unwrapping the leather strapping from my calf.

Although its touch was surprisingly gentle, only an urge to appear tougher than I felt stopped me moaning and screaming. But I had to check the damage, though I feared seeing a compound fracture. Gritting my teeth, I propped myself up. My calf was a mess of swelling and bruising from ankle to knee, but at least it looked straight, and no jagged bones poked out. The worst injury was a long, deep gash that was oozing blood.

The shorter Yeti gave it a gentle poke, peered into my face and grunted.

The meaning was clear.

'Yes,' I said, wincing, and allowing myself a groan for effect, 'it does hurt.'

The Yeti nodded and looked sympathetic, just like a doctor, though no doctor I'd seen before had been so smelly or so hairy. I hoped it had washed its hands—or were they paws?

Doctor Yeti emitted a staccato grunt, and four of the larger ones stepped forward.

'What are you doing?' I yelled, as they held me down. 'Let me go. No!'

Doctor Yeti prised open my wound with one hand and poured in a pungent brown gloop.

I screamed and yelled and fought and swore and passed out.

They still had me pinned down when I came round. Doctor Yeti was binding the wound with black wool and yarn, and the pain was not as bad as it had been—it was a hundred times worse, and far too bad to scream about. There was nothing I could do but take it like a man. I whimpered, and as I did, a Yeti from the supporting cast pushed a hollow bamboo tube between my teeth and poured in a bitter potion. Within seconds, the pain receded as if the volume had been turned down, and I was giggling like an idiot.

They released me, covered me up, and left me in a weird state, halfway between waking and dreaming. At the back of my mind was concern about Daphne, but everything felt far away and all things in my world were wonderful. All worry, fear and pain evaporated as I journeyed down strange, beautiful paths, which a small part of my brain knew weren't real. Now and again, Yetis would visit, and I would smile and chuckle. Now and again, they'd give me delicious, cool fruit drinks that were so beautiful I wept for happiness.

I have no idea how long I was out of the real world, but when I was more or less back, an enormous Yeti came to see me. It stared in my face, stuck out its long pink tongue, and grinned before engaging in a bout of grunting with other, smaller Yetis. Although their speech sounded no more coherent than the noises a wild boar had made in Hobbes's kitchen a couple of years back, it was clear they were discussing something and by the way they kept glancing at me, I could guess the subject. Although paranoid Andy insisted they were discussing recipes for cooking me, rational Andy wasn't much worried—why would they bother looking after me if they intended to devour me?

I couldn't quite shut up paranoid Andy, who insisted that I test my leg to see if it was up to running away. As soon as I was alone, I tried to move it.

A stab of agony nearly killed me.

But, the pain receded, leaving me comfortable and drowsy. I dozed and thought I saw Daphne in an enormous cave, lit by electric lamps. She was smiling as she talked to a tall, bearded man, but I couldn't make her see me and she was shrinking, growing smaller or further away.

I jerked awake in utter darkness. It took a few moments to understand that I'd been dreaming, or hallucinating, and that I was still stuck with the Yetis. My bladder was full, and I wasn't sure what to do, because there was no way I could stand up or even turn onto my side, and I was all alone. Even if a Yeti had been to hand, how could I explain my predicament in mime? My bladder resolved the problem by cutting through the niceties and emptying itself. Despite expecting a warm pool of piss to lie in, I heard it trickling onto the floor—my hammock had drainage holes. A little urine would not make the place stink any worse. I slept again.

When I awoke, I was swaying. The dim, smoky flames of lamps that smelled of hot butter dazzled after the blackness, but I could see my hammock was dangling from a hefty wooden pole stretched between the broad, hairy shoulders of two huge, hairy Yetis. They were carrying me along a rough-hewn rock tunnel. Whatever they had planned for me was happening.

'Where are you taking me?'

The grunts in reply might have been reassuring. Then again, they might have been threats. Either way, there was nothing I could do about it.

The eerie journey continued for hours. At last, while I was puzzling out the mystery of why the flames from the smoky little lamps appeared to be dimming, even though I could see more, we turned a corner into light. We'd reached a wide, open-fronted archway with the dazzling, low, red sun shining right in. Someone had painted the walls with depictions of local animals: wolves, leopards, yaks, things like donkeys, goats, and a great variety of birds. Bizarre little humanoid idols of translucent green stone and weird bowls and jugs that gleamed as if made of gold covered half the floor.

Moments later, we were outside, and I concentrated on breathing in the cool, breezy air, and expelling the stink of the Yetis' lair from my body. My stretcher bearers were carrying me along a rough, terrifyingly narrow path with a precipitous drop to a white-watered river hundreds of feet below. I gasped and grabbed the edges of the hammock. The two Yetis made a familiar sound—they were laughing at my fear. Although I tried to relax, nothing could break my white-knuckled grip on the hammock, though I knew it was futile—if one slipped or tripped, we would all plunge to our deaths. I tried not to think about it and failed.

Although I'd assumed we'd emerged from the tunnel at dawn, it soon became clear that night was falling. After an all-too-brief period of twilight, the lingering tendrils of sunlight slithered away, and I pulled the smelly furs up around my face to combat the chill. I hoped the Yetis could see where they were going, because I couldn't, but at least, the darkness hid the horrible drop. Myriad stars glittered in an ocean of velvet black, and the swaying and the fresh air were soothing.

I must have dropped off because it felt as if no time had passed before I made out the faint silhouettes of the mountains again. The Yetis' occasional grunts sounded more urgent, and I felt them speed up. Soon, the rosy light of early dawn was all around. After a brief exchange of grunts, the Yetis stopped, laid me on a flat area of rock-strewn ground, and bounded away. I turned my head and saw them slip behind an enormous boulder. Then they were gone.

It wasn't until I turned my head back that I noticed they'd left me beside a weathered wooden gate set in a crumbling stone wall.

I lay where I was for a few minutes, wondering what was going to happen next.

Nothing happened.

A few minutes later, still nothing had happened and since just lying there seemed futile, I thought I'd shout for help.

'Help!' I shouted.

A few moments later, the gate opened a crack and a red, weather-beaten face peered out. The gate shut.

'I could do with some assistance here,' I cried. 'I've hurt my leg. Can anybody speak English?'

I had a moment of horror that they would just leave me there, and then the gate opened again. A tall, slim, pale-faced middle-aged woman with a no-nonsense short haircut emerged.

She smiled. 'Fancy meeting you here, Mr Caplet.'

8

My jaw dropped into a gormless gape. I must know her, but from where?

'What brings you to these parts?' she asked.

'Umm?' It was not the most intelligent response, but the last thing I'd expected was that anyone would recognise me. But who was she? My brain rallied and dragged up a memory of Hobbes's spare bedroom and a doctor treating me for a fever I'd caught off Violet, the werecat I believed I was in love with. (To be clear, I had only loved her in her human form—I'm not weird.)

The name came back to me. 'Doctor Procter!' I said. 'I've had a fall and I've hurt my leg.'

'We'd better take you inside.' She glanced back at the gate and called out in a language I didn't understand. Two young men, locals in appearance and dress, ran out, picked up the hammock and carried me into a broad courtyard with a small orchard on one side and a well-tended garden on the other. They took me into a squat, stone structure that looked rather like an old fort, and set me down in a room with whitewashed walls. Everything stank of antiseptic, and everything looked medical.

With practised gentleness, they removed my fur blanket and rolled me onto a gurney, leaving me cringing with embarrassment—I was still naked.

Doctor Procter said something and a small woman who'd followed us in rolled a white cotton sheet over my middle.

'Let's look at that leg,' said Doctor Procter, picking up a pair of scissors. She cut off the Yeti's dressing and bent to examine it. 'It does not appear to be broken. This might hurt.'

She poked.

I yelped.

'Excellent,' she said, straightening up. 'That suggests there's no nerve damage. What happened?'

'I fell into a ravine. It might have been worse if I hadn't landed in water.'

She sniffed and frowned.

'What's the matter? Tell me the worst, doctor—is it gangrene?'

She smiled. 'No, the wound looks clean, there's no sign of infection and it appears to be healing. There's an unusual smell, though. Who's been looking after you?'

'A Yeti. I didn't catch its name.'

She stared into my eyes. 'Did you hit your head when you fell?'

'No ... well, I probably did ... but what are you implying? A bunch of Yetis looked after me and two of them carried me here. They were very hairy and not very clean.'

The doctor smiled. 'Some local villagers must have looked after you. The traditional ones still wear yak skin cloaks—that would explain the hairiness. You were in shock and confused.'

'Yes, doctor,' I said, in case she thought I was mad.

She looked around, saw we were alone, and whispered in my ear. 'It's best not to mention our hairy friends when the staff are about—relations between the locals and the Yetis are rather delicate at the moment.'

'Okay,' I said.

She resumed her usual brisk voice. 'I'll apply surgical strips to keep the wound closed and put on a fresh dressing. It may hurt a bit. When that's done, we'll get you to the ward. You'll need a few days' rest before you're back on your feet.'

A few minutes later, my leg a throbbing inferno of agony, but with its wound conventionally dressed, and with me wearing a baggy cotton nightshirt, the two young men carried me to a small ward and laid me on a hard bed. I fell asleep almost at once.

A wrinkled raisin of a woman with gentle hands woke me. 'Eat!' she said with a gap-toothed grin.

Taking care not to jar my leg, I sat up. My bed was one of five lined up against the wall and was the furthest from the window. The fierce burning torment of my leg had diminished to a mild soreness while the swelling below the knee was barely noticeable. I smelled food and hoped for the best. The little woman presented me with a large bowl on a battered aluminium tray—I was not too surprised to see tsampa again. But I was famished and, after mumbling thanks, I stuffed my face until I feared my stomach might explode. There was also a glass of water—its sparkling icy freshness, a pleasant contrast to the buttery tea I'd expected.

When I'd finished, I lay back on the pillow and worried about Daphne. Was she worrying about me? My eyes closed.

When they opened again, it was late afternoon to judge by the light, and I'd gained a room-mate, an elderly white man with a deeply tanned face, or at least the bits I could see—the rest of it lurked behind a magnificent white beard and moustache. He was snoring gently in the bed at my side.

Doctor Procter appeared. 'How are you feeling, Mr Caplet?' she asked, popping an old-fashioned thermometer into my mouth before I could reply.

'Mmfeelingoaky.' I said like a bad ventriloquist.

'Good.' She touched my forehead, stared into my eyes and made a note in a battered leather-bound book before removing the thermometer. 'Still no sign of fever, I'm glad to say.'

'Good.'

'How's the leg?'

'A lot better, thanks.'

'Excellent.' She sat at the end of the bed and smiled. 'What brought you to this neck of the mountains?'

I was on the verge of telling her when I remembered we were on a secret mission—even if that was all I knew about it. 'I'm here on … umm … a walking trip with my wife, Daphne.'

'You're married?' The good doctor looked even more astonished than she had been on recognising me outside the gates.

I nodded.

'Are you here with an organised tour group? I only ask because the guides don't tend to bring tourists to these parts—there are bandits.'

'No, there are just the four of us … or five if you include Flossy.'

'Flossy?'

'Our yak. Otherwise, it's just me and Daphne, Akar and Hobbes.'

'Inspector Hobbes?'

'Yes.'

'That explains a lot.' She smiled. 'But where are they

now?'

I shook my head. 'I have no idea—I'm not even sure where I am. Daphne must think the worst—they'll have returned to camp and found I wasn't there. I should have stayed near the tents, but I didn't really go that far away.'

Doctor Procter stood up. 'I'll mention it to Dolma, our secretary. She'll work something out.'

'Thank you, but what are you doing here?' I asked.

'I'm on a year's sabbatical. I always wanted to see these mountains and jumped at the opportunity when it arose. Medical facilities are sparse here, and medical problems are rife. I trust you have insurance?'

I nodded—the department had made provisions for accident or illness.

She glanced at her watch. 'Good. I have a sick child to visit in the next valley and I must go. I'll see you when I get back.'

She bustled away, and I lay in my bed, worried, helpless and bored. As evening crept into the ward, the tiny, wrinkled woman reappeared with two mugs and handed one to me—it looked and smelt like British-style tea. She placed the other mug on the cabinet by my neighbour's bed. The old man woke as it chinked against a glass of water. He sat up, murmured a few words in what I took to be the local language, and gave me a curt nod.

'Hello,' I said and took a sip of tea—it was good.

'English?' he asked.

I confirmed the diagnosis.

'M'name's Twilley,' he said, his voice brittle and breathless.

'Mine's Caplet. Andy Caplet.'

He took a quick swig from his mug and grimaced. 'It'll

do, but I'd kill for a whisky.'

I smiled and took another sip. It was like nectar after the yak butter variety.

'What brings you to this place?' asked Twilley.

I explained my fall, leaving out any mention of Yetis.

He looked sympathetic. 'I've taken a few tumbles in my time—it's a hazard of mountaineering.'

'Is that why you're here?'

He shook his head and took another gulp of tea. 'I'm afraid my climbing days are long gone. The quack says I shouldn't even walk upstairs—my heart, you know?'

'I'm sorry to hear that.'

'Just one of those things. Reckon I'm not long for this world, though it'll be a wrench to leave these mountains. Stayed on after the last expedition and haven't been home since. Still, mustn't grumble—life's been fun so far and I wouldn't change anything ... well, not much anyway. Where are you from?'

'Sorenchester—it's a small town in the Cotswolds.'

'Sorenchester, eh? Name rings a bell. Can't think why.'

Old Mr Twilley lay back on his pillows, an expression of deep concentration on his face. Within a few seconds, he was snoring again. I finished my tea and fretted about Daphne. Though I was confident Hobbes would ensure her safety, she'd no doubt be distraught at my disappearance. And what if bandits had ransacked the camp in my absence? I fell into a troubled sleep.

Doctor Procter's brisk voice woke me. 'Come along, Mr Twilley, it's time for your medication.'

She was standing over him, an exasperated frown crossing her brow.

'Shan't,' said Twilley. 'What's the point?'

'Because it's keeping you alive,' she said.

'Sorry, but all these damned drugs you've got me on aren't giving me anymore life, they're just stretching out the little I've got left. Whatever you do, the thread of life is going to break soon and I can't see the point of just being when I can't do anything. I've enjoyed what life I've had, but I've had enough now.'

The doctor shrugged. 'I won't force you if you're sure—but on your own head be it.'

'Thanks, doc, much appreciated. How long have I got? Without the drugs, I mean.'

She shrugged. 'A week, perhaps a month, but you could go any time if something upsets you.'

Twilley smiled. 'That'll do.'

The doctor nodded and turned to me. 'How are you?'

'Much better,' I said.

She checked my temperature and pulse again and smiled. 'That all looks good. Any pain?'

'Not much, unless I move.'

'Excellent. Your leg will take some time to fully heal, but I think the worst is over. I'll dress it again in a day or two. Goodbye.' She walked away, her walking boots incongruous below her white coat.

After that exhausting exchange, I thought I might take a nap, but Mr Twilley had other ideas.

'Just remembered why Sorenchester rang a bell—a chap in a climbing party I led came from there. Name of Squire—Clarence Squire, if I recall rightly. D'you know him?'

'Umm ... no ... I don't think so. I know a Colonel Squire, but I think his first name is Toby.'

Twilley beamed. 'That's right—Clarence sometimes spoke of a young rogue of a nephew with that name. The black sheep of the family, as I recall—mucked up his army career and made a living from second-hand cars.'

I nodded and thought back to some dark times at home. 'Toby Squire is still a rogue, Mr Twilley—I've had dealings with him myself.'

'Now we're friends, you may call me Piers.'

'And you can call me Andy.' I smiled.

Piers continued. 'Clarence was a good man. Our group was climbing in the Karakorams—must be forty years or more ago. Anyway, a boulder broke free from a glacier and rolled straight at us. I had my back to it and it would have killed me but for Clarence, who shoved me out of harm's way. Trouble was, it smashed his leg. Gad, the blood! We thought he was a goner, but he was tough. We did what we could, and carried him to the nearest hospital. It was about four days' march away and Clarence was in a bad way with the pain and an infection. He became delirious, and we thought we were losing him until an old monk appeared out of nowhere and dosed him with some evil-smelling gloop. It kept him going until we got him to the doctors.'

'What happened to him?' I asked.

'They air-lifted him out when he was strong enough. Turned out he was rich—owned half of Sorenchester, I believe. Never heard from him again.'

A deep memory surfaced. 'I heard that Colonel Squire inherited his estates when his uncle died in a climbing accident.'

'Poor blighter must have succumbed on the way back,' said Piers. 'That's tragic—he seemed so much better. Explains why he never got in touch though.' He blew his nose and shook his head.

'I'm sorry.' I said, wishing I'd kept quiet.

'No, don't be,' said Piers. 'Best to know. When he didn't write, I thought he'd blamed me for the accident.'

He sounded so sad and frail that I tried to change the

subject. 'Umm ... why did you stay here?'

'Liked it. Friendly people. Food's not bad when you're used to it. And no one bothers me. Back home there was always someone making fun of my name, but I could be myself here. Worked as an engineer for local projects—pay was terrible compared to what it is in the so-called civilised world, but stuff is cheap. Bought a house, lived well, indulged my passion for climbing. Life's had its ups and downs, but on the whole, I've been lucky.'

Rather late in the day, I realised I'd got another story for the *Bugle* if I played my cards right. Ralph would be pleased, and it would make up in part for having lost my camera in the fall. 'Have you climbed with anyone famous?' I asked.

'Expect so,' said Piers. 'A film star or two, a former president of the USA, the king of ... '

'Oh,' I said and chuckled, 'I've just got what you meant about your name! Piers Twilley—it sounds just like Pierced Wil ... '

'I know damned well what it sounds like. Shut up and leave me alone.' He turned away.

'I'm awfully sorry.' I could have kicked myself.

When I woke next morning, his bed was empty—he'd died in the night. Although he'd not had long left, I couldn't help suspecting that my thoughtlessness had been the final straw. In fact, I felt so guilty and sad that I almost refused breakfast. Had it been tsampa again, I might well have done. However, when the wrinkled little lady came in and offered me a plate of primrose-yellow scrambled eggs, I felt it would seem churlish if I refused.

Although Doctor Procter checked on me after the little lady had cleared my breakfast things, I was alone for most of the morning, apart from when a cheerful local chap cleaned the little ward with a pungent antiseptic that made my eyes run. There was nothing to do, nothing to read, and nothing to write on. All I had left was to try enjoying my own company, which turned out to be rather boring. I couldn't help thinking about Piers Twilley and regretting my thoughtless remark, though I moved on to worrying about Daphne. I'd progressed to wondering if it was nearly lunchtime yet when a shadow darkened the window.

I looked up to see a pair of dark eyes beneath a thicket of eyebrows on an ugly, grinning face.

Hobbes had found me.

Two minutes later, the ward's door opened and Daphne rushed in with Hobbes a respectful few paces behind. I smiled and raised my hand. 'Hi!'

'Are you alright?' Daphne asked, reaching for my hand.

I nodded. 'Yes, but my leg is sore. It's not broken though.'

'I'm just so relieved to see you in one piece,' she said, tears in her eyes as she bent to hug me.

'It's so great to see you,' I said when she released me. 'How did you find me?'

'Lhamo, told us where you were,' said Hobbes.

'Lhamo?'

'The young Yeti who treated your leg. She seemed very kind.'

'So, she was a she!' I said. 'I thought she was. How did she know where to find you?'

'We were negotiating with representatives of her people.'

'You know,' I said, 'I knew at once they were Yetis.'

Daphne smiled. 'Well done! I was sceptical about their existence, despite the briefing. But we met them!'

'Doctor Procter told me to keep quiet about them,' I said. 'She said there'd been trouble.'

'Yes,' said Daphne, 'and it would have got worse if Mr Hobbes hadn't persuaded the parties to compromise.'

'That was on the day when you were meant to be guarding the tents,' said Hobbes, looking stern. 'What kind of job do you call that? Bandits took all our stuff.'

'I'm sorry,' I said, hoping he wasn't too angry. 'It wasn't my fault. A leopard scared me and I slipped and fell. I woke up in a Yeti cave.'

'Mr Hobbes is teasing,' said Daphne. 'Lhamo told us everything that happened. That's how we found you, though it was a mighty long trek.'

'Good, but ... umm ... how? She didn't seem to know any English; none of them did.'

'Mr Hobbes is fluent in Yetish.'

'Hardly fluent,' said Hobbes, 'but I get by.' He glanced at the window. 'Pleasant though this cosy chat is, we need to get moving.'

'What d'you mean?' I asked.

'We have to be back at the airfield by midday tomorrow,' said Daphne. 'Otherwise, we're stranded for at least another week.'

'But I can't walk. And it must be nearly lunchtime!'

'Where there's a will, there's a way,' said Hobbes with a smile.

That sounded alarm bells. 'What do you mean?'

'Nothing, but I need to think how we're going to proceed.'

He looked innocent, in so far as he could ever look innocent, but I'd had enough experience to suspect he already had something in mind, and that I wouldn't like it. A thought occurred. 'If you're in so much of a hurry, what would you have done if you hadn't found me in time?'

'We'd have kept on looking for you, of course,' said Daphne.

'We couldn't leave you behind,' said Hobbes, though I was sure a guilty flicker crossed his face.

'Ah, Mr Hobbes!' Doctor Procter entered the ward with a smile. 'The way the staff were talking, I thought it must be you. Thank you for sorting out Andy's insurance and for your donation—it will help us continue our work.'

'Dr Procter,' said Hobbes, and gave a low bow of the type that must have been fashionable two centuries ago. 'We've come to collect him.'

'Of course.' She turned and smiled at me. 'It's been pleasant to see an old patient, and I've no doubt we'll meet again when I'm back home. Look after that leg of yours. Keep it clean and dry and it should heal without any problems. If it hurts or bleeds or if there's any discharge or fever, then contact a doctor.'

'Goodbye.' She shook my hand, said farewell to Hobbes and Daphne, and bustled away.

'Let's go,' said Hobbes.

I pointed out a problem. 'I lost my clothes. All I've got is this nightshirt.'

'What's this then?' asked Daphne, pulling a yak-hair bag from under my bed and upending a load of clothes. 'They look like yours.'

They were, too, and someone had washed them, though they retained a faint smell of Yeti.

I started to dress with Daphne's help, but my bandaged leg wouldn't fit into my trousers.

'I'll rip it off,' said Hobbes, causing a gasp of alarm

until I realised he meant the trouser leg. He tore a bit off and I tried again.

One-legged trousers on a two-legged man looked weird, but I had no choice.

Daphne checked the rest of the contents of the Yeti bag. My camera was there, as was a tiny figurine of a homunculus carved from translucent green stone.

Hobbes picked it up and grinned. 'It's a Yeti idol—it's a gift for good luck.'

I liked the look of the thing—I'd keep it on my desk at work.

'And we might need it,' said Hobbes. 'I've worked out how to get to the plane on time. My plan should work, but a little luck will be helpful.' He chuckled and slapped me on the shoulder in a way I supposed he meant to be reassuring.

'What is the plan?'

'A little cruise,' he said. 'But there are a few things I need to arrange first. I'll speak to Dolma, the secretary—she knows what's what.'

He left Daphne and me alone.

'A cruise will make a nice change after all the walking,' said Daphne.

'It won't be,' I said.

'Cynic!'

'I'm not—I just know what he's like.'

9

Hobbes returned after about half an hour. He was smiling. 'Everything's arranged, and it's time to go.'

'And quickly?' I said, joking—there was no chance of me going anywhere fast.

'And quickly!' he confirmed.

I did not expect he would grab me and sling me over his shoulder like an old sack, though it wasn't the first time he'd treated me in such a cavalier fashion. My protests that this was no way for an injured man to travel were ignored, and he lugged me outside, where the hospital staff had gathered in awed silence. He deposited me on the back of a small grey yak.

'This is Nak,' said Hobbes. 'She's agreed to carry you. Comfortable?'

'Not really,' I said, despite the padded saddle.

'How's your leg?' asked Daphne.

'Alright, I suppose.'

'Good,' said Hobbes. He handed us bars of Kendal Mint Cake. 'In case you get hungry—there'll be no time for cooking.'

My stomach groaned. It was already missing its lunch, even though I suspected it would have been tsampa again.

'Backpacks on and let's go,' said Hobbes.

Daphne did as he asked without complaint—she was

still in awe of him, despite having known him for a couple of years and having got to know some of his odd ways.

I thanked the staff, waved, and clutched the saddle as Nak set off.

Before us was a flat, dusty, grey plain with only the occasional shrivelled plant to break the monotony. Snow-capped peaks hemmed us in on three sides.

'How far away is that meadow where we landed?' I asked after half an hour of swaying on Nak's back had made me a little seasick ... or it might have been the mint cake I'd wolfed.

'Thirty-five miles, more or less,' said Hobbes. 'That's as the crow flies.'

'And how fast are we going?'

'Nowhere near fast enough to get there on time—it's more like a hundred miles as the yak walks and it's mostly up hill.'

'But Dilip will be expecting us tomorrow,' I said. 'He won't stay long.'

'So, we're making for the airfield in town. I've contacted him, and he'll wait, so he can fly us from there to the airport. If all goes well, we should be in time to catch our flight home.'

'So, how far away is the airfield?'

'That's also a little over a hundred miles if we walked it.'

'There may be a flaw in your plan,' I said.

'You mentioned a cruise?' said Daphne.

Hobbes grinned. 'There is a more direct route.'

She nodded. 'I get it. We'll go there by boat. That'll be fun.'

'Don't be silly,' I said, shaking my head. 'There aren't

any cruise boats up here. Haven't you seen the rivers? Nothing could sail up here against the current, and even if it could it would be smashed to matchwood on the rocks on the way downstream.'

'Wooden boats would,' said Hobbes, 'but the one I'm thinking of is made of yak hide.'

'That's no better,' I said. 'It'll be smashed anyway, and we'll be smashed too, and I've already had more than enough of that sort of thing for one expedition ... and I'm hungry.'

'I'm sure Mr Hobbes knows what he's doing,' said Daphne with sublime, naive confidence. 'We'll soon be approaching the foothills where the rivers won't be quite so wild.'

I wasn't as trusting as her. 'It's still not going to be what I'd call a cruise—the three of us and that yak in a flimsy skin boat is not my idea of fun. Don't forget my bad leg.'

'Which matches your attitude, Grumpy,' said Daphne with a grin.

'Nak, of course, will not be coming with us,' said Hobbes. 'Yaks don't do well at lower altitudes. Three in a boat will be fine—we should be able to buy one in the next village.' He glanced at the sky, sniffed the air and led us onto a side path.

Swaying in my saddle with my leg throbbing but bearable, I hoped he wasn't so mad as to try it.

But I knew he was.

After another hour or so, we reached a squalid scattering of twenty or more stone huts lounging around a square of compressed earth that was redeemed by a fragrant, blossoming almond tree in the middle. Several ill-favoured men loafed in its shade, watching with cold eyes and hard faces. Chickens scratched in the dirt, a goat stared from a window, and a handful of wide-eyed children gathered around, watching our every move as if we were aliens just arrived from Mars. At the end of an alley just wide enough for a yak to pass, a river grumbled and roared. On its bank, like giant beetles basking in the sun, lay several small, upturned boats.

'Oh, no!' I said.

'Oh, yes!' said Hobbes with an evil chuckle as he swept me from Nak's back and sat me on a low stone wall. Nak sauntered across the street to a patch of wiry-looking grass and started grazing.

'What'll happen to her?' I asked.

'She'll find her own way home,' said Hobbes. 'She's a clever beast. And now, it's time for some haggling.'

He beckoned to one loafer, a villainous-looking man with a scar splitting his face from brow to chin. The man shrugged, stood up and swaggered over. Hobbes greeted him by sticking out his tongue and smiling before engaging him in a conversation that involved a great deal of gesticulation, posturing and raised voices. At one point the talk turned angry, and the group under the tree got up. I feared trouble, and hoped there wouldn't be, because the little hospital wouldn't have room for all of them—the poor innocents had no idea what Hobbes was capable of. Then he handed over money, smiles returned, and peace was restored.

'Isn't this exciting?' said Daphne, grinning.

All I could manage in response was a sickly smile while I fretted about the horrors to come. I didn't explain my worries—she'd find out soon enough, and why should I spoil her mood?

Leaving us to rest in the shade, Hobbes sauntered to the river bank, turned a boat the right way up, ensured it was secured to the old jetty, and shoved it into the water.

'Our craft awaits,' he said, coming back to join us. 'By the way, those chaps under the tree were the ones who stole our stuff. I have retrieved our passports and this— a souvenir for you.' He handed me the monk's flask. 'I told the chief it was a cure for baldness, and that he had such a fine head of hair that he'd never need it.'

'Thanks,' I said, and put it into my hairy Yeti bag.

Daphne stared at the villains and turned to me. 'It was just as well you fell down that ravine.'

'Why?'

'Because, you might have tried to stop those guys, and they might have really hurt you.'

'I *was* really hurt,' I said, peeved by her callous attitude to my suffering.

'I know, but they could have killed you and then what would I have done?'

Mollified, I gave her hand a gentle squeeze.

'So, all's well that ends well,' said Hobbes. 'And now I declare boating season is open.'

Daphne and Hobbes loaded our bits of baggage into the boat—no more than a rickety framework of sticks, with skin stretched over the outside.

Luxury it was not.

Primitive it was.

Hobbes returned, picked me up beneath one massive arm, carried me to the boat and put me down in the narrower end.

'Is this thing safe?' I asked, appalled that we were trusting our lives to such a tiny, flimsy craft. Perhaps the river wasn't as mad as the ones I'd seen in the mountains, but it still looked pretty wild to me.

'It's perfectly safe … ' said Hobbes, ' … until we reach

the rapids.'

'And then?'

He shrugged, and stepped into the blunt bit with a cheerful cry: 'All aboard the Skylark!'

It dismayed me how much the little craft swayed, and how close was the water. Daphne propped me up with a bag so I could see what was going on and made sure my leg was as comfortable as it could be in such a confined space.

'How are you going to row this thing?' I asked, looking in vain for oars or paddles.

'No need—with luck, the current will take us,' said Hobbes. 'Let's hope that idol of yours works.'

I hoped so too, for although I didn't believe in lucky charms, I knew how hopeless he was in any boat that required rowing. Furthermore, he couldn't swim, and should he fall in, he'd plummet straight to the bottom. In fact, swimming was the one area where I could bask in superiority over him—I'd earned a bronze swimming certificate at school and, more recently, Daphne had given me lessons in the local pool that had transformed my feeble splashing into near competence. Not that it would help, for when the inevitable smash happened, I doubted my leg would let me swim. Yet, that did not worry me—the rocks would pulverise us long before we could drown.

Hobbes reached onto the bank and pulled a long wooden pole from a rack. He tested it for weight and balance and nodded. Then, after sniffing the air and gazing at the current, he cast us off, waved at the children, and poled the flimsy boat into midstream.

There was a moment of calm before the current struck. Then my head jerked back, and we were careering through foaming water, the green banks zipping by in a blur. Like so often when I was with Hobbes, my life was suddenly out of my control. Although I should have been used to it, it didn't stop the utter terror. Even my worst imaginings had not envisaged the river hurling us along at such a breakneck speed. Daphne knelt by my side, a massive grin splitting her face whenever I turned to check she wasn't too frightened. Hobbes stood at the back end (stern seemed far too grand a word), wielding his pole like a lancer, fending off rocks and keeping us away from the shallows.

I sprawled on the bottom, gripping the side with one hand and moaning as spray wet my face. 'We'll be dashed to pieces! How fast are we going?'

Hobbes glanced at the river and then at the banks. 'I would estimate a little over five miles per hour.'

'Nonsense. We must be doing at least fifty!'

'I don't think so, Andy.'

'It feels fast,' said Daphne, her face aglow.

'Hold on,' cried Hobbes. 'Boulders ahoy!'

He jabbed at one massive rock, stepped forward to fend off another, and whooped like a cowboy in the old Western films he loved when the squalid little tub scraped and juddered against some unseen obstacle. 'This is the life,' he said.

'It'll be the death of me,' I muttered.

I did what I could to relax, which proved far more effective than I could have imagined, for after perhaps an hour of sheer terror as our flimsy craft bucked, span, sped and lurched, the rocking motion got to me and I dropped off. Or fainted through fear. In any case, when I opened my eyes, it was dark, and I could feel Daphne asleep at my side. Hobbes, silhouetted against the starlit sky, jabbed the pole as if he was a knight fighting off a horde of ogres. I yawned and gasped as a spray of icy water dampened my face.

'Sleep well?' asked Hobbes.

'Not bad. How long was I asleep?'

'Six or seven hours.'

'Are we nearly there yet?'

'No, we're about half way. If we keep going like this, I'd estimate another eight hours.'

'Eight hours! With nothing to eat? Is that any way to treat an invalid?'

'Probably not,' he acknowledged, shoving us away from a rock and spinning the bobbing boat, 'but it can't be helped.'

'Is there any more of that mint cake?'

'I'm afraid not. The bandits took most of it—they liked it. Perhaps a drink of water will quell your hunger pangs for a while.'

'Perhaps,' I said, more than a little sceptical since I felt empty enough to devour a whole yak. 'Where's the water bottle?'

'I gave it to the bandit as part of the price for his boat. We still have a tin mug.'

'How will that help? It's like saying there's no dinner tonight, but never mind, here's a plate.'

My sarcasm was wasted on Hobbes, who pulled the mug from his string bag and dipped it in the river. The boat lurched as he bent and, for a moment, I feared he might go in. 'There you go.'

'I can't drink river water!'

'It's clean and quite safe … '

I took it and sipped. It was icy cold.

' … unless there's a dead yak upstream.'

I nearly spat it out, but chose to believe he was joking. Besides, the water tasted fresh, as if drawn from the first river when the earth was still young, and it tingled on the tongue like soda water. I drained the mug and dozed again.

Next thing I knew, the rosy glow of dawn was all around. Our little boat still rocked and rolled, though not in a such a frantic manner. Daphne slept on, and Hobbes was still at his post. It surprised me to see the mountains so far behind us, though we were still in hill country. My bladder was crying out for relief—a predicament since I could not stand.

I told Hobbes, whose swarthy face glistened with a fine film of dew.

He handed me the mug.

'I can't use that—we'll want to drink from it.'

'You can rinse it.'

'Yeah, but it's not nice, is it?'

'No,' he admitted, 'but unless you want to flood the boat, the only other option is that I dangle you over the side. There're risks in that: we might capsize, we might strike a rock when I'm busy, or I might drop you.'

I filled the mug, tipped the contents overboard, and repeated the procedure. Then I rinsed it out as well as I could. How Hobbes and Daphne managed their lavatorial requirements, I didn't care to find out.

The rising sun cleared the hilltops, golden light enveloped us, the temperature rose, and little biting bugs beset me. We were passing through a land of lush green forests, alive with bird song and movement. Not that I cared—my rumbling stomach took up too much of my attention.

Daphne woke and stretched. 'Morning. Andy, where's my coffee?'

'Umm … ' I responded, confounded by the question.

She chuckled, sat up and turned to Hobbes. 'How are

we doing?'

'Very well,' said Hobbes, 'though the current has slowed. We should be on time if we carry on like this.'

'And if we don't?' she asked.

Hobbes shrugged. 'We'll improvise, but I think we'll make it.' He began using the pole to push us onward.

To my horror, Daphne picked up the mug, filled it and drank deeply from the river. I never let on what I'd done in it.

As the temperature soared and sweat soaked my clothes, we passed a ramshackle village overflowing with goats and scrawny chickens. A small child sitting on the bank rubbed her eyes, gaped, and shouted. People emerged from every house, pointing, waving and yelling as if the circus had come to town.

'What's up with them?' I asked.

'They didn't expect to see anybody on the river,' said Hobbes.

'Why not? There were plenty of boats upstream.'

Daphne grinned. 'I think we're the first to come down this year.'

'Why?'

'Because the river is still in spate with all the melt water. It's far too dangerous for most. Give it a couple more weeks and it will be relatively placid.'

Hobbes nodded. 'According to the old villain who sold me the boat, only a madman would attempt the river at this time of year.'

I felt sick as I glared at them. 'Why didn't you tell me?'

'We didn't want to worry you,' said Daphne.

I gasped. 'You risked our lives!'

'But we survived,' said Hobbes, 'and you've slept most of the way, so where's the harm?'

'Well ... umm ... ' It was difficult to argue against this,

though I wasn't happy they'd kept me in the dark, even if it had been for my own good.

Daphne ruffled my hair and soothed my rattled nerves. Hobbes sniffed the air. 'We should be there in a little over an hour.'

We were now drifting on a placid flow beneath a warm sun with the white-capped peaks far behind. Overhanging trees lent us a little welcome shade and the earthy scent of the forest came as a shock after the mountain air. I reached for the camera to capture the scene, but it didn't work. I guessed the batteries were flat.

Daphne took a few snaps on her mobile. 'I've got a signal at last,' she said a few minutes later.

It was the first sign of our return to civilisation and I could have cheered—the mountains, though awe-inspiring and majestic, were too dangerous. Even so, deep down, I wouldn't have missed the trip for all the world.

After about an hour, the reek of decay and smoke warned us that we were approaching a small town.

'We're here,' said Hobbes as we rounded a bend. He punted our trusty boat toward a solid-looking concrete and steel jetty. 'This is where we say farewell to the river. Everybody out and let's get moving.'

This time I was expecting it when he slung me over his shoulder. He sprang ashore, sat me on an upturned wooden barrel, and helped Daphne to unload our stuff—so much less than we'd started with. A curious crowd gathered, jabbering in the local language. Hobbes greeted them and spoke to a rotund, dark-faced individual with a mouthful of gold. After a few minutes of gesticulating, the man grinned and led us into the village. The crowd howled with laughter when Hobbes tucked me under his arm like a baby, despite my best efforts to look cool and composed. Daphne walked alongside, chuckling to herself.

The rotund man led us towards a battered, rusty, black Mercedes with 'Taxi' painted on its side in shaky yellow letters. He shouted, and a dozy-looking man emerged from a shack to greet us. Following a few moments of haggling and an exchange of cash, Hobbes placed me inside the taxi. The cracked and discoloured black vinyl of the back seat could have done service as a barbecue, and the hot air felt suffocating with its overwhelming odours of sweat, garlic, spice and farmyard. It all came as a shock after the clean air we'd enjoyed. Our few bits of baggage went into the boot, which the driver tied shut with a length of frayed rope. Hobbes sat in the front, Daphne sat beside me, and the driver hopped in and started the engine.

My limited experience of foreign taxi drivers had led me to expect a certain amount of madness, disregard for traffic conventions, and a cavalier attitude to the lives and well-being of his passengers. Our man did not let me down. The only consolation was that it only took a few heart-stopping minutes before we reached the airfield where Dilip was checking his Cessna. The taxi pulled up in a cloud of dust and, ten minutes later, we were airborne. In a little over two hours we'd be at the international airport.

'That went according to plan,' said Hobbes, looking pleased.

'Great, but when do we get to eat?' I asked.

'At the airport,' he said. 'We'll have time for a good meal. There is a fine restaurant there.'

'Excellent,' I said, steeling myself against the gnawing hunger. 'Then what?'

'Then we fly home,' said Daphne. 'Thank you, Mr Hobbes, for asking us on this trip. It's been amazing, hasn't it, Andy?'

Amazing was not the word I'd have chosen, but I nodded and smiled.

I should have been a diplomat.

10

I couldn't stop yawning, Daphne seemed dazed, and even Hobbes looked bleary. We'd just disembarked from the Airbus into a drizzly, blustery afternoon at London Heathrow after what had felt like an interminable flight, battling headwinds and turbulence. Even though I was in an airport wheelchair being pushed by Daphne through the bustle, the sense of comparative space was a delight, despite the thought of the long queues at immigration and customs.

A youngish, but otherwise nondescript woman in a smart grey suit appeared as if from nowhere. 'Mr Hobbes and party?'

Hobbes nodded.

'Nicola Smethurst.' She showed some ID. 'Would you follow me, please?'

She led us through an unmarked side door into a small room.

'Please, take a seat.' Nicola gestured at the soft-leather sofa along one side and picked a tablet computer from a table.

'How was your trip?' she asked as Hobbes and Daphne made themselves comfortable.

'Successful,' said Hobbes. 'I mediated between the opposing parties, banged a few heads together, and helped them achieve a satisfactory settlement.'

'Excellent.' Nicola tapped away at her tablet. 'Were there any problems?'

'Many,' said Hobbes, 'but nothing my team couldn't handle.'

I grinned, happy he regarded me as part of the team, though I couldn't help wondering if I'd been more trouble than I was worth.

Hobbes continued. 'As you can see, Mr Caplet received an injury to his leg during his official duties, and we lost some equipment to marauding bandits.'

Nicola smiled. 'How is your leg, Mr Caplet?'

'Oh ... umm ... it's getting better.'

'Mrs Caplet's archaeological skills and knowledge were crucial to the success of the mission,' said Hobbes. 'Akar fulfilled his transport and guiding role to perfection.'

'And yaks are nice,' I said. 'They've got lovely ... '

'Quite,' said Nicola.

Daphne nudged me and I shut up.

'One other thing,' said Hobbes.

Nicola raised her eyes.

'As a consequence of his accident, Mr Caplet has become acquainted with our friends.'

'I see.' She ran her gaze over me and didn't appear much impressed. 'Can we trust him?'

'I'll guarantee it,' said Hobbes, fixing me with a look that made me nod, though I wasn't sure what I was agreeing to.

'Don't talk about the friends who looked after you when you fell,' Daphne explained.

'You mean the Yet ... '

'Shh!' said Daphne.

'Why?'

'Because I say so,' said Hobbes.

'I'll keep quiet.'

'Good,' said Hobbes, smiling like a friendly crocodile.

Nicola nodded. 'In that case, thank you for your help. Your car is waiting outside. Goodbye.'

'I'll join you in a day or two,' said Hobbes, turning to Daphne and me. 'I must make my report.'

Nicola opened another door, helped Daphne push me through, stepped back inside, and shut it behind us. We were outside, and the first hints of evening were already darkening the cloudy sky. A damp, chilly breeze raised goose pimples on my bandaged, but trouser leg-less leg, and I hoped we wouldn't be out there for too long. But within seconds, a large grey car pulled up and a morose-looking driver got out, showed his ID and said he would drive us home. He helped me from the heavy airport wheelchair and onto the back seat without causing my leg too much discomfort. As Daphne got in beside me, he stowed our baggage, took his position at the wheel and set off. Despite roadworks and heavy rain along much of the M4 motorway, we reached Sorenchester in under two hours.

I dozed much of the way, and it was only when the car pulled up outside our house that it struck me that there would be problems. 'How am I going to get into the house? How do I get upstairs to bed? And ... umm ... what about the bathroom?'

'Mr Hobbes has arranged something,' said Daphne through a yawn.

The tiny, frail-looking figure of Mrs Goodfellow welcomed us from the doorway of our house. 'Hello, dears,' she said in her quavering voice. 'Did you have a pleasant holiday?'

'Lovely,' I said, 'but I can't walk.'

'So, the old fellow said. Don't worry though, I'm here.

He asked me to stay until you are more mobile.'

She prised me from the car seat, and, despite Daphne and the driver's attempts to help, insisted that I use her bony shoulder as a crutch. She was much stronger than she looked, and I had few qualms about this, except that it seemed undignified and wrong for a grown man to be seen leaning on a little old lady, even if that man had only one functioning leg. Still, I doubted many people would be out in the rain. I'd probably get away with it.

The harsh voice of Len 'Featherlight' Binks, proprietor of The Feathers, the town's grottiest pub, shattered that hope. 'Nice trousers, Caplet. Now, hop it!'

'Hi, Featherlight,' I said. Despite the downpour, he was wearing his habitual stained vest and saggy-waisted trousers with his bellies flopping over the top.

Featherlight smiled at Mrs Goodfellow and bowed to Daphne—he appeared to admire her, despite her poor taste in marrying me.

'Such a nice man,' said Mrs Goodfellow, as he left us in peace. 'Always so polite!'

That she believed it was annoying, yet it was a peculiar quirk of Featherlight's character that he treated women with old-fashioned courtesy, a complete contrast to the way he treated men, in particular the lowlifes that drank in his pub.

Mrs Goodfellow lugged me into the house and set me down on the sofa in the lounge.

'It's good to be home,' I said.

Daphne nodded. 'And it was great to be away too.'

'Apart from the boring food,' I said. 'And the hardship … and the pain … and the danger.'

'But we wouldn't have seen the mountains, the rivers, the lakes or the snow leopard. We wouldn't have enjoyed the company of our friends, and the history, and the mysticism of the place. We wouldn't have such wonderful memories.' Her brown eyes shone. 'We should get out in the wild more often.'

I nodded some sort of agreement. She was right, of course—we had seen wonderful things, but there was something about home comforts and safety and not getting altitude sickness, and not being frightened into ravines by leopards that held more appeal. Nevertheless, I felt I should offer some encouragement. 'Great idea,' I said, 'but can we wait until my leg's better?'

She smiled. 'Of course. I'm going for a shower.'

'I'll put the kettle on,' said Mrs Goodfellow, and started for the kitchen.

'Umm ... before you do that, I need the bathroom, but how will I get upstairs?'

'You won't, dear.'

'So, what do I do?'

'The same as usual, except down here.'

'I can't!'

'Don't worry—I've borrowed Mrs Fothergill's commode. The poor old dear is in hospital with her feet and doesn't need it.'

Poor old dear, indeed! I'd met Mrs Fothergill at Blackdog Street and was sure she was only in her late sixties—decades younger than Mrs G.

There's little dignity in using a commode, but the relief was worth any embarrassment, and at least the old girl left me alone until she returned to take it away.

'Thank you,' I said when all was back to relative normality.

'Always pleased to help, dear. It takes me back to my nursing days.'

Daphne, clean, fresh and changed, came back down

ten minutes later, just in time for the old girl's tea, which was infinitely more welcome than the greasy stuff we'd endured in the mountains. And there was another treat—the old girl had baked a dark and succulent ginger cake to welcome us home. My world, shattered by journey and injury, began rebuilding around me.

'Has anything happened round here over the last few weeks?' I asked when my mouth was at last empty, and the cake was a fragment of its former glory.

'Not much,' said Mrs Goodfellow, 'other than a horrible murder—the old fellow won't be happy about that when he gets back.'

'A murder?' I said, aghast.

'What happened?' asked Daphne.

'A young boy called Timmy Rigg went missing after school,' said Mrs G. 'They didn't find him until the next morning. He was in someone's back garden, shot through the head.'

'How awful,' said Daphne, echoing my thoughts, though I could imagine the excitement the crime must have caused at the *Bugle*. No doubt Ralph, despite his fondness for positive stories, had splashed it across the front page.

'Have they caught the murderer yet?' I asked.

'No, dear. Since the old fellow was away, the police brought in a detective from the city, but Constable Poll told me there've been no leads so far.'

'When was this?' asked Daphne.

'Five days ago, dear. The killer used a high-velocity rifle.'

'Why would anyone want to shoot a child?' asked Daphne.

The old girl shrugged. 'Who knows the manifold wickedness of the human heart?'

We sat in silence, digesting the news for a few moments.

'Mr Hobbes will catch the murderer,' said Daphne.

'I hope so, dear, if he's allowed to. The man they brought in outranks him and has a ... reputation.'

'But surely,' I said, 'he'll want all the help he can get, and what better help than Hobbes?'

'In a sane world you would be right, dear,' said Mrs G. 'But no one shoots children in a sane world and I know some senior police officers get jealous of a big case and hate anyone to share in the glory of solving it.

She smiled. 'More cake?'

'No, thanks,' said Daphne.

'Yes, please,' I said, pleased with my wife's restraint, since there wasn't much left and I fancied it all. 'It's delicious—especially after living on tsampa for weeks.'

Mrs Goodfellow cut another slice, and I allowed myself to appreciate the rich, spicy, tongue-tingling aromas before sinking my teeth into it. 'This,' I declared, 'is a masterpiece. It is the king of ginger cakes.'

Mrs G smiled and handed me the last slice.

'I shouldn't,' I said.

But I did.

'Any more news?' asked Daphne as I stuffed.

The old girl nodded. 'The council has agreed to allow Colonel Squire's development, despite local feeling. The SODs are still doing whatever they can to oppose it, though it looks hopeless.'

Since my feelings about all this were disappointment, sadness and anger, I realised I'd made up my mind—and I was too late to do anything about it.

All the travelling and the time difference caught up with us. Daphne yawned, which started me off. Within a minute, it was clear that sleep was our only option.

'How am I going to get to bed?' I asked.

'You'll have to sleep here,' said Daphne.

'On the sofa? I suppose I could, but what about washing and ... other things?'

Mrs G took charge. 'I anticipated your needs. There's the commode, and I'll bring in a bucket for you to wash in. If you're lucky, dear, I'll give you a bed bath in the morning.'

It was not an idle threat, and I blushed and squirmed until Daphne brought down a spare duvet and pillows and converted the sofa into a cosy bed. Despite her obvious exhaustion, she helped me wash before tucking me in, kissing me goodnight, and heading upstairs. If I hadn't got used to roughing it, I might have found the sofa uncomfortable, and might not have dropped into a deep sleep before I could even say 'goodnight' to Mrs G.

Thanks to the combined efforts of Daphne and Mrs G, and my gift for putting up with adversity, I survived the night and the next day. I was, however, puzzled when Daphne remarked that I could be a miserable git, for in my opinion, I was behaving heroically in a stressful situation. Anyway, she wasn't the one forced to spend days on a sofa, having to use a commode, and having to wash in a bucket. All in all, I considered I was coping well in very trying circumstances.

Now and then, I experimented with my leg—it was still tender and sore but was regaining movement. In fact, by the third morning after our return, the bruising, swelling and discomfort had reduced enough that I could stand up and lurch around downstairs with the help of a stout wooden walking stick—the tooth-marks in it suggested Mrs G had taken it from Dregs. I missed that big, bad dog, but he'd been banned from visiting on account of his galumphing great feet and lack of bedside manner. Mrs G looked after my wound, changed the dressings when required, and expressed her approval at the way it was healing. I had an inkling her cooking took much of the credit—her cream of chicken soup with warm crusty bread fresh from the oven would have drawn any latter-day Lazarus from his tomb. And as for the Eton Mess she made at Daphne's request, paradise was regained during the eating of that sweet dish.

I filled my convalescence with boredom, including watching television and reading newspapers. Most of the time, I didn't even bother to turn on my laptop or charge my phone. I suspected that despite everything, I was missing the mountains. Occasionally, television news provided snippets about the murder, but there was no indication of how the case was progressing.

As the pain in my leg faded, my mobility increased. When I could hobble around without too much difficulty or swearing, Mrs G returned to Blackdog Street, and Daphne went back to work, suggesting she needed a rest.

Since I was getting back to my normal self, and the tiredness of travel had passed, there was no longer a reason why I shouldn't start writing my exciting account of the expedition. I rummaged through the bits of baggage I'd brought home and pulled out my notebook, only to find the pages damp and clumped together—the monk's flask had been squashed in transit and the potion had run over everything. Still, my camera, though battered, appeared to have survived. However, when I turned it on, nothing happened. I replaced the batteries and tried again. Still nothing. I opened the back, and gasped as water splashed into my groin.

The doorbell rang.

I struggled to the front door and opened it.

It was a salesman, with a bag full of invaluable tools for old folks. After giving me a quick glance and a canny grin, he offered to sell me patented incontinence pants. I shut the door in his face and retreated to the sofa.

I'd just made myself comfortable when the bell rang again.

Muttering, I got up to answer. 'It was just an accident. I am not incontinent,' I said, as I tugged open the door.

'Glad to hear it,' said Hobbes.

'Oh … umm … sorry. I thought you were someone else. You're back.'

'Evidently. How are you?'

'Much better, thank you.' I glanced down my front. 'I spilled some water. Come in.'

Hobbes ducked under the door frame and followed me inside.

'Take a seat,' I said, and slumped back onto the sofa.

Hobbes sat in an armchair and sighed.

'When did you get back?' I asked.

'About an hour ago. I thought I should check on you before going to the station.'

'Thank you. I've been well looked after and I'm getting around after a fashion. How about you?'

'I'm fed up with filing reports and answering questions. However, that is the nature of the job and the department appears pleased with the results of our expedition. I'll be happy to get back to some proper police work, though.'

'You've heard about the murder?'

He grimaced. 'I've read the lurid account in the *Bugle*. I gather DCI Steve Kirten from the Met has taken charge.'

'Do you know him?'

'I've met him,' said Hobbes.

'Is he any good?'

'He's been promoted rapidly.'

I thought for a moment. 'What does that mean?'

Hobbes grinned. 'It means he's good at getting promotions.'

'But you're not impressed,' I guessed.

'I'll speak no ill of the man as long as he gets results. In this case, he should, because there are relatively few legally held rifles around here. Of course, there may be illegal, unregistered weapons too.'

'And the killer might have come from somewhere else,' I said.

Hobbes shook his head. 'Possible, but unlikely. Anyone walking around town with a rifle would attract attention. Anyway, why would anyone come to town to shoot a small boy?'

'And why Timmy?' I asked.

Hobbes's expression was grave. 'That's a good question. There's something strange about this case.'

'What are you suggesting?'

'I don't have enough information to suggest anything.'

His mobile rang. 'Inspector Hobbes ... Hello, Mr Catt ... Yes, I know what they are ... When did it escape? How dangerous? ... OK, I'll see what I can do, but I can't come round straight away because I have to look in at the station first—I've been away.' He ended the call.

'The Wildlife Park?' I asked. I'd met Mr Catt, its manager, on a number of occasions.

Hobbes nodded. 'He was letting me know that one of their rheas escaped two weeks ago and hasn't been caught yet.'

'Aren't rheas those big birds from South America?'

'Big birds indeed—distant relatives of ostriches. Mr Catt said they can disembowel a man with a single kick. He's got staff out searching, and the local police are aware but he thought I should know.'

'Quite right,' I said. 'We can't have monstrous birds disembowelling the public—it wouldn't look good in the tourist brochures.'

'Indeed not,' said Hobbes, getting to his feet. 'I'm glad to see you on the road to recovery, but there's constabulary duty to be done.'

'I was going to offer you a cup of tea,' I said, realising I'd failed in my duty as host.

'And I was going to refuse it,' said Hobbes with a chuckle. 'I've tried your tea before. I'll see myself out. Goodbye.'

He left me to my own company, and finding I didn't much enjoy it, I turned on the telly, which soon confirmed that I liked its daytime output even less. I picked up my laptop, rested it on my knees, and after wasting a few minutes browsing social media and news sites, got down to some writing.

I drafted a light-hearted article about the pleasures and pitfalls of yak butter tea, including a recipe. The first lines gave me particular pleasure: 'First, milk your yak. Then churn the milk for forty minutes and scoop out the butter.' I wasn't much concerned with accuracy—I doubted anyone would try it.

After finishing, I emailed the piece to Ralph and glanced at the clock—it was approaching midday and time to look forward to Mrs Goodfellow's visit. She'd said she'd call round at one o'clock. My stomach put up a convincing argument that this was far too late and to take my mind off it, I started writing, 'My Life among Yetis by A. C. Caplet'. I hadn't forgotten that I'd signed the Official Secrets Act, which forbade me from revealing anything Yeti-related to any uncleared person, but I had no intention of letting anyone other than Daphne read it. It started well, and I was so thrilled by my adventures I lost track of time.

'Paella!'

The shrill, sudden voice would have caused me to leap to my feet had my leg not let me down. As it was, a convulsive twitch launched my laptop into the air. It came down face first on the arm of the sofa.

Mrs Goodfellow had just come in, carrying a stoneware bowl that looked as if it weighed more than she did.

'Hello,' I said, shaky of voice and fearing for my poor heart. My laptop slid to the carpet. 'You startled me.'

'I noticed. I did ring the bell.'

'I was busy,' I said.

'That's not like you, dear. Are you ready for lunch? I've brought some paella.'

'Yes … I am.' My stomach groaned, reproving my previous neglect.

'I'll warm it up,' she said, heading for the kitchen. 'It'll be ready in a few minutes. Do you need to wash up or anything?'

'I'm fine for now. I'll just sort out the laptop.' I picked it up.

The screen was blank, and despite a flurry of random key poking, it was dead. I abandoned my efforts with a shrug and a hope that Ralph's budget might buy me another. Giving up on it, I examined the camera, which was a sorry sight—the plastic housing had split and a crack bisected the lens. When I shook it, it rattled and something clunked. My stint as the *Bugle*'s roving photographer had ended in failure and, although I didn't consider it my fault, Ralph would not be impressed.

Delicious scents wafted from the kitchen to soothe me, and it wasn't long before Mrs G walked back in, bearing my lunch on a tray. I'd been a little worried when she mentioned paella, having once suffered a bad one in a tourist trap in Marbella, but, of course, with the old girl at the pan, nothing could go wrong. Even before I'd tasted it, the aromas told me it would be brilliant. I took a tentative taste and realised I'd been mistaken—it was more than brilliant, it was stupendous. Once I'd got over the initial delight, I was amazed she'd found so many types of seafood in Sorenchester. I ate in rapturous silence, appreciating every morsel, every nuance, every flavour, the way the golden threads of saffron wove through the dish, the way the different textures balanced each other out. I could have eaten it forever—but I would have said much the same for almost every meal she'd made.

When I could stuff no more, she handed me a mug of hot tea. I sat back, feelings of smugness and privilege overwhelming me. Still, I spared a compassionate thought for the unfortunates she hadn't cooked for. No king or emperor ever lunched so well as I had.

Mrs Goodfellow was washing up, and I was resting my eyes, when distant shouting disturbed the peace.

11

'What's going on out there?' I asked as Mrs G came back into the room—as if she could know.

'No idea, dear, but it's coming from the town centre. Let's go and take a look—you've been cooped up in here since you got back and could do with some fresh air.'

My response was peevish. 'You can, but there's no way I can make it that far!'

'Where there's a will there's a way, dear.' Her false teeth beamed at me.

'What way?'

'Old Mrs Brodie passed away last year, and left me her wheelchair. It's parked outside—I thought you might need it.'

'Mrs Brodie?'

'She was a friend, I suppose ... though she was an old sod.'

I laughed. 'That's not a nice thing to say about a friend, I suppose you mean she opposed the development.'

Mrs Goodfellow shook her head. 'Not that sort of sod, dear. She was a mean, cantankerous old biddy and never had a kind word for anyone—especially for me.'

'If she was so nasty, why did she let you have the wheelchair?'

'Because she didn't need it. She was dead, dear, a

victim of the Glevchester Knitting Emporium collapse—she died in the wool. Here's your stick.' She handed it to me, helped me to rise, and led me to the front door.

The bright spring sunshine dazzled eyes that had not seen the light of day since our return. I blinked and gaped in horror. The late Mrs Brodie's wheelchair was a wooden relic, with a latticed-cane seat, two large wheels on the sides and a smaller one at the back. It reminded me of a squat penny-farthing tricycle.

'Umm ... is that thing safe?' I asked, unwilling to risk my weight to it.

'Probably, dear.'

'But it's an antique!'

She shook her head. 'No, it's not that old. Mrs Brodie got it during the Blitz so she could keep calm and carry on working—she'd broken both ankles when her bus drove into a bomb crater. The chair has weathered the years better than she did. She drank, you know?'

I hesitated and was lost.

'Why not try it, dear?'

I sat, and although the seat creaked, nothing fell off. 'Are you sure you'll manage?' I asked, embarrassed that people would see me being pushed by a stick-thin little old lady—few would know how tough she was.

She laughed. 'There's only one way to find out. Let's roll!'

We set off faster than felt safe, but I said nothing, too busy trying to look nonchalant as the wooden wheels clattered on the paving.

At the end of The Boulevard, we turned up Moorend Road and crossed toward The Shambles, the noise growing louder as we approached the junction with Vermin Street. The road was full of shouting people, though there seemed to be little actual trouble until a beer bottle flew over the top of the crowd and shattered against a shop wall. I would have stopped and retreated, but Mrs G headed straight into the danger zone.

An almost spherical woman emerged from the Cake Hole bakery, clutching a chocolate sponge the size of her head in pudgy hands.

'Good afternoon, Fenella,' said Mrs G.

'Hello, Mrs Niblett,' I said. 'What's happening?'

Fenella acknowledged us with a regal smile and a dribble of drool. She took a bite from the cake, masticated for a few moments with a look of sheer bliss on her moon-like face and said, 'I don't rightly know.'

'Skeleton' Bob Niblett, her emaciated husband, emerged from her shadow. 'It's a demonstration against the new development.'

I'd first met the pair of them when I'd visited their cottage with Hobbes while we were investigating a big cat sighting. Although nearly always in trouble, there was something likeable about Bob—his regular law-breaking was petty, unsuccessful, and performed with no malice aforethought or, indeed, much thought of any kind. Fenella scared me.

Another bottle flew from the crowd. It was coming straight at my head. Unable to move in the cramped wheelchair, I covered up, cringed and expected pain. But, in one effortless movement, Mrs G leaned forward, caught the bottle by its neck and tossed it into the nearest litter bin.

'The demo was all well-behaved and respectable when we got here, ten minutes ago,' said Bob. 'There were a lot of older folk, a bunch of students with placards, and a lady with dreadlocks collecting names for a petition.'

'Then what?' I asked.

'We went in there,' said Fenella, gesturing at the Cake Hole, 'because we wanted a cake.' She engulfed another great mouthful, leaving chocolate smears around her lips.

Something was happening. The crowd surged backwards and forwards in waves, and lost in the middle, Constable Poll's lanky frame swayed like a yacht's mast in a storm. A fat, ugly, young man, his short hair like suede, swung a punch at a mild-looking, bespectacled old man who was looking the other way. Faster than I'd ever seen him move before, Constable Poll blocked the blow with his truncheon. The young man swore and sucked sore knuckles.

'Jolly well done, constable,' said a smart middle-aged lady, wielding a rolled umbrella to whack the miscreant on the ear.

There was a moment of quiet.

And then, a mob of at least twenty burly young bullies charged into the crowd, roaring and threatening. Constable Poll rocked, tipped, and went down in the storm. But before the charge of the heavy-brigade caused too much damage, it stopped. Dead. Several of the bullyboys took flight—one moment, they were causing mayhem, the next, they were airborne, arms and legs flapping like chicken wings. Within seconds, the trouble was over, and the troublemakers were grovelling in the road like worms on a rainy night. Except that most were groaning.

Hobbes was strolling through the crowd. He raised the crumpled figure of Constable Poll and shook him out. 'Are you all right, Derek?'

Poll, a little dazed, nodded, and Hobbes set him back on his feet.

'Good man,' said Hobbes. He bowed to Mrs Niblett,

who'd buried her face in her cake again. 'Did anyone see what started this?'

'Not really, Mr Hobbes,' said Bob. 'Some rough guys was hanging round outside the church when we got off the bus. I reckon they came from out of town because I didn't know them. We kept out of their way, though they weren't doing much. We went into the cake shop and heard the SODs start a chant when Fenella was inspecting the comestibles.'

'What were they chanting?' I asked, getting details for the story I might write.

Bob screwed up his face to squeeze out a memory. 'A skinny woman in dreadlocks yelled, "What don't we want?" and the others shouted, "Development on the common!" Then she yelled, "When don't we want it?" and they roared back, "Ever!"'

'Then what?' asked Hobbes.

'I looked out the window and a tall, nobby-looking bloke in a suit nodded at the rough guys, and they all began shouting and throwing things at the poor old SODs.'

'Did you recognise the nobby-looking bloke?' asked Hobbes.

Bob shook his head. 'Never seen him before in all my life, but I reckon I'd know him again 'cause he was wearing dark glasses.'

'Thank you for your help, Bob,' said Hobbes, before saluting Fenella, who acknowledged the gesture with a faint tilt of her head and a chocolate smile.

People were checking the casualties, but apart from one old gentleman with a bloody nose and another with a black eye, no one was much hurt—thanks to Hobbes I suspected. Even the bullyboys were sitting up with dazed expressions. Bob's suggestion that they were from out of town looked plausible—they looked like Pigtonites to me, though it might have been my prejudice against the knuckle-dragging inhabitants of that godforsaken town.

'Albert Herring,' said Hobbes, clamping the heavy hand of the law onto the shoulder of a man who was getting to his feet, 'what brings you to town?'

Albert, tall, overweight and over-tattooed, cringed and attempted a friendly smile. 'Hello, Mr Hobbes ... I didn't see you there. They told us you was out of town— I wouldn't have been here otherwise. I'm ... er ... very sorry for the trouble.'

'And why did you cause trouble, Albert?'

'Say nothing,' said one of his mates, trying to look tough, though his piggy eyes were wide with fear.

Albert squirmed under Hobbes's stern expression. 'I don't know.'

'Are you sure?' asked Hobbes, towering over him like a thundercloud over a picnic.

'Say nothing!' roared piggy eyes.

Hobbes seized Piggy's ear and invited him to join the conversation. 'Who are you?'

Although the man squirmed, he was going nowhere. 'None of your business. Aargh!'

Hobbes, I gathered, had increased the twist on his ear.

'They call him Mad Mick,' said Albert, sparing his mate further pain.

'Good afternoon, Mad, or do you prefer Mr Mick?' asked Hobbes.

An engine revved. Tyres screeched. The crowd panicked as a red pickup truck sped through them from the direction of the church. As people raced to get out of harm's way, Hobbes released the two bullies, scooped up three elderly ladies and a snappy dachshund, and carried them to safety. Mrs G rolled me clear.

The pickup slowed, Albert, Mad Mick and the other bad guys scrambled aboard and it screeched away.

'How very ill-mannered!' said Mrs Goodfellow in her cross voice. 'It's as if they didn't care that someone might get injured.'

Hobbes, after setting the flustered old ladies down, calmed the dachshund, who was howling like a soprano wolf. When he'd restored peace, he turned to us. 'Did you see the driver?'

I shook my head.

'I did, but I didn't recognise him,' said Mrs G. 'He was wearing a grey suit and dark glasses.'

Hobbes nodded. 'Not much to go on, I'm afraid—I suspect he was the one pulling the strings behind this little incident.'

'Those guys were his puppets?' I said, thinking it an astute remark—none of them had looked like thinkers.

Hobbes nodded. 'It's likely, if they're anything like Albert Herring. He's been getting into trouble since he was a lad, though he never knows how he got there. He's incapable of planning anything and never starts anything himself.'

'How do you know him?' I asked.

'He lived next door, dear,' said Mrs G, 'which was handy for keeping an eye on him. Back then, the old fellow kept him away from the worst troublemakers, which made his mum happy. Sadly, when the family had to move, he got into bad company.'

Hobbes turned to the crowd. 'Did anyone get the pickup's number?'

I was surprised he hadn't noted it himself, though in fairness, he'd had his hands full.

'I did, sir.' Constable Poll eased through the crowd and handed Hobbes the number plate. 'It came off when the pickup hit the speed bump.'

'Thanks, Derek,' said Hobbes, taking it in his huge, hairy hands. 'It was only held on by a bit of gaffer tape. I'd guess it was stolen from another vehicle. That suggests forethought.'

I pondered this for a moment. 'So, it'll be a waste of time tracing the number?'

Hobbes shook his head. 'Not necessarily.' He handed the plate back to Constable Poll. 'Would you take this to the station and check it out? Get it dusted for prints, too.'

'Yes, sir,' said the constable.

Hobbes said 'goodbye', took out his notebook, and talked to witnesses.

'The excitement seems to be over all too soon,' said Mrs Goodfellow, sounding disappointed. 'I'll take you home.'

We said our farewells to Bob and Fenella, who was eyeing another cake and dead to all other considerations. The old girl whisked me homeward.

'Why would anyone cause trouble at a SODs protest?' I said. 'They're such a peaceful bunch.'

'True, dear,' said Mrs G. 'But, maybe, this will get them some publicity. The *Bugle* has barely even mentioned any opposition to the development.'

'Are you suggesting they organised the whole shebang for publicity? How irresponsible! Someone might have been badly hurt.'

But part of me was thinking what a great story if it were true.

'Not at all,' said Mrs G, 'though I wouldn't blame them if they had. And, as the old fellow says, it's best to get all the relevant facts before jumping to any conclusions.'

'That makes sense—for a policeman,' I said, aware my profession often took the opposite approach.

I thought about it. According to Ralph, the primary task of a reporter was to sell newspapers. Although I could see sense in his point of view, I still believed we should aim for the truth—my previous editors had insisted on it, up to a point. However, I suspected Ralph's integrity, though I was still giving him the benefit of the doubt because he claimed he was doing his best to save the newspaper from bankruptcy. Like many others, it had experienced a sharp decline in paper sales. It worried me, though, that even historic articles were not immune to his striving for positivity—he'd tweaked some to be more favourable to companies that advertised with us, claiming it was vital not to drive away income. I was a little uncomfortable with the notion.

'Hiya!' Billy Shawcroft, miniscule in stature though massive in ability, waved and directed his motorised skateboard towards us from the other side of the road.

'Good afternoon, Billy,' said Mrs Goodfellow as he approached.

'What have you been up to?' he asked, examining the wheelchair.

'There was this leopard and some Yet ... ' I began.

Mrs Goodfellow interrupted. 'He fell over and hurt his leg.'

I realised how close I'd come to letting slip a detail of my secret journey.

'Yes,' I nodded. 'I was checking out ... umm ... some yet to be opened restaurant ... near Tode-in-the-Wold ... and I fell down the steps. The ... umm ... leopard turned out to be a cat.'

'Were you drunk?' asked Billy.

'A little tipsy, perhaps,' I said, pleased how well I'd covered up. 'I'm a lot better now and expect to be getting around on my own in a day or two.'

'And how is Mr Binks?' asked Mrs Goodfellow.

Billy sighed. 'Featherlight is not in the best of moods.'

In my experience, Featherlight Binks was never in the best of moods, unless he'd just flung an unfortunate customer into the street. But for some reason, Billy got on well with him and even worked behind the bar at The Feathers.

'He won't say why,' Billy continued, 'but he's been like it since that development got accepted. And learning that a child had been murdered made him even more morose. Well, I can't stay long—I said I'd help him clean the beer pipes.'

'He cleans the pipes?' I was astonished—having drunk more than my share of lager there, I could testify that it was the worst kept in Sorenchester.

'I said I'd do it,' said Billy. 'It's high time someone did, and he's not to be trusted with cleaning fluid and, with a few exceptions, I'd rather we didn't poison our customers. See you!' He skated away.

Mrs G pushed me home, helped me inside, and left me to my own devices.

I slumped onto the sofa and mulled things over—I'd seen no other reporters at the trouble, so I'd probably got a scoop if I wanted it. But, if I wrote an honest account of what I'd witnessed, I had an idea Ralph would twist it so that it appeared the trouble had really been a cynical publicity stunt by the SODs, even though I suspected the thugs had been acting for the developers.

Despite all the claims that the development would be good for Sorenchester, bringing not only new houses, but jobs and countless other benefits, I was increasingly opposed to it. Sure, I could see that having more potential *Bugle* buyers might help keep the paper going and, thus, keep me in a job, but the downsides seemed massive: the disruption, the huge change to the town's character, the lack of available jobs for the newcomers, the need for new facilities to cater for them. These things barely got a mention in the plans or the publicity, and the list of minor problems went on and on. However, what really bothered me was building over the common. It struck me as an act of vandalism that such a wild, secluded area could be buried beneath concrete.

The doorbell rang. I got up, opened the door, and a big, black, hairy dog storm engulfed me, leaving me flat on my back, getting nuzzled and licked, despite my yelps.

'Glad to see you up and about,' said Hobbes, retrieving Dregs.

'I'm actually down and licked,' I retorted, though it was good to be appreciated, if only by a delinquent canine.

Hobbes helped me up. 'How's the leg?'

'Weak and still tender, but much better. Is the trouble in town over?'

He nodded. 'It is. Derek Poll checked the number plate from the pickup—it was stolen from a similar vehicle in Pigton. The owner reported the theft three days ago, but he'd been away for a month so had no idea when it had happened. There were no useful prints on it.'

'So, not much use as a lead,' I said and sat back down.

He shrugged. 'You're probably right, but it does tell me the thief has been in Pigton within the last month, and since the vehicle the plates came from was kept out of sight behind a locked gate, it suggests local knowledge.'

'Maybe,' I said, 'but the thief might have been intending to commit a burglary, found he couldn't get in to the house, so took the number plates as a trophy or something.'

Hobbes smiled and shook his head. 'Unlikely—there were no signs of an attempted break in.'

'So, the number plate was taken specifically to disguise the pickup,' I said, cottoning on at once. 'Get down, Dregs!'

To my astonishment, the dog, who'd just settled his lumpy head like a lead weight on my groin, bounded away. Seconds later, he returned with one of my walking boots. He took it to a corner and lay down, sniffing it like a connoisseur with a fine wine.

'Is he going to eat it?' I asked.

Hobbes smiled. 'I doubt it. It's more likely he's just interested by the exotic odours picked up on our excursion. Excuse me.'

His mobile was ringing. He answered, saying little except 'thank you' and 'goodbye'.

'What's up?' I asked, seeing his frown.

'That was Derek Poll. Keith Brown turned up at the station and confessed to shooting Timmy.'

'That's good,' I said, before noticing his exasperated expression. 'Isn't it?'

'No. Keith confesses to everything—he once claimed he'd shot Archduke Ferdinand and started the First World War.'

'Why would he do that?' I asked.

'He has what they call "issues", though I think he just enjoys being the centre of attention. The lads call him Culpability Brown. Whenever he turns up at the station, they give him a cup of tea, listen to his confession, pretend to take notes and send him on his way.'

'Won't they do the same now?'

'They would have,' said Hobbes, 'if DCI Kirten hadn't overheard him. Despite what everyone has told him, he is taking it seriously. I'd better go over and sort things out. See you later.'

He called Dregs to heel and left me to my thoughts.

I might have decided to write the article had my laptop been working. The thought of having to use pen and paper put me off, and, although I could have tapped something out on my mobile, its insane autocorrect function had scared me off.

12

Daphne returned from work. I stood up to give her a welcome home kiss, and mentioned that I'd broken my laptop. She picked it up, pressed the on button, and handed it back. It started. 'It must have turned itself off when you dropped it.'

The camera, however, as I'd successfully diagnosed, was beyond all hope, no matter how much I grimaced at it.

'I was hoping I'd got some awesome photos,' I complained as I sat back down. 'My stunning stories of a *Bugle* reporter in the wild will seem a bit lame without them.'

'Don't despair yet,' she said.

'Despairing early gets it over sooner,' I said, sharing the benefit of experience.

She removed the flash card, patted it dry on a tissue, and inspected it. 'It looks okay—let's give it a go.'

She sat beside me, slotted it into the laptop, and I had my photographs. Despite my lack of talent, many of the snaps looked amazing: rugged snow-tipped mountains, verdant valleys, rushing rivers, and rocky ravines, barren plains ... and Yetis in their cave!

I gaped. 'I don't remember taking that!'

Daphne pointed to the edge of the picture. 'You didn't—that's you, isn't it?'

A pathetic, crumpled figure was lying on the fur-covered hammock in the background. 'So it is,' I admitted. 'Umm ... so who took it?'

'A Yeti,' she said. 'It probably pressed the button when it was checking out the camera. There are a few more photos.'

'They're not very good, though,' I complained as we scanned them. 'They're all a bit blurry. I expect they didn't know to focus ... and the light wasn't great.'

'Despite all that,' she said, 'you have photographs of Yetis at home—I especially like the group portrait. As far as I know, no one's obtained anything like it before. If only you were allowed to sell them, you'd be rich and famous!'

I sat back, dreaming of what might have been—me, Andy Caplet, going down in history as an intrepid mountaineer and friend of Yetis. It would have been fantastic. On the other hand, back in the real world, the infamous Andy Caplet going to prison for breaching the Official Secrets Act was not such a pleasing prospect. I sighed. 'Oh well. But at least I can use the other photos.'

Daphne nodded and brought some other pictures up on screen. 'Look at this!'

The unmistakable shape of a big cat was looking down at me from a crag.

'I remember taking this one,' I said, surprised, 'but I thought it was just scenic—I never spotted the leopard. I think it was the day before it pounced on me.'

She laughed and nodded. 'That was just after you'd started taking the monk's magic medicine. Do you have any left?'

'No, the flask got squashed. A pity.'

'Why, do you want to attract more cats?'

I smiled. 'No, but I miss the way it made me feel. I've

never felt so full of energy.'

'So, I noticed in the tent,' she said with a wink that made me grin like a naughty schoolboy. She changed the subject. 'Are you hungry?'

A foolish question, as she well knew. I nodded.

'I'll order something,' she said. 'What do you fancy?'

'Umm ... don't know ... Chinese, maybe?'

'Yeah, why not?' She reached for her mobile and brought up Aye Ching's takeaway. However, a message apologised that the shop was closed for a family holiday.

We settled for ordering from the Leaning Tower of Pizzas. Our meal arrived within twenty minutes. It was nothing to write home about, but it was filling.

When we'd finished eating, I washed up while Daphne started up her laptop to prepare a lecture for the morning. After finishing my chores, I took the opportunity to bang off a piece of lurid prose describing how I'd battled adversity, terror and injury in the mountains, to bring the glories of nature in the rough, to *Bugle* readers.

After that, since Daphne was still busy I decided, it was time to write something about the afternoon's trouble—it was my job. I bashed out a quick five hundred words, without apportioning blame, though I did mention the SODs and the involvement of out-of-towners. At the end, I thought it an engaging and honest piece. I pushed the button and sent it on its way, though I suspected Ralph would edit it into something more compact and, to my mind, less readable.

I couldn't stop thinking about the afternoon. Who would favour the development so much that they'd want to disrupt a protest against it? Colonel Squire? It seemed plausible—he had form. Or Valentine Grubbe? Other than that he was handsome, suave, and rich, I knew too little about him to speculate. So, I turned to Google.

My first search brought up only an article about a long-dead, but well-respected philanthropist of the same name. A second search including the word 'developer' got me my man—Valentine Edward Grubbe.

It turned out that he was thirty-nine (though I'd have guessed a little older), and had been born in Ogborne St Lukes, an obscure village in Wiltshire. Following an undistinguished academic career at a minor public school, he'd joined the army, rising to the rank of captain, where he'd seen action and won medals for gallantry. In addition, he'd played rugby and cricket for the army and won trophies for target shooting. He'd married a Helen Fry, and his career had been on an upward trajectory until a court-martial for theft. Although acquitted, he'd left the army soon after.

It was interesting enough stuff in a gossipy kind of way, but told me little about the man.

The doorbell rang.

'Who's that at half-past eight on a Sunday night?' I asked.

'There's only one way to find out,' said Daphne, getting to her feet.

I half expected Hobbes.

I did not expect Valentine Edward Grubbe.

'Apologies for intruding,' he said, with a nod at me and a smile at Daphne as he came in, 'but I was wondering if you might reconsider my proposal.'

'What proposal?' I asked.

'The one I discussed with your wife,' said Grubbe, sparing me a brief glance.

'Eh?' I said, succinct as ever.

'Mr Grubbe offered me some paid work when we met him at Colonel Squire's house,' said Daphne.

'Please, call me Valentine,' said Grubbe.

She smiled. 'I'm sorry I didn't get back to you, Valentine. We've been away and only came home a few days ago. I've been busy catching up since them.'

'A holiday?' asked Grubbe with a pleasant smile.

I hoped it was the trip that interested him rather than my wife. He seemed to be standing a little too close to her, oozing charm and affability, the bastard.

'It was great,' she said, 'but it was work.'

Grubbe nodded as if to say that he knew all about working trips.

'Please, take a seat,' I said before he could say anything else. I indicated the armchair in the corner.

'No thanks, I'm fine. So, Daphne, what do you say?'

She looked thoughtful. 'Well, the money would be welcome, but I am rather busy at the moment—apart from the day-to-day stuff, there are loads of school trips to the museum at this time of year and they take so much preparation—I've had to work this afternoon.'

'Of course,' said Grubbe, smoothing back a hair on his immaculate haircut. 'However, I would not expect the work to impinge on your time very much.'

'What work?' I asked.

'Valentine wants me to research old records about Sorenchester Common.'

Grubbe smiled. 'For which your training makes you a perfect fit. Plus, of course, you have access to the museum's records.'

'I don't understand why you haven't engaged solicitors to do this,' said Daphne.

'We have, of course,' said Grubbe. 'They scanned

Land Registry documents and deeds and covenants and so forth. However, the common is ancient and we are just ensuring there are no charters that might still apply and which might delay our development. I'm also interested if there's anything strange I should know.'

Daphne frowned. 'I must think about it a little more.'

'Of course,' said Grubbe, 'but I'll need your answer soon—if you say "no", I'll have to find someone else. Tell you what, why not discuss it with your husband, sleep on it, take a day or two to consider, and let me know your answer?'

'Alright.' She nodded.

Grubbe continued. 'I've an idea—why don't I take the two of you to lunch tomorrow? We can talk about it then. I understand Le Sacré Bleu is decent. Do you know it?'

'Isn't it the one at the bottom of Helmet Hill by the river?' said Daphne. 'I suggested going there on our last anniversary, but Andy wasn't keen.'

I said nothing because the last time I'd been there, the food had been delicious, the wine had been amazing, and the ambiance had been perfect until Violet, my girlfriend at the time, had rather spoiled it by murdering someone. I'd never gone back in case they recognised me.

'It's quite a long way to go for lunch,' I said, hoping to change Grubbe's mind. 'How about Bombay Mick's in town? It does a fine lunchtime buffet.'

'Nonsense,' said Grubbe. 'I'll send a car round and pick you up. Shall we say at twelve-thirty?'

'All right,' said Daphne and glanced at me. 'What do you say?'

'Umm ... ' I dithered, caught between wishing to keep an eye on Grubbe and memories of that horrible summer evening. I shifted my gaze towards him. 'Yes, alright. Will your wife be joining us?'

Grubbe glared. His fists curled into tight balls, and then he smiled. 'I'm not married.'

'But ...' I began and stopped. Perhaps the information had been wrong—he ought to know, after all. 'Sorry. I was making assumptions.'

'No problem, Andy,' he said. 'Sadly, I've never been lucky in love like you. Perhaps one day.'

'It's true,' I admitted. 'I am lucky.'

But what, exactly, did he mean? Did he hope to get lucky with Daphne? Or was I reading too much into an innocent comment?

'Well, I must be on my way,' he said with a glance at his Rolex. 'Where is the best place for my driver to pick you up? At the museum?'

'Here would be better,' said Daphne. 'It's difficult to park in town during the day, and Andy can't get there—he hurt his leg when we were away.'

'That's settled then.' Grubbe got to his feet and swaggered towards the door with Daphne. 'I'll see you tomorrow.'

The front door closed and Daphne returned. 'He seems nice,' she remarked.

'If you say so.'

'But I suspect a streak of ruthlessness underlies his charm.'

'I hadn't noticed the charm,' I said. 'What are you going to do about his job offer?'

'It's not a job as such. It's just a few hours' work.'

'But you're busy.'

'I am. However, I'm sure I can arrange things so I've got the time. He's offering good money.'

'How much?'

'Two thousand pounds plus a bonus.'

That took the wind from my sails—it was a lot for just a few hours' work, and would help towards the new windows our house needed. 'Bonus? How much?'

She smiled. 'Another thousand if I turn up what he's looking for.'

'And what is he looking for?' I asked.

'That is not entirely clear. It's something to do with cryptids and land rights.'

'Cryptids, eh? But ... umm ... didn't Hobbes ask you about them?'

She nodded. 'He did. I thought that was to do with our trip, though Yetis can hardly be said to be mythical creatures now my husband has lived with them and captured pictures on his camera.'

'But there are no Yetis here,' I pointed out ... or were there? I thought of the masked face on Sorenchester Common. But, no, it hadn't been a Yeti, though, perhaps, it had been something similar.

'No Yetis,' Daphne agreed, 'and it's probably just a coincidence that Valentine is also interested in cryptids. I guess the only way I'll find out what he wants is by taking on the work.'

I nodded. 'Grubbe may have a point though—there are plenty of folk in town that aren't what you might call mainstream ... like those ghouls I told you about.'

A shudder shook me as I recalled falling into an opened grave, and the hideous faces contemplating me as a future meal. Back then, it had been my darkest hour, though I'd survived a few similar experiences since, which was a hazard of hanging around with Hobbes. I'd often wondered why I kept getting involved in his adventures, but deep down and against my better judgement, I'd become addicted to excitement.

Although I feared it would be the end of me one day, at least I would have lived—my old life had been safe, dull and disappointing.

Daphne hugged me and the horrors, as well as my unwarranted fears of losing her, melted away. At least I hoped my fears were unwarranted.

'So, you will do it?' I asked.

'I think so. There are no real downsides as far as I can see. I'll do a search through the archives and let him know what I turn up—if anything. The money will certainly come in handy.'

I nodded, though I didn't trust Valentine Grubbe—he was too smarmy. Nor did I trust his partner, Colonel Squire, who was devious and ruthless, though I had one reason to feel gratitude to him—had he not employed an unhuman thug to intimidate Daphne, I might never have summoned up the courage to ask her out.

Daphne and I returned to our laptops.

I supposed it was writing about the mountains that had brought the late lamented Piers Twilley to mind. Recalling his story, I searched for anything about the fate of Clarence Squire, the injured mountaineer. The results suggested that Clarence, younger brother of General Aloysius Squire, Colonel Squire's grandfather, would now be eighty, if he'd survived. Then, noticing the time, I turned on the TV news.

Little interested me, until an update on Timmy Rigg's murder.

They cut from the studio to The Shambles, where local reporter, Jeremy Pratt, introduced DCI Steve Kirten, a tall, weasel-thin man with a smug expression, a sandy moustache and a fashionable business suit. Standing in front of the floodlit church, Jeremy shoved the microphone in Kirten's face and asked what progress the police had made.

Kirten grabbed the mic and faced the camera. 'Our investigations are progressing well and we already have a man in custody. Since he has confessed to the heinous crime, I consider the case solved, though we are still tidying up a few details.'

'What details?' asked Jeremy, trying to regain control of the mic.

Kirten nudged him aside and smiled. 'We need to know such things as why he targeted an innocent child, and where he disposed of the murder weapon. I regret that since his confession, he has become less co-operative and is apparently incapable of understanding why I won't let him go home.'

'Why would that be?' asked Jeremy, on the edge of vision.

'However, highly trained police officers are interviewing him,' Kirten continued, turning away from the frantic reporter, 'and I'm convinced he will break soon. In the meantime, I would like to reassure residents of Sorenchester and the surrounding districts that this type of crime is extremely rare, and that since we have the culprit—I should, of course, say suspect—in custody, they should go about their normal business with no concerns. I am gratified to have resolved this case so quickly. Thank you.'

'And thank you,' said Jeremy, wrenching the mic back. 'So, there you have it—the suspect is in custody, and the good people of Sorenchester can sleep safely in their beds. And now, back to the studio.'

I snorted. 'Hobbes says he's got the wrong man.'

Daphne closed her laptop. 'I thought he wasn't on the case.'

'He isn't, but you know what he's like.'

She yawned. 'I'm too tired to think. Would you like a drink or anything before I go to bed?'

'A glass of water, please,' I said, playing the invalid, though I could have got it myself.

As I turned off the telly, she placed the glass on the table beside me and helped me ready the sofa for the night. After a kiss, she left me, but though my body demanded sleep, my stupid brain wouldn't shut down. Thoughts kept churning in my head: the murder, the trouble in town, my position at the *Bugle*, Valentine Grubbe. Half an hour of restless fidgeting later, I sat up and reached for my laptop.

After scanning several pages of nothing, I discovered that Grubbe had first lived in the area ten years earlier. He'd been a member of an obscure group called the Old Boars Club, but I could find little about it recently, just a historical note. It seemed the Old Boars was an exclusive dining club for local businessmen, dating from the eighteenth century. The name came from the Old Boar Inn, where they used to hold their meetings.

I dug a little deeper and found that the Old Boar Inn had been on The Shambles, just a few doors down from the *Bugle* officers. An old black-and-white photograph showed a picturesque, though ramshackle, Cotswold stone building with a broad archway at the entrance. The place had burned to the ground in 1927, during a rowdy dinner—I wondered if the Old Boars had been to blame.

Further investigations suggested the club might still exist, but my eyes were growing heavy. I closed my laptop, lay back, and crashed out.

13

The telephone was ringing. Grumbling about the sort of person who makes calls in the middle of the night, I groped until my fingers closed on it. 'Hello?'

'Hi, I'm on my way,' said Daphne.

'You what?'

'I'm on my way home,' she said. 'I'm just making sure you haven't forgotten.'

'Forgotten what?' I asked, sitting up, shaking my head, and trying to make sense of the world. What was I doing on the sofa?

She clicked her tongue. 'Mr Grubbe's driver will pick us up in fifteen minutes.'

The name 'Grubbe' rang a bell, but I was still lost in the fog of sleep. 'Where are you?' I asked.

'At the museum, of course. I'm just leaving.' She sounded a little exasperated.

'What are you doing there in the middle of the night?'

There was a pause. 'Andy, it's quarter past twelve.'

Dimly, through the haze came a hint that something might be wrong.

'Are you feeling alright?' she asked.

'I'm fine,' I said, 'but isn't he coming round at lunchtime?'

The room was not as dark as it ought to be. At last, the penny dropped.

'It's lunchtime now, isn't it?'

'Of course. Are you sure you're alright?'

'I've just woken up.'

She laughed. 'I thought you weren't your usual lively self when I left this morning.'

'Was I awake?'

'You said "Thank you" when I brought you tea.'

I glanced at the table where a mug of tea looked cold and scuzzy. Getting up, I drew back the curtains and blinked in the midday brightness. I mumbled an apology.

'That's alright,' said Daphne, 'but, if you intend coming with us, you'd better get a move on. I have a feeling Valentine won't look kindly on unpunctuality.'

'I'm coming.' No way was I letting her enjoy lunch with Grubbe, unless I was there too—it had not escaped my notice that she'd called him Valentine. 'See you in a few minutes.'

I ended the phone call, dashed upstairs for the bathroom, and then scurried to the bedroom. Flinging open the wardrobe, I grabbed my best trousers, a smart tweed jacket, and a shirt. As I hurried to dress, a glance at the clock showed time running out.

But I was almost ready.

Then I glanced in the mirror. There was a horrible, sticky yellowish stain down the front of my trousers— it was the orange juice spilled at Colonel Squire's bash. Only an idiot would have hung the trousers back in the wardrobe without getting them cleaned first. I cursed myself and grabbed an old pair that looked unblemished and not too creased. After peeling off the stained trousers in record time, I stepped into the clean ones. Both feet ended up in the same leg hole, and despite three or four desperate bunny hops, I lost my balance. My shoulder crashed into the wardrobe door, which rebounded off the wall, and smacked my head as I went down.

I heard the front door open and shut.

'Are you ready?' Daphne shouted.

I groaned.

'What on earth are you doing?' she asked, after running upstairs.

'I got in a bit of a pickle.'

'No kidding.' She freed my feet and helped me stand.

The doorbell rang as I was pulling up the clean trousers.

'That'll be Valentine's chauffeur,' she said. 'Hurry up.' She ran to answer the summons.

I pulled a flamboyant tie from Mr Goodfellow's collection, hoping it would lend me an air of sophistication, and hurried downstairs, still somewhat flustered. Daphne gave me a quick once over, adjusted the tie, smoothed down my hair and suggested I button up my fly. She nodded. 'You'll do.'

I was only three minutes late, and what was three minutes in a lifetime, or indeed, a lunchtime?

'How's your leg?' asked Daphne as she pushed me out the front door.

I'd not given it a thought, but now she'd drawn my attention to it, I could feel it was still tender though no longer painful. 'A little better,' I said.

A big, black Mercedes was parked by the side of the road, and a tall, uniformed chauffeur saluted before opening the passenger doors. Daphne and I slid in and onto leather seats, the colour of rich Jersey cream. Despite myself, I was impressed.

'My name's Corbett,' said the chauffeur as he took his position at the wheel. 'Please, fit your seat belts.'

'Where's Valentine ... Mr Grubbe?' asked Daphne. 'I thought he'd be with us.'

'The boss has an urgent matter to attend to,' said Corbett. 'He will meet you at the restaurant. Your reservation is for twelve forty-five, so we should be there in plenty of time. Please, relax and enjoy the journey.'

I might have relaxed more, but for Daphne calling Grubbe by his first name again. The journey was smooth, pleasant and unalarming, and I almost missed the terror of being Hobbes's passenger.

We reached Le Sacré Bleu five minutes ahead of our reservation.

Corbett stopped at the front and let us out. 'Please, go straight in and let the headwaiter know you are Mr Grubbe's guests. You'll be well looked after.' He saluted again and turned back to the car.

I hesitated on the door step, a maelstrom of memories from my last visit swirling around my head: Violet looking so beautiful, the man bleeding out before us, the shock of discovering that she was the culprit. Though I would never have admitted it to anybody, least of all my wife, I still had some feelings for Violet, who I believed had cared for me in her own way.

'Are you alright, Andy?' asked Daphne.

'Umm ... yes.' I forced a smile, pretending I'd been admiring the view, which, to tell the truth, was stunning—the ivy-clad, honey-coloured stone mansion snuggled in a dip below Helmet Hill where the little River Soren wandered between reed-strewn banks. The emerald green lawn in front would be snow white with daisies in a week or two.

'Let's go in.' I steeled myself, pushed open the door, and held it for her.

148

As before, my impression was of dark beams, white tablecloths, sparkling glasses, and gleaming silver. The rich aroma of good French food tingled my taste buds.

The headwaiter, a plump, greying man in a sombre black suit, greeted us with a smile. 'Bonjour, madame, monsieur. Welcome to Le Sacré Bleu.'

He was new and wouldn't recognise me or remember the dark events of that evening. 'Thank you,' I said and relaxed.

'Are you here for luncheon?' he asked.

'We are,' said Daphne. 'We are meeting Mr Grubbe.'

'Of course,' said the headwaiter. 'Your table is ready, but Mr Grubbe has not yet arrived. Perhaps you'd care to take a seat in the bar and enjoy a drink while you're waiting?'

Daphne nodded, and he escorted us to a comfortable, old-fashioned alcove with deep leather seats around gleaming dark wood tables.

'Marie!' He called to a young woman in a neat black skirt and crisp, snow-white blouse. 'Our guests would like a drink while they're waiting.'

He returned to his station to greet a smart elderly man and a rather lanky, long-haired, middle-aged woman who'd just arrived.

Marie took her position at the bar. 'Bonjour,' she said, her accent betraying her as a local girl. 'What can I get you?'

'I'll have a small dry sherry,' said Daphne, to my surprise—she didn't like dry sherry.

'And for you, sir?'

Although I fancied a pint of lager, I thought I ought to appear more sophisticated, and remembered what I'd drunk last time. 'A pastis, please.'

'Of course, sir. Take a seat and I'll bring your drinks

to you.'

'Umm ... ' I said, fumbling for my wallet, 'how much?'

'No charge, sir. Mr Grubbe said to put everything on his account.'

'Oh, good,' I said, wishing I'd opted for a bottle of vintage champagne, even though it gave me gas.

We sat down by the window, overlooking the river, where ducks dabbled among the reeds and a pair of sedate swans patrolled. A minute later, Marie brought us our drinks. Daphne picked up her sherry and took a sip.

'I thought you didn't like that stuff,' I said.

'I don't, but I need to keep a sober head today. It's a trick I learned in Blackcastle. There often wasn't much to do except watch television or go to the pub, but having a full glass usually stopped people pestering me to have another.'

I smiled as I recalled the fateful day when I'd walked through the Blacker Mountains to the Badger's Rest, the only pub in that godforsaken town. I was trying to find the local police and report finding a skeleton, which turned out to be the mortal remains of Daphne's husband, Hugh. That's what had led to my meeting her for the first time.

I picked up a dainty water jug and poured a few drops into my glass, changing the clear pastis to a yellow, milky consistency and releasing the scent of aniseed. It stirred more memories of Violet, who'd introduced me to that drink, though I hadn't touched it since. Forcing away her image, I concentrated on chatting to Daphne about work, house repairs and mountains. When I finished my drink, she'd barely wet her lips with hers. Hunger was growling in my breakfast-deprived stomach, and it was one o'clock already. Where was that dratted Valentine Grubbe? At least the pastis made me feel better. I ordered another. After all, he was paying, and should have had the common courtesy to turn up on time.

'Are you sure that's a good idea on an empty stomach?' asked Daphne.

I shook my head and grinned, hoping a little alcoholic lubrication might help lunch slip down.

One-fifteen came and went. Where the hell had Grubbe got to?

I'd finished my second pastis, and was considering a third, when he appeared.

'Sorry I'm late,' he said, looking ruffled.

'I should bloody well think you are,' I said, the alcohol taking over my voice. 'What kept you?'

'Andy!' Daphne nudged me.

'I had an accident,' said Grubbe.

'Are you alright?' she asked.

'I'm fine, but my car is a mess.'

'What about Corbett?' I asked.

'Corbett?' Grubbe paused, looking puzzled, and then smiled. 'Corbett is using one of my other cars. I was driving myself.'

'What happened?' Daphne asked with, I thought, a little too much interest.

'It was strange,' said Grubbe. 'I'd completed my business and was back on schedule, when this sodding great bird ran out in front. I slammed on the brakes and swerved, but a wheel clipped the verge and the car flipped into a ditch. I crawled out and called a taxi.'

'You were lucky to walk away,' said Daphne. Looking shocked.

'I'd have been even luckier if that damned bird hadn't shown up,' he said with a laugh.

'Was it a pheasant?' I asked.

'No, it was about the size of an ostrich, though I'm not an expert.'

I laughed. 'An ostrich? In the Cotswolds? You're joking!'

He shook his head. 'It was huge—the last thing anyone would expect.'

I gave him my best quizzical look. He was clearly lying ... or mad. Of course, he might have encountered the missing rhea, but I preferred to consider him a mad liar.

'What about the car?' asked Daphne.

Grubbe shrugged. 'It's a mess. I've got one of my people retrieving it and seeing if it's worth salvaging. Not that it matters. I was intending to replace it, anyway.

'But enough of that, no one got hurt and I expect you're hungry—I know I am.'

'I've found brushes with death tend to sharpen the appetite,' I said with the wisdom of experience.

Two minutes later, we seated ourselves around a table by the window, with great views of the river across to Helmet Hill and Loop Woods for the two who were facing that way. My view was of Daphne to my right, which was nice, and Grubbe to my left which wasn't, though his ruffled hair did at least make him seem a bit more ordinary.

'Since we were running late, I rang ahead and ordered for us all,' he explained. 'I hope that's alright?'

'I should think so,' said Daphne.

'Depends on what you ordered,' I said.

'Oh, have I made a faux pas?' he asked. 'You don't have any food allergies or unusual dietary requirements, do you?'

I shook my head. 'It's just that I don't like a few foods: pigs' trotters, surströmming, Casu Marzu and the like.' Admittedly, I'd never eaten the latter two, a Swedish fermented fish dish and a Sicilian maggot-infested cheese, but I'd read about them. I had, though, tried trotters—too bland and chewy for me.

'Have no fear,' said Grubbe, 'I ordered a selection of what I consider their finest dishes, and can assure you there will be nothing like that, though they do have trotters on the menu—their Pieds de Cochon Farci au Foie Gras et aux Langoustines is one of their signature dishes. I have also taken the liberty of ordering wine—the Chateau Jacques is a passable Burgundy.'

Although Daphne appeared relaxed about his presumption, I was not. I'd have much preferred to peruse the menu, pretend to ponder deeply, despite my weak grasp of French, and order something expensive—why not if he was footing the bill?

The headwaiter brought over a bottle of wine and poured a drop into Grubbe's glass. The pretentious git held it up to the light, swirled the ruby red liquid, took a lingering sniff, sipped, and rolled it around his mouth. 'That will do,' he said.

The headwaiter nodded and filled our glasses.

I had a taste. If Grubbe had been hoping to impress me, he'd failed. Not that there was anything wrong with the Chateau Jacques, it was just that I'd often enjoyed far better—Hobbes received an annual crate of fantastic wines from a mysterious count he'd helped during the First World War, and he was generous with it. This got me thinking of Hobbes's age, for although he could have passed for a fit man in his early fifties, I knew him to be far older. Sometimes, I glimpsed the depth of time in his eyes and was amazed.

'Does the wine meet with your approval?' asked Grubbe.

I came back to the present. 'It will do,' I said, echoing him.

He grinned. 'It bloody well should do at ninety quid a bottle.'

Daphne took a sip and smiled. 'Nice.'

I smiled the complacent smile of a man who knew better—last time I'd been there, Violet, who knew what she was doing, had ordered far superior wine at half the price. As the second drink kicked in, my mind drifted back to the short period when, despite her beauty, sophistication and wealth, I'd hoped she might be the woman for me. It all seemed so long ago, and so much had changed since then. Most of it for the better. I was so happy with Daphne: her kind, dark eyes, her soft brown hair, her neat figure, her intelligence, her humour and, most of all, her continuing tolerance of me. With Violet, there'd always been a touch of terror. Still, sometimes I wondered what might have been.

When I emerged from my reverie, Grubbe and Daphne were discussing his offer, but before I could work out where they'd got to, the first dish arrived. It was French onion soup with a sourdough crust smothered in Comté cheese. The rich, savoury aroma was seductive.

The waiter served us. 'Bon appetite,' he said and merged into the background.

The soup came close to matching one of Mrs Goodfellow's masterpieces—perhaps Grubbe's judgement had been sound in this case, though all the food at Le Sacré Bleu had a reputation for excellence. I decided to enjoy the meal on its own merits and thought I might write an article—Ralph would be delighted with a positive review, especially when it wouldn't cost the *Bugle* a penny in expenses.

'That's most generous, isn't it?' said Daphne.

'What?' I said, as I chased the last drop around the bowl.

'Valentine's offer.'

'Oh, yes,' I said, hoping it was. 'And the soup's good, too.'

'Glad you like it,' said Grubbe with a condescending smile. He turned back to Daphne. 'Are you happy to sign a contract?'

She shook her head. 'Not now. I need to take a step back, think about what you've said, and read through it in slower time.'

'Very wise,' said Grubbe. 'Ah, here's the next course—I ordered a selection.'

The waiter set down a tray and distributed the dishes around the table, pointing out moules marinières, baked goat's cheese, pork rillettes, smoked aubergine roulade with spinach and sun-dried tomatoes, steaks frites and an assortment of light vegetables.

'That all looks jolly nice,' said Grubbe as the waiter departed. 'Please, help yourselves.'

It was good, but we hadn't made much of an inroad when a shadow fell across the table.

The lanky, middle-aged woman I'd noticed earlier was standing there. I recognised her—it was Rosemary Crackers. This time, her eyes were wild and her face was flushed. 'You disgust me,' she said, leaning towards Grubbe.

'I expect I do,' he said and sighed. 'Sorry.'

'Don't sorry me, you swine,' she said, her voice slurred. 'You are a despoiler of the countryside, a ravager of beauty, and a total bastard to boot.'

'Guilty,' said Grubbe with a nonchalant shrug, 'but people need somewhere to live. I give them houses. What do you do?'

Rosemary snorted, her narrow nostrils flared, and her voice changed to a shriek that made everyone stare. 'Give?' she laughed. 'You don't give, you charge ridiculous prices for your shoddy little boxes.'

'I can assure you that we will build our homes to the highest standards.' Grubbe smiled. 'Look, I know we'll never agree, but you've made your point, so would you kindly allow me and my friends to enjoy our lunch?'

In response, Rosemary tipped the bowl of moules marinières over Grubbe, who squeaked like a dog's toy. I sniggered, and then gasped as she grabbed the wine bottle, wielding it like a club as the ruby fluid ran down her sleeve.

As the headwaiter rushed towards us looking horrified, the tall, older man, who had a clipped moustache and a military bearing, marched from the dim recesses of the restaurant.

'Stop that, Rosie!' He took her by the shoulder and relieved her of the bottle.

'I must apologise for my daughter's outrageous behaviour,' he said as she hung her head like a naughty child. 'She's passionate about nature, but can get carried away, and she's not been herself for the last few days. She's taken far more wine than is good for her, though that's no excuse. Please, allow me to pay for your meal and for the cost of cleaning your suit.'

Grubbe's smile was rueful, but forgiving as he contemplated his crotch. The pile of mussels there reminded me of a rocky shore at low tide, and I couldn't suppress another heartless snigger.

156

'Don't worry about it,' he said. 'It's all part of life's rich tapestry.'

'Most decent of you,' said Rosemary's father.

'Not at all,' said Grubbe. 'Your daughter clearly cares about the environment, and I can understand that. However, my company will be doing its utmost to mitigate any damage to the area.'

'Liar!' said Rosemary.

'Enough!' said her father.

'Sorry, Daddy.'

'I'll take her home. I don't know what's come over her. Once again, I apologise. Good afternoon.' He nodded and propelled Rosemary away.

'That was exciting,' said Grubbe, mopping his lap with a napkin. 'Sorry about that.'

'Are you all right?' asked Daphne, looking shocked.

'I'm fine,' he said with a cheerful grin, 'but I'll be better when someone helps me clear up these molluscs.'

The waiter and the headwaiter brought a bucket, napkins, and profuse apologies to our table.

14

Once the staff had mopped Grubbe down, they left us to enjoy the rest of the meal. And, although I hated to admit it, he'd chosen well. In particular, the sensational, succulent pork rillettes slathered over crisp, toasted slices of baguette was heavenly. Furthermore, now business was complete, he proved a genial companion—even if he did exude an overwhelming fishy odour.

'What's your connection to this town?' I asked after stuffing myself rigid on dessert, a scrumptious tarte tatin, with beautiful, buttery pastry, and wonderfully sweet, caramelised apples. 'That is to say ... umm ... why did you choose Colonel Squire as a partner?'

'I was looking for business opportunities in the region and heard that Toby Squire needed ready cash for urgent repairs to his manor. I've known Toby for years, so I brought him to this restaurant for lunch and suggested a development would be mutually beneficial. He put forward Sorenchester Common as an ideal location.'

'But why? There are already enough homes and few homeless people.'

Grubbe shrugged. 'But housing is expensive, and many young people struggle to afford anything. I like to help them.'

'So, you intend to build affordable housing?' asked Daphne.

He nodded. 'Yes ... well, some of it will be. The idea is that other properties will be more exclusive and the profits from these will help pay for the affordable ones.'

'What about jobs?' I asked. 'Unemployment is low round here.'

'That,' said Grubbe, 'is an excellent point. However, it is rising. For instance, many shops have closed recently. My development includes space for industrial units which will attract new businesses, and, of course, new businesses need new workers. The project will be a great boost to the local economy.'

It sounded great as he told it—apart from the environmental aspects, where all the new people would come from, who would pay for the infrastructure, and a sack load of other questions. I'd have liked to ask more, but he glanced at his Rolex and stood up. 'I must be on my way—I have a meeting in half an hour and need to change my suit.'

'It's time I was getting back too,' said Daphne.

'And me,' I said, 'but I need the loo first.'

Grubbe signalled the waiter, took a credit card from his wallet and paid. 'Corbett will take you back to town. He's waiting in the carpark. Goodbye and thanks for agreeing to the work ... in principle, Daphne. Andy.' He nodded and was gone.

So was I—my bladder could wait no longer.

When I rejoined Daphne, she was standing in the doorway, staring towards Loop Woods and frowning.

'What's the matter?' I asked.

'There's a funny noise up there.'

A deep boom resounded from up the hill.

'What do you think it is?' she asked.

'No idea ... it sounds a bit like someone blowing over the top of a jug.'

Something burst from cover and came hurtling down the hill.

It was a huge, brownish bird with long, powerful legs and a neck like an ostrich's.

'That must be the rhea,' I said. 'It escaped from the Wildlife Park.'

'I bet that's what made Valentine crash,' said Daphne. 'I'm surprised you never mentioned it.'

'It crossed my mind,' I admitted, 'but I didn't think it could have reached here—the Wildlife Park is miles away.'

'If it always runs like that, it wouldn't take long to get anywhere,' she said. 'Someone ought to catch it—it's clearly a danger to traffic.'

I nodded. 'Not just to traffic. According to Mr Catt, they can disembowel a man with a single kick. Look at it go!'

Each stride was bringing the rhea closer. Its long legs were pumping like the coupling rods on a speeding steam locomotive, and I watched, entranced by its tiny head which never wobbled or bobbed despite the rough ground.

'It's coming this way, isn't it?' Daphne sounded a little nervous.

'Yes,' I said. 'Umm ... what's that?'

It was Hobbes, his loose mac flapping like bat wings as he pounded down the hill in pursuit. Since I didn't think Daphne had seen him in full charge before, it must have been a shock to her, as it had once been to me—I reckoned he could have outpaced any Olympic sprinter. A few moments later, Dregs appeared, following with grim determination, trying to keep up, though neither he nor Hobbes was a match for the rhea.

'Perhaps, we'd better take cover,' I suggested as the bird drew nearer—getting disembowelled seemed such a waste of a fine lunch.

She nodded and took a step back. But there was no need, because the rhea changed course on reaching the foot of the hill and bounded along the side of the Soren. Within no time at all, it was out of sight.

Moments later, Hobbes leapt across the river and joined us. 'Good afternoon, Andy, Daphne,' he said, breathing a little heavier than usual. 'We almost had him in the woods when he was booming, but he gave us the slip. He's a fast one, isn't he?'

'Very,' said Daphne. 'Do you know he ran into the road earlier and made Valentine Grubbe crash? You need to catch him before he kills somebody.'

'Before Grubbe kills somebody?' I asked with a facetious grin.

'The rhea!'

'Oh, right ... umm ... is Dregs alright?'

The dog who'd slowed to a tongue-lolling trot, reached the river and slumped into it as if he'd collapsed.

'He's just cooling off,' said Hobbes. 'That was an invigorating chase.'

'Though the rhea got away,' said Daphne.

Hobbes nodded. 'He did, but at least I learned something.'

'What?' she asked.

'How not to catch him,' he replied with a wolfish grin. 'Since I can't match him for speed, I'll have to come up with a better method.'

Dregs emerged from his wallow and sauntered towards us, tail wagging. I'd forgotten his sense of humour and thought he was just pleased to see us until he shook and showered us with river water.

'Bad dog!' said Daphne with a smile.

Dregs snickered.

'Sorry about that,' said Hobbes. 'He lacks manners.'

'But I can't stop now, I've got a bird to catch, and then I intend to find the killer. DCI Kirten does not appear to be making any progress.'

'I didn't think it was your case,' said Daphne.

'Any crime on my patch,' he said, 'is my case, and if Kirten can't catch young Timmy's killer, then I will. However, getting that bird under control is my primary concern at the moment.'

'I'll see you later. Come on, Dregs.'

As he and the dog loped away, Corbett turned up with the car.

'Home, please,' said Daphne as he opened the doors.

On getting back to our place, Daphne changed her clothes and popped her dress into a laundry bag. 'I'm going to get this dry-cleaned—some of that mussel juice splashed it, and then Dregs made his contribution. Does anything of yours need cleaning?'

I checked my jacket and trousers. They looked alright. 'No,' I said.

'What about those trousers with the orange juice?'

'Oh, yeah.'

'Where are they?' asked Daphne.

'Umm ... '

She rummaged through the wardrobe—I'd hung them up again.

'What are you going to do for the rest of the afternoon?' she asked, holding out the bag.

I threw in the trousers. 'I'll write a review of Le Sacré

Bleu.'

She smiled, kissed me, said 'goodbye', and hurried back to the museum. I went downstairs and started my laptop.

My intention was good, though I could still feel the alcohol in my brain. I typed in a title, 'C'est fantastique, Le Sacré Bleu!', and was forming a first line along the lines of 'You are guaranteed a warm welcome at Le Sacré Bleu ... ' when thoughts of Grubbe's alleged wife distracted me. Since a run-of-the-mill Google search only turned up the same references I'd discovered earlier, I tried all sorts of different searches. In the end, I'd skimmed through pages of irrelevant stuff before I came across a twelve-year-old archive edition of St Stephen's Parish magazine.

It looked more promising than the other stuff, though it started with an unhinged and bizarre article from the vicar at the time, Henry 'Hellish' Mellish. (Henry went on to posthumous fame when struck down by a bolt from the blue, or to be more accurate, part of a satellite, during the church fete.) Then came a report of a wedding: Edward Valentine Grubbe, bachelor, had married Helen Jane Fry, spinster of the parish. A blurry photograph of the happy couple being pelted with rice outside the church made me as certain as dammit that I'd found my man. So, he had been married! So, what had happened to his wife?

I resorted to Google again, but turned up very little on Helen Fry or Helen Grubbe as I supposed she might have become.

One article distracted me, a totally irrelevant historical account of the trial of an earlier Helen Grubbe, who was arrested for witchcraft in 1645. Luckily for her, an enlightened judge saw through the imaginative 'evidence' against her, realised the accusation was nothing more than a scheme to gain control of her land, and declared her innocent. Then, in a rare display of poetic justice, he'd sentenced her accusers to the pillory. The playful populace of Sorenchester had pelted them with sheep dung for two happy hours. It was a fascinating tale and I made a note to write about it for the *Bugle*—there was often a need for historical filler.

The front door opened and Daphne was home—I'd wasted three hours when I should have been working.

'A good afternoon?' I asked, getting up to give her a hug.

She smiled. 'It was okay, but quiet. I was intending to finish something for a school visit, but it turned out to be poor Timmy Rigg's school, and unsurprisingly the head cancelled the trip. Still, it gave me time to look around for material for Valentine.'

'Did you find anything?'

'Not much. So far, it's only a few bits I'd already dug out for Mr Hobbes. I can't really believe it's a coincidence that they're both interested in local cryptids.'

I shrugged. 'I should think it is. Grubbe's interest must be connected to his development, and Hobbes is probably looking for something to do with crime—he's not interested in history without a good reason.'

'That makes sense if you've already lived through a good chunk of it,' said Daphne. 'Have you ever asked how old he is?'

'I once asked Mrs G, but she didn't know. I've never dared ask him.'

She sat down on the sofa and nodded. 'I get that—it might offend him. The thing is, I've come across loads of old photos in the archives, and some of them look just like him. If I didn't know better, I'd have assumed they were his ancestors.'

'It's best not to think about it too much,' I said. 'I don't anymore. Not often, anyway—it hurts my head.'

'You're right,' she said. 'But, I'm worried. What if Mr Hobbes is one of the cryptids? I don't want to make things awkward for him.'

'That's a good point,' I said. 'And there are others: Featherlight and Sid and … '

Daphne bit her lip. 'That's true—I'm now wondering if I was a little hasty in suggesting that I'd accept the work. I was thinking about things like the Loch Ness Monster and dragons, not people we know. I'm just glad I didn't sign the contract.'

'Well,' I said, 'you could always leave our friends out of your report.'

'I could, but would it be right or fair to expose the others? Whatever you want to call them.'

'Unhumans,' I suggested.

She nodded. 'Would it be right to expose them? I'm sure Valentine means no harm, but … I'm not sure what to do.'

'Umm … you could give him a bogus report. Something he'd like to read.'

'That wouldn't be ethical. I'd be taking money under false pretences.'

'You'll never become a newspaper reporter with ideas like that,' I said, intending it as a joke, though it contained a massive dollop of truth—I'd met a number of reporters who'd based lucrative careers on pandering to their readers' prejudices rather than in revealing the truth. I had a nagging fear Ralph was one of them, and though I maintained a naive belief in

165

honest journalism, I had no wish to lose my job. How far would I compromise my ideals to keep it?

'I'm going to think about it,' said Daphne.

'It's often best to sleep on a problem.'

She nodded, but looked sceptical. 'But am I delaying when I've already decided in my heart? Am I just making things more difficult than they are? If you have to swallow a frog, it's best not to look at it for too long.'

'That reminds me,' I said. 'What would you like for supper?'

'Not much—I'm still quite full from lunch. How about you?'

'I am a little peckish. Perhaps I'll make some beans on toast.'

'That would be okay—just one slice for me. Is your leg up to standing?'

'Probably—I've barely given it a thought today. It's still tender if I poke it, but other than that, I think it's almost better.'

'Good.' She smiled. 'I'd suggest not poking it, and sleeping upstairs tonight.'

Next morning, I woke in bed—it was so much comfier than the sofa and I'd slept heavily. Daphne was already sitting up. She looked tired.

'What's wrong?' I asked.

'I woke early and couldn't get back to sleep.'

'Are you still worrying about Grubbe's contract?'

She nodded. 'We really could do with the money, but I don't want to put our friends and others in the spotlight. Mr Hobbes hates publicity, and what if people find out about Sid? Many are scared of difference, and it's easy to whip up their fears, even though Sid's harmless.'

I nodded, though I would never have described Sid Sharples, our bank manager and friend, as harmless. He was, for sure, a charming, kindly man, but unlike Daphne, I'd seen him fight—he also happened to be a vampire.

'If the wrong people find out,' Daphne continued, 'there might be trouble—I keep thinking of those old films when the townsfolk take up flaming torches and pitchforks to kill the monster. What would you do?'

I came close to saying that I wouldn't have had any dealings with Grubbe in the first place, whether or not we needed the money. However, I figured out just in time that this might not be tactful. 'Umm ... you could talk to Hobbes.'

'But he's always busy, and he's helped us so much already.'

'He won't mind,' I said. 'He won't bite your head off.'

Daphne nodded and gasped. 'Look at the time! We'd better get a move on or we'll be late for work.'

After a quick shower, a shave and a bite of breakfast, I headed towards the *Bugle*, my leg giving only the occasional mild twinge. I was approaching the office when a rusty white minibus packed with tough-looking men stopped at the kerbside. The driver, wearing stained jeans and a grubby white t-shirt, leapt out holding a large brown envelope and rushed into the building. I reached the front door and was pressing down on the handle, when he ran back out, apologised for bumping into me, jumped back into the minibus and sped away. I was halfway upstairs before I realised it had been Corbett, the chauffeur. Why was he driving an old minibus? Not that it was any of my business what he did in his spare time.

'Morning, Andy!' Ralph's hearty voice boomed round

the office as I entered. 'What time do you call this?'

I checked the clock—I wasn't late, but I still felt guilty. 'Time I was at work,' I said.

'Quite right.'

Something looked different. A desk was empty. Not mine, but Duncan Donohue's. 'What's up with Dunc?' I asked. Our crime correspondent was always punctual.

'I've had to let Drunken Duncan go.' Ralph made a drinking-from-a-bottle gesture. 'His replacement starts next week. In the meantime, Andy, I'd like five hundred words to reassure our readers that the police are close to an arrest in the Timmy Rigg case and that there is nothing to worry about.'

Shocked at Duncan's fate, I nodded, accepting the assignment with the assurance of one who'd once been the *Bugle's* temporary deputy stand-in crime-reporter. Back then, I got fired by Rex Witcherley, the editor, because, instead of reporting a case, I'd got myself involved in it. That was when I'd first met Hobbes.

'Now that's sorted out,' said Ralph, 'I have a meeting. I'll be back in an hour or two. If anyone wants me, tell them ... oh, just make up something.'

Basil Dean was lurking behind his computer screen. As Ralph left, he leaned across, fixed his non-revolving eye on me and whispered. 'He didn't fire Dunc. Dunc resigned—he didn't like what our esteemed editor had done to his piece about shady dealings in Squire's new development.'

I raised my eyebrows.

Basil continued. 'By the time Ralph had finished with it, possible criminal activity sounded like a harmless, schoolboy prank, nothing more than a naughty, but understandable, bending of the rules to cut through the tedious bureaucracy and ensure the smooth running of a project that will benefit the whole of Sorenchester, if not the whole of humankind.'

'I can see why that annoyed Dunc,' I said.

'Annoyed is not the word! He had a meltdown, called Ralph all the rude names in the dictionary plus several I hadn't heard before, and resigned on the spot.'

'That's drastic,' I said. 'What's he going to do?'

'Not a clue, mate,' said Basil.

'I expect he'll look for a job elsewhere.'

Basil nodded. 'But there aren't so many these days, and word gets around, if you know what I mean. Dunc will be lucky to get anything in newspapers at his time of life.'

'You have got to admire him, though,' I said.

'Have I?' said Basil. 'Well, I don't blame him—I might do the same myself if I wasn't within a year of retirement. I did a piece about the town's infrastructure not being able to cope with the development, the roads being too small for the increased traffic, the sewers and drains already being near capacity, and the requirement for a whole new supply of water, gas and electricity. Our idiotic editor changed enough to make them seem minor points that are all dealt with in the planning documents. They aren't, though—I've gone through them line by line, and ... '

'Rather you than me,' I said.

' ... and there's not a mention of these factors. They'll cost this town and district millions, and the developers will barely pay a penny.'

The door burst open and Ralph marched in, flanked by two heavies.

'I heard all that, Mr Dean,' said Ralph. 'If you don't want to work with my methods, I don't want you on my team. Pack your things, you are out. Now!'

'You've been bugging us!' said Basil.

'No, just listening in.' Ralph pointed towards the phone on the desk. It was off the hook. He held a mobile in his hand. I desperately tried to think if I'd said anything out of turn.

Basil, pale of face, his eyes angry, swept his belongings into his backpack. 'If I were you, Andy, I'd get out of this.'

All I could do was to risk a sympathetic smile as the two heavies escorted him from the building.

'Sorry you had to witness that,' said Ralph, 'but I'd suspected Mr Dean was undermining my authority.' He smiled. 'The office will be a much more harmonious place without his disruptive presence.'

'But who's going to find the stories and write all the articles?' I asked. 'Duncan and Basil were our chief reporters.'

'Mr Donahue's replacement will do most of that when she gets here. In the meantime, Andy, you must fill in for them. I'll lend a hand when I have a few minutes.' Ralph smiled.

My stomach lurched. How could I do three people's jobs? I barely had the time to do my own.

'Don't worry about it,' said Ralph, reading my panicked expression. 'It'll be easy. All we have to do is work smarter, not harder.'

He grinned as if the vacuous remark meant something. I grinned back, humouring the maniac.

15

It became the busiest day of my newspaper career. No sooner had I bashed out an optimistic and ill-informed draft about the investigation into Timmy's murder than Ralph demanded it, edited it, and posted it on the *Bugle*'s web edition, one of Phil Waring's innovations. Before I'd had time to look at the finished article, Ralph had me writing up my review of Le Sacré Bleu, which I did without mentioning Grubbe or Rosemary Crackers. Next, I wrote five hundred words in praise of Councillor Ranulph Sydney for his sterling work in ensuring the potholes in the town's roads were fixed. Although I'd not noticed any improvements, Ralph insisted it would make our readers happy. I began to understand his point of view—saying something was better was almost as effective and was far cheaper than doing anything. Lunch was a sandwich and a can of lemonade at my desk, while typing a few words about the ongoing rhea hunt with my free hand.

Having finished both sandwich and the rhea story, I stood up and reached for my jacket.

'Where do you think you're going?' asked Ralph.

'Out, to see if I can find some stories to report.'

'No, no, no, no, no!' said Ralph, slamming his fist on his desk with every syllable. 'That's not working smarter—you'll waste all your time doing nothing before coming across anything of interest, and there's still half a paper to fill.'

'Umm ... what should I do then?'

'Google other news sites and social media and find something interesting about the area.'

'Alright, and if anything turns up, I can go there—that's not a bad idea.'

'No!' Ralph shook his head. 'Cut and paste the good bits and puff them out a bit with local knowledge and imagination. Add names when you can, and if it's not opening the paper up to a libel case—people love to read about themselves and their friends. We need to make the *Bugle* profitable again, and we'll do that by pleasing our readers and our advertisers.'

'Okay,' I said, too flummoxed to resist.

'Good.' Ralph nodded and smiled. 'Start with Twitter.'

I spent the next four hours browsing, cutting and pasting and making stuff up. It filled the paper, but it was light years away from what I'd always considered reporting—there was no time to reflect or delve. In truth, I hadn't always lived up to my own standards, but I couldn't help feeling that there ought to be some meat in a story, seasoned, if possible, with a little unbiased analysis. I didn't complain, though—Basil's abrupt firing had unnerved me. He was a solid, experienced reporter, far better than me, and had often helped out in my early days at the paper. Looking back to when I'd been a cub reporter for an embarrassing length of time, I would have lost my job on several occasions had he not quietly come to my rescue. I would miss him. Duncan, too, though he'd been inclined to keep himself to himself.

The *Bugle* felt different. Of course, all businesses

must adapt, but in the past, new technology and the slow flow through of staff had driven the change. Now, I was astonished and terrified to be the only reporter other than Ralph himself. However, Ralph had already enrolled two new people into our advertising section, since he believed ads brought in far more revenue than actual sales of the paper. He demanded that staff treat companies who'd paid for advertising with respect at all times. Although I'd thought this reasonable when he'd first said it, I'd now glimpsed what it meant in practice and was worried.

'That's me finished for the day,' said Ralph at six o'clock. 'You've done well, Andy—I knew you would!'

I mumbled my gratitude.

He stepped towards the door. 'I'm off now. Don't stay too late.' He paused. 'You do have the office keys, don't you?'

'No,' I said—I'd never needed them and, I suspected, no one had trusted me with them before.

'You can have Basil's.' Ralph reached into his desk drawer and handed me a bunch of keys. 'There you go. Have a nice evening.' He was off.

I finished plagiarising a story about wasps in a log pile, locked up and trudged home.

Daphne was in before me—a rare event.

'Are you alright?' she asked as I slumped onto the sofa.

'I suppose so.' I told her of the day's events.

She gave me a sympathetic smile and a hug, brought me a mug of tea, and I revived. 'How was your day?'

'Quiet.'

'And ... umm ... did you do anything for Grubbe?'

'Sort of. I searched during my lunchtime and found something that might be interesting, but I'm still worried about sharing it. I took your advice in the end.'

'Good. What advice?'

'I called Mr Hobbes—he's invited us for supper.' She glanced at the hideous cuckoo clock on the wall, a wedding gift from my parents. 'We don't want to be late.'

I nodded. 'We'd better get a move on—he can get rather wild when he's hungry.'

She smiled. 'So, move yourself—and quickly!'

A brisk walk through town took us to Number 13 Blackdog Street. Daphne rang the bell, and Mrs Goodfellow opened the door a few seconds later. I braced myself against Dregs, but he didn't show. I missed his enthusiasm. Still, I was more than compensated by the smell of cooking as the old girl led us into the sitting room.

'Come in, dears, and make yourself comfortable.' She gestured towards the worn but comfortable red velour sofa that must have occupied the spot for decades. It looked even more threadbare than I remembered. The room, neat and tidy as always, smelt of polish, though there was also the faint feral scent I associated with Hobbes.

'The old fellow will be home in a few minutes—he and Dregs are out having a friendly little chat with a fraudster who tricked old Mrs Diogenes out of her week's pension.'

From my experience of being an observer of Hobbes's friendly little chats, the fraudster, if he had any wits left afterwards, would devote the rest of his life to charitable works.

'I'd better check on the supper,' said Mrs Goodfellow. 'It won't be long.'

'Smells good,' said Daphne.

'Better than good,' I said. My sad lunchtime sandwiches seemed a century ago.

The front door opened. There was a woof, and I was engulfed in Dregs who, for reasons only he understood, loved to rough me up. I didn't mind, unless he knocked me into a puddle, or worse. Daphne, on the other paw, he treated with gentle friendliness.

'Evening all,' said Hobbes, closing the front door and hanging up his raincoat. 'Glad you could make it.'

He pounded upstairs and returned a minute or two later, washed and wearing new slippers—novelty ones that looked like rabbits. I hoped they were slippers.

'Supper's ready,' said Mrs Goodfellow, making me jump, though not very high, since Dregs had draped himself over my legs.

Trying not to rush, I allowed Daphne and Hobbes to lead me into the kitchen. We sat around the scrubbed wooden table and Mrs G carried over an iron casserole dish that looked as if it weighed as much as Dregs.

'I hope Lancashire Hotpot is alright?'

'Of course,' Daphne and I said in unison.

The old girl served us, Hobbes said grace, and we were allowed to eat. Succulent chunks of lamb melted in the mouth, the vegetables were magnificent, and the crisped, browned potatoes on top were perfect. The food at Le Sacré Bleu had been exceptional, but this went way beyond it for taste and comfort. I'd sometimes thought it was just as well she'd never opened a restaurant because all the others would have given up in despair, and I would never have got my job. I still found it strange that she never ate with us—in fact, I couldn't recall ever seeing her eat at all, unless she'd have a taste to ensure a meal met the mark. It always did.

We ate as ever in reverential silence.

Afterwards, she gave us mugs of tea, cleared the table and started washing up.

It's often been said that it's the thought that counts—I thought I might offer to help her, but my mobile vibrated in my pocket.

Hobbes rose to his slippered feet and said to Daphne. 'Let's go through to the sitting room. I believe you have a question for me?'

She nodded and stood up.

'I'd better just check this,' I said, taking my mobile out as they walked away. It was rare for me to receive a text, and most of the ones I did get I could have lived without.

It was from Papa's Piri-Piri Palace. 'Thanks for your great review of our restaurant—much appreciated. Glad you enjoyed it. Come back anytime.'

'What the!'

'A problem, dear?' asked Mrs Goodfellow, scrubbing a plate.

'Umm ... not exactly ... it's a mistake, I think. I hope so.'

With all the haste my clumsy fingers would allow, I clicked onto the *Bugle*'s website and scrolled through until my review. But, despite having my name on the by-line, it was not mine at all—Ralph had changed it beyond recognition. I'd expected him to tone down my righteous fury, but he'd murdered it! Most of the words were mine, but re-arranged so that the piece now read like fulsome praise. It was appalling! Forgetting where I was, I swore.

'Language, dear,' said Mrs G, giving me her cross look.

'Sorry,' I said, 'but I didn't know what else to say. The

editor has completely changed the meaning of what I wrote.'

'Then, I'll forgive you. My husband only swore if it slipped out. A change of tailor solved the problem.'

I wondered what she was rabbiting on about, but didn't care—it stunned me that Ralph would do such a reckless thing. A sparkling review like that would draw my readers to Papa's Piri-Piri Palace, where they'd all get sick or die and my reputation would be ruined! And what if they sued me? Would a judge believe I hadn't written it when my name was at the top, next to that excruciating photo from when I'd been more than a little tubby?

Getting up in a seething daze, I wandered through to the sitting room and slumped beside Daphne on the sofa. Hobbes was in his armchair, his slippered feet resting on the coffee table, alongside the latest edition of *Sorenchester Life*. I groaned, because my reviews were syndicated in that esteemed publication. Swarms of my readers would drop like flies, and any survivors would sue me en masse.

'What's up?' asked Daphne.

I showed her.

'I thought you'd given that place a rotten review?'

'I had!'

Hobbes held out his hand for my mobile and looked. 'Papa's Piri-Piri Palace—that's the new place on Rampart Street. Isn't that where you got food poisoning?'

'Yes. The editor's changed what I wrote—it's my words but in a different order with some bits added and all the criticism removed.'

'Why would he do that?' asked Hobbes.

'He says he wants positive articles, but what's

positive about poisoning people?'

'Depends on the people,' said Hobbes with a grin. 'However, if the restaurant is dangerous, it needs immediate improvement or to be shut down. Adequate hygiene and proper cooking is not difficult—even Featherlight can manage it sometimes.'

Daphne nodded. 'If we stayed healthy in the Himalayas without even basic facilities, anyone should be able to do it.'

'But the point is,' I said, 'if anyone gets sick now, they'll blame me. It's going to be the end of my career!'

Hobbes shook his head. 'Poisoning people is the real point, but I understand what you mean. Do you still have your original version of the article?'

'Yes.'

'Then don't lose it. I doubt there'll be a legal problem, but it's best to err on the side of caution and that will prove you weren't to blame.'

I felt a little better. 'But people will flock to the restaurant and blame me when it's no good.'

'Calm down,' said Daphne. 'Reviews don't come with a guarantee.'

Hobbes's mobile rang. 'Inspector Hobbes. How may I help you? I see ... where? In what direction? Okay, I'll be there as soon as I can.'

'A call out?' asked Daphne.

'I'm afraid so,' said Hobbes. 'The rhea has turned up near Hedbury and caused a flock of sheep to stampede. They broke through a hedge in their panic and ran into the town where they are now creating mayhem.'

He stood up. 'This should be interesting. I'd better go—you're both welcome to come along if you fancy a bit of air.'

Daphne shook her head. 'I need a little time on my

178

own to think about what you told me. You go if you want, Andy.'

'You don't mind?'

'Of course not.'

Hobbes strode towards the door and pulled his old raincoat from the coat stand. 'Come along, Andy. And quickly. Dregs!'

'Umm ... aren't you going to put your boots on first?'

'Good idea.' He ran upstairs.

Dregs, still smacking his lips from dinner, bounded from the kitchen, alert and ready for anything. He hurtled around, tail wagging, until Hobbes clumped downstairs wearing his usual big, shiny boots. 'Let's go,' he said and opened the door.

I kissed Daphne and followed them out, adrenaline flowing—there was nothing like the rush of a good hunt with Hobbes, despite the chances of terror and pain. However, this time would be easy—we were only dealing with a runaway bird, albeit a big one with a lethal kick, and one that could outrun a racehorse.

Dusk was settling in.

Hobbes's little car wasn't parked in Blackdog Street, and he was jogging away with Dregs, leaving me to gallop after them. I was panting and wishing I hadn't eaten quite so much when, at the end of the road, we turned into Pound Street. We crossed over and approached a small gate set in the old stone wall along the edge of Church Fields. Hobbes opened it with a small key, and led us into a courtyard, almost enclosed by garages. Dregs cocked his leg against a door.

'Where's your car?' I asked between gasps.

'In pieces,' he said, pulling the gate behind me. 'It got in the way of a Pigton drug pusher's attempt to escape. Billy reckons he can put it back together—possibly even in the right order.'

'But how are we going to get to Hedbury?'

He pulled another key from his pocket and opened a garage door. 'Sid said I could borrow this.'

'Gosh!' I hadn't known Sid Sharples owned a small collection of vintage vehicles.

Hobbes tugged a dusty tarpaulin from a gleaming black motorbike and sidecar combination.

'Wouldn't a car be better?' I asked.

He shook his head. 'All of his are too big for present purposes—I might need something I can manoeuvre and use off-road.'

'Do you know how to ride a motorbike?'

'I expect so.' Hobbes's big, yellow teeth gleamed in a broad grin as the streetlights came on. He rolled the bike from the garage and locked the door behind him. 'It's all to do with controlling the throttle.'

Butterflies massed in my stomach and started fluttering. I wasn't so sure this was a good idea. I was even less sure when he reached into the sidecar, pulled out an old-fashioned peaked helmet, and jammed it onto my head. Although I'd never been one to fear confined spaces as such, the smell of old leather, the muffled hearing and the restricted vision gave me a sense of massive claustrophobia. I could have said something, remembered an urgent imaginary appointment, or something, but it was too late. He picked me up and dropped me onto the pillion. Dregs leapt into the side car. After checking we were secure, Hobbes straddled the seat, turned a key and stomped hard on the starter. The engine throbbed into life, the front wheel lifted, and we were off.

In a heap.

On our backs.

'A little too much throttle,' said Hobbes, picking himself up. 'Are you okay?'

I nodded—I was only a little winded. He pulled me back on board and we tried again. Despite a wild lurch at the start, he controlled it this time and, keeping to a moderate speed, steered us out of the courtyard, along a narrow lane and back onto Pound Street. We kept to a slow pace as we proceeded along Rampart Street, but as soon as we reached Hedbury Road it was time for me to shut my eyes, cling to the grab rail as if super-glued, and pray.

Motorbiking with Hobbes was not for the faint-hearted, so what on earth was I doing there? Dregs, on the other hand, was sitting up in the side car, his ears flapping in the wind, his mouth open as if grinning. There was nothing faint about his heart.

I clung on and tried to stay positive—I was positive death was imminent.

16

We roared down the main road. When at last I sensed we might be slowing down, I risked opening an eye. Then the other. Streetlights shone all around, and although I couldn't see much beyond Hobbes's broad back, I craned my neck and caught glimpses of the modern housing estates encircling the ancient centre of Hedbury. He brought the bike to a standstill, stopped the engine, and stepped off. Disgruntled householders and passers-by had gathered in small groups to argue and gesticulate at the woolly animals that were flocking in gardens and ignoring everything except tasty flowers.

'Hey, ewe,' said Hobbes as he approached the nearest sheep, 'what's going on here then?'

In response, the sheep, who had just finished decimating a flower bed, gave a peevish 'baa!' and turned her back on him. Clearly affronted by this display of insolence, Dregs sprang from the sidecar, barking and bristling.

'Remember what I said about sheep?' said Hobbes.

Still growling under his breath, the dog sat and stared until the sheep grew uncomfortable and rejoined her friends.

'Is anyone in charge of this lot?' asked Hobbes, turning to the people.

'Well, sir,' a short man with dark, curly whiskers around a pink face loafed towards us, 'I reckon that'd be me—in a manner of speaking.'

The man, whose features reminded me of a very intelligent monkey, looked familiar. I prised the helmet from my head for a better look.

It all came back. 'Charlie Brick! It was your pig that made Violet crash!'

My mind took me back to that night when the ambulance had carted Violet off to the hospital, leaving me to face the wrath of the furious man whose hedge she'd driven through. That and memories of the long trek home afterward caused a shiver—I'd walked through a storm with a werewolf on my trail.

Charlie stared at me for a moment and grinned. 'And how is your young lady?' he asked.

'She's probably fine,' I said, 'but we ... umm ... split up soon after. I'm married now.'

'I congratulate you on your nuptials, sir,' said Charlie.

'Enough,' said Hobbes. 'Are you responsible for these sheep or not?'

Charlie scratched his chin with a long, hairy hand. 'Yes, sir ... in a manner of speaking I am, though they're not mine, except insofar as I'm looking after them for Mr Foulkes.'

'And Mr Foulkes is?' asked Hobbes.

'The owner of the flock, sir.'

'So, he's responsible?'

'Normally, sir, he would be. Only he's had to go to the hospital. You would scarcely credit it, sir, but he got hurt by the bird that was scaring the flock.'

Hobbes, who was staring at a sheep as if ravenous, pricked up his ears. 'Can you describe the culprit?'

'It was a bloody big bird, sir,' said Charlie, 'if you'll

pardon my French. Some sort of ostrich, I'd say, with huge, clawed feet and a beak that'd make you think twice about wrestling it. Well, sir, it made me think twice, but not Mr Foulkes. He tried to tackle it and got a good stomping.'

'Are you Mr Foulkes's shepherd?' asked Hobbes.

'No, sir. I'm a pig man, myself. Always have been, always will be. My mam foretold it when I was knee high to a piglet. "Charlie," she said, "you're only a little fellow now, but you'll be a pig man someday" and, sir, she was right.'

'Then, how come you're looking after the sheep?' I asked.

'Because, sir, I was taking Cuthbert for his evening constitutional when we saw what was happening.'

'Cuthbert?' asked Hobbes.

'My prize boar, sir. He likes a walk of an evening after a hard day's eating and … doing what prize boars do.'

'Enough chitchat,' said Hobbes. 'I have two questions. First, do you require help to get the sheep back into Mr Foulkes's field?'

'I would appreciate a hand, sir. Whereas sheep may not be as wilful as pigs, they will insist on snacking and spreading out as they go.'

Hobbes nodded. 'And second, where did that bird go?'

'There you have me, sir. I last saw it zigzagging through town.'

'Thank you for your help,' said Hobbes. 'Let's get the flock out of here while there's still a little light.'

'Thank you kindly, sir,' said Charlie, pressing a grubby knuckle to his forehead. 'Their field is along Darkling Lane.' He pointed to a narrow entrance between high stone walls.

Hobbes nodded. 'Dregs!'

The dog ran towards him. Hobbes dropped to one knee, pointed, and muttered something. Dregs, tail wagging, darted behind the sheep, drove them into a single flock and, with Hobbes and Charlie blocking the main road, hurried them along the lane into the gathering darkness. Within ten minutes, they were all back in their field.

'I didn't know Dregs knew how to be a sheepdog,' I said, impressed.

'He didn't,' said Hobbes, 'but he's a quick learner.'

Charlie made running repairs to the damaged hedge. 'That ought to hold the woolly buggers—excuse my language,' he said. 'Now, where on earth did Cuthbert go?' He looked around, but there was no sign of a pig. He shrugged. 'I expect he's found his own way home. I'd best have a look. Thank you for your assistance, sirs.'

I smiled and nodded, though all I'd done was follow the flock at a safe distance.

'Where do you live?' asked Hobbes.

'Mr Brick's cottage is a couple of miles away on the road to the arboretum,' I said.

'That it is,' Charlie confirmed.

'In which case,' said Hobbes, 'may I offer you a lift?'

'Umm ... ' I said, 'don't forget we came here on Sid's motorbike. There won't be room for another.'

'I'm sure we'll manage—you'll just have to share the sidecar with Dregs.'

'Will I?'

Hobbes nodded. 'Let's get going.'

Dregs lead the way back to the motorbike combination and bounded into the sidecar.

'I thought so,' said Hobbes, taking a close look. 'There's plenty of room.' He picked me up, folded me in half, and wedged me into the space in front of Dregs, so I was facing backwards. 'You'll be fine there—just as long as you don't both breathe in at the same time.'

Unable to see, I awaited my fate with as much dignity as I could, which was not much. A thought occurred. 'Is this safe?'

'We'll be fine,' said Hobbes. 'I have no intention of crashing.'

The sidecar dipped and rocked. I guessed it was Hobbes and Charlie getting on.

'Hold tight,' said Hobbes.

'There's nothing to hold on to, tight or otherwise!' The throb of the engine drowned out my moans.

Squatting on the floor while wedged inside a sidecar with a large dog is not as much fun as it's cracked up to be. Still, the journey to Charlie's was not too terrifying since my only view was Dregs's undercarriage, and all I could hear was the thrum of the engine and the rumble of the tyres on the road. It was only a few minutes before the engine stopped. Dregs bounded out, and wriggling forward on hands and buttocks, I hauled myself to freedom. I'd been hoping for fresh air, but the pungent aroma of pig dung overwhelmed everything. Hobbes had parked the motorbike on the grass verge outside Charlie's little stone cottage. They were walking towards the front door.

'Wait for me!' I said, attempting to leap out and follow, only for my cramped legs to let me down. My leading foot snagged the rim. For a moment, I fought for balance before surrendering to gravity.

The ditch was not full of cold water, but it was full of glutinous mud that soaked through my clothes and chilled my skin. I struggled to get free, dragged myself out, and was getting to my feet when the headlights of a passing coach lit me up. The coach stopped, and the amplified voice of a guide rang out into the gathering darkness. 'Ladies and Gentlemen, before we reach Haunted Hedbury and begin our ghost tour, I'm delighted to bring you this bonus sighting of the legendary Dirty Dunderhead of the Dismal Ditch.' A powerful torch dazzled me, laughter erupted, and all I could do was stand there, drip and look gormless. After a few seconds, the coach drove away.

I couldn't see the others, but heard Dregs bark from round the back. Dropping gobbets of mud, I followed the bark as the stink of pigs grew stronger. 'What's happening? Has Charlie's pig come back?'

I squelched around the side of the cottage into the backyard, where an electric bulb dangling from an upstairs window lit up a row of concrete pens. Tail wagging, Dregs ran towards me, stopped, sneezed, and retreated. The stench was overpowering.

An enormous snoring boar dozed by the back door.

'That's my Cuthbert, sir,' said Charlie with pride in his voice. 'He won best of breed in the Sorenchester Old Spot category at last year's Sorenchester Show. He's a good lad.'

'Well done, him,' I said.

I looked at Hobbes. 'So, all's well that ends well. Can we go home now? I'm covered in mud.'

Charlie scratched his head. 'Begging your pardon, sir, but that's not mud.'

'What do you mean?' I asked, foreboding rising.

'Well, sir, did you happen to fall in the ditch?'

'What of it?'

'Well, sir, it might've been mud ... it would've been mud, only I had a bit of an overflow the other week and ...'

I knew what he was going to say. 'It was pig faeces that overflowed, wasn't it?'

Charlie looked mournful. 'No, sir—it was pig shit what overflowed. I had it all nicely rotting in a lagoon, only that rain we had made the wall fail. Well, sir, I was going to clean it up but never got round to it. I'm very sorry.' He turned to Hobbes. 'You ain't going to report me, are you, sir?'

Hobbes thought for a moment. 'It's not my department, but I will have to inform the authorities— unless you clear it up as soon as possible. We can't allow that sort of stuff into the waterways.' He contemplated me and rasped his big, hairy thumb over the stubble on his chin. 'And we can't allow you on Sid's bike like that—it wouldn't be fair.'

I shivered as the liquid dung began to dry in the light breeze. 'I'm cold and I stink and I want to go home.'

'Let me think,' said Hobbes. 'Do you have a bath, Mr Brick?'

'Of course, sir.'

'Good,' said Hobbes. 'And do you have any spare clothes that might fit him?'

'Well, sir,' said Charlie, screwing up his face with the effort of examining me, 'he's a bit bigger than me so my normal apparel will be no good, but I reckon he might just fit into my old work overalls. It'll be a pinch, mind.'

'There you are,' said Hobbes. 'If Charlie has no objections, you can have a quick wash.'

'I don't mind at all, sir,' said Charlie. 'I'll grab the bath and heat the water.'

Until then, I hadn't noticed the galvanised steel tub hanging from a nail in the wall next to the back door. Charlie took it down and let us into the kitchen, which wasn't much to write home about: a stained enamel sink with a single dripping tap, a battered Formica table, two worm-eaten wooden chairs, some shelves, and a corner cupboard standing on the chipped red-brick floor. A wood-fired range that looked as old as time covered one wall and supplied a little welcome warmth. Charlie took a blackened cauldron from a shelf, filled it with water, and plonked it on the range.

'Won't be long now, sir,' said Charlie. 'I'll go and find a pair of my old overalls. I think there's some clean ones somewhere.' He wandered away, shaking his head and humming to himself.

Hobbes and Dregs stayed in the yard with Cuthbert, who'd woken up and was watching proceedings with interest. I just wished they'd shut the door—a nasty draught was blowing in, raising countless goose pimples on my skin. I moved nearer to the range's warmth.

Charlie had placed the bath in the middle of the red-brick floor. I compared it to the size of the cauldron. 'I'm not going to get much of a wash—I'm used to lots of hot water.'

Hobbes shrugged. 'Do the best you can. In the meantime, Dregs and I are going to nose around for that rhea—it must have been heading in this general direction. Put your filthy clothes in a bag and let's hope Charlie's overalls fit.'

They left me in the company of Cuthbert, who was now lying half-on, half-off the doormat, propping open the back door with his bulk. He seemed to find me fascinating and followed my every move with curious eyes.

'What are you looking at?' I asked.

'What was that, sir?' asked Charlie, ambling back into the kitchen with a set of patched and stained khaki overalls and a large, rather threadbare towel.

'Nothing,' I said. 'Just clearing my throat.'

'Oh, I thought you were talking to Cuthbert. I often do, sir. He's a good listener.'

I nodded. 'I expect he is. Do you think you could make him move so we can shut the door—there's a horrible draught.'

'I'll see what I can do, sir,' said Charlie, 'but I can't make him do anything unless he wants to—he's far too big, if you get my drift.' Charlie took an apple from a shelf and placed it in the corner. 'Come on in if you want it.'

Cuthbert raised his head. After a moment's contemplation, he got to his trotters and skipped across the kitchen to the apple. Charlie closed the door, and Cuthbert ate, savouring every delicate bite like a gourmet.

'There you go, sir. He's very partial to a bit of fruit.'

'Thanks,' I said, though I'd hoped Cuthbert would be on the other side of the door—I'd never shared a bathroom with an enormous pig before and wasn't entirely comfortable with the idea. Still, I'd endured worse—Mrs Goodfellow had once tricked Dregs and me into sharing a flea bath when we became infested after a visit to some werewolves we knew.

'Water's hot, sir,' said Charlie, covering his hands with an old rag and lugging the cauldron over. He upended it and filled the tub to a depth of about half an inch. 'I'll just cool it off,' he said, refilled the cauldron with tap water, and added it. 'There you go, sir,' he said with a contented smile. 'I'll leave you to it. There's a bar of soap in the sink—you can use that. Put your shitty clothes in this.' He pulled a black bin bag from the cupboard and left me.

Cuthbert, having finished his apple and, seeing no more, gave a regretful sigh and lay down next to the bath, staring through round, piggy eyes as I stripped off. The intensity of his gaze was embarrassing. I stepped into the water—it would have been pleasant to wallow, but it barely covered my feet and was only tepid. I might have collapsed into misery, if experience with Hobbes hadn't taught me to make the best of things. Sitting down with my knees up to my chin, I splashed myself, much to Cuthbert's amazement, and set to work with the soap. Charlie had exaggerated by calling it a bar—it was a misshapen lump of old scraps in various shades of grey. I did my best to sluice the rancid pig stink from my body and was pleased to see and smell a difference.

When decontaminated as well as possible in the circumstances, I stood up, towelled down, stepped out, and finished drying myself by the range, performing a weird jig to ensure neither foot had too much contact with the chilly brick floor.

Rather to my surprise, Charlie's old overalls fitted, though they were a little tight here and there, mostly across the buttocks. I was grateful that he'd also brought a pair of thick woollen socks. I must have looked a horrible sight, but there was no mirror in the kitchen. It was just as well.

Cuthbert decided it was a crime to waste good bathwater and drank it.

'Desist, you daft bugger!' said Charlie as he dawdled in. 'Excuse my language—he's a charming pig, sir, but he's an idiot.'

Cuthbert ignored him.

'Would you care for a cup of tea, sir? I like to have one this time of an evening and I was going to put the kettle on.'

'Yes, please,' I said with some trepidation, uncertain about Charlie's hygiene—he had a pig in his kitchen!

'Would Earl Grey tea be to your taste, sir?'

I nodded, astonished at the sophistication—there was clearly more to Charlie than met the eye.

He put the kettle on the range, rummaged in the blue-painted cupboard, and emerged with a delicate bone china tea set on a silver tray, and a magnificent tea caddy. After going through the entire ritual—warming the pot, counting out three spoons of tea into the pot, inundating them with boiling water, and waiting for four minutes, he stirred it and pronounced it ready.

'How do you take it, sir? I usually have it with a dash of milk, but they tell me some people prefer lemon.'

'Milk would be great.'

'That's good, sir, as I appear to be right out of lemons.' He grinned and gestured towards the least wormy chair. 'Take a seat, sir.'

'Thank you.' I sat down, and Charlie lounged against the wall with Cuthbert at his feet like a monstrous lap dog.

'What's the news from Sorenchester, sir?' asked Charlie. 'Only I don't get to the big town too often these days.'

I told him of Timmy Rigg's murder.

He looked shocked. 'How horrible! Why would anyone want to shoot a child?'

I took a sip of my tea. It was perfect—Mrs G herself might have made it. 'Nobody knows,' I said.

'Somebody knows, sir,' he said, shaking his head. 'The one who pulled the trigger.'

I nodded and told him about Colonel Squire's development on Sorenchester Common.

'That's not right, sir,' said Charlie, his simian face

outraged. 'He shouldn't be doing anything there.'

'What do you mean?'

'I mean, sir, that the land doesn't belong to him.'

'I'm sure it does,' I said.

'No, sir, it does not. General Squire, I mean General Redvers Squire, not General Arthur Squire, gave it away when Queen Victoria was still a slip of a girl.'

'How would you know about that?' I asked.

'I know more than you might think, sir,' said Charlie, looking serious, 'because I was General Arthur's pig man when I was a youngster. The old man was a proper gent—he insisted I called him Arthur, and he was very fond of his pigs. He liked nothing more than to chat about them over a cup of tea—he'd fortify his with a nip of whisky. Arthur was a good man and so was his son— nothing like the present Colonel Squire. If only Mr Clarence had stayed in charge ... '

He sighed. Cuthbert was snoring.

'What does this have to do with the development?' I asked, more out of politeness than interest.

'I was coming to that, sir. One day, when Arthur had enjoyed more than his usual nip of whisky, he started talking about his grandfather—that was old General Redvers.'

I sighed—this was going to be a long job. I hoped Hobbes would be back soon.

'He told me all about the campaigns the old General had fought—exciting tales they were, too, for a young country lad like me. Then he dozed off.'

'And the common?' I said.

'Oh, yes, sir. When he woke, he said General Redvers would often ride on the common. It was more open then and still the property of the Squire family, sir.'

'Are you saying they don't own it anymore?'

'That's right, sir. The old man said his grandfather had signed it over to ... '

There was a scuffle at the back door.

It burst open and Dregs bolted in, as if pursued by demons.

A moment later, Hobbes rolled in on his back, grappling with something wrapped up in his raincoat.

The rhea's head emerged through the raincoat's sleeve and aimed a vicious peck at Hobbes's nose. A huge, clawed dinosaur foot emerged from somewhere else and tried to kick him.

Hobbes, twisting to avoid the attacks, established a firm grip on the bird's neck and looked over his shoulder. 'Andy, would you be so good as to shut the back door? My hands are a little full at the moment.'

As I pushed the door shut, Charlie picked up my discarded towel and draped it over the rhea's head. The bird relaxed.

17

Hobbes, never the best groomed of men, looked even more like someone who'd wrestled a giant bird than normal. He got to his feet, brushed off a few downy feathers, pulled out his mobile and made a call.

'Mr Catt? ... Hobbes here ... I have your bird in my custody ... Yes, there was a severe pecking in Hedbury.

'No, sir, I'm aware of no further injuries since then ... When can you get here? Good ... We're at Pigsty Cottage on the main road out of Hedbury, assuming you're coming from the direction of Sorenchester. If you pass a hedge with a car-sized hole in it, you will have gone too far.'

Dregs lay down behind Cuthbert, keeping a wary eye on the rhea, and growling whenever it twitched.

Hobbes finished his call. 'Mr Catt is on his way.'

'Good,' I said. 'I'll be delighted to see the back of that thing—it scares me.'

'I wouldn't be too alarmed,' said Hobbes. 'Mr Brick has him tamed for the present. How did you know what to do?'

Charlie grinned. 'When I was a lad, sir, my friend, General Arthur, kept geese for the Christmas market and I looked after them. Covering their eyes always kept the mad buggers quiet—I thought it might work on that too.'

'Well done,' said Hobbes, and accepted a cup of tea.

Cuthbert chose that moment to investigate the strange phenomenon. Snuffling the air, he sauntered across the kitchen, prodded the bird with his snout, and trod on the bottom of the towel. The rhea took a step back, and the towel slid to the floor.

'Umm ... ' I said, in the moment of calm before the rhea opened his wild brown eyes and glared around the room.

Dregs yelped. Cuthbert sat down in shock. The rhea went bananas. It charged anything that moved, and anything that didn't, flapping, pecking and kicking without discrimination.

Being of sound mind, and full of fear, I dodged behind Hobbes and Charlie and wedged myself into a corner where Dregs joined me. 'It's only a bird,' I said. He didn't look reassured.

One of the few facts I knew about rheas was that they were flightless, and maybe that was true, but no one had told this one. Somehow, it got a grip on the walls, and circled the kitchen, its stubby wings flapping, its vicious, horny feet knocking plaster from the walls, and pots and pans from the shelves. As Dregs and I cowered, Hobbes dived for it but missed by a feather.

'Duck!' I yelled as the rhea hurtled towards Charlie.

'No, sir, it ain't,' said Charlie.

'Umm ... What?'

'It ain't a duck, sir. Oof!'

In attempting its most ambitious circuit so far, the rhea had slipped. Charlie had caught it—right in the midriff.

Hobbes pounced.

The towel went back over the bird's head.

Peace reigned once again.

196

Hobbes removed his belt and trussed the rhea's legs.

Charlie, groaning, used Cuthbert's stolid solidity as a prop to get to his feet. 'Crikey, sir, that's a fast one and no mistake!'

Hobbes nodded. 'I'm sure it was a valuable learning experience for us all. Now, where did I put my teacup?'

There was a knock on the door.

'That'll be Mr Catt, I expect,' said Hobbes at the same time as his mobile rang. 'Would you let him in, Andy?'

I walked through Charlie's sparse sitting room: one battered sofa, one old-fashioned radio, one moth-eaten rug, and one naked light bulb dangling from the ceiling. When I reached the door, Mr Catt was waiting but something looked different—it was the smart lounge suit. I'd never before seen him without a crumpled safari suit.

He responded to my quizzical look. 'I had to look my best today—I was in court.'

'Why?'

'You remember that cold snap at Christmas?'

I nodded.

'Well, the heating in the insect house broke down. Many of them died ... it wasn't swarm enough.' He smirked at his lame joke.

'But ... umm ... I don't understand why you were in court.'

'Because of how I disposed of the dead ones—I dumped them in a lay-by and got charged with fly-tipping.' He chuckled like a schoolboy as I groaned. 'Now, I believe you have something of mine.'

'Yes,' I said. 'We have your rhea.'

Mr Catt grinned. 'You always have my ear if you need to talk.'

'You'd better come in,' I said. 'The rhea is at the back.'

'The rhea should always be at the back,' said Mr Catt, and tittered.

Mr Catt entered the kitchen and beamed. 'Mr Hobbes, you really have caught Dai the rhea! I hope you'll be better soon.'

'This is Mr Brick,' said Hobbes, ignoring the quip, and introducing our host.

'Arfur Brick?' asked Mr Catt.

Charlie shook his head. 'No, sir, that was my old man. I'm Charlie.'

'Mr Brick subdued your rhea when he was proving to be a handful,' said Hobbes.

'Then I thank him,' said Mr Catt. 'I'd better take Dai home.'

Hobbes nodded. 'And make sure he doesn't escape again. He has put the public at risk and it is only through good fortune that no one was seriously injured or worse.'

Mr Catt looked solemn. 'You are absolutely right, Inspector. *Rhea americana nobilis* and other rheiformes can be dangerous, but they are at risk from traffic. And there are hunters—one escapee got shot and made into sausages. I'm grateful no such fate has struck Dai—we have great hopes for him as the basis of a captive breeding flock. The species is near threatened in the wild.'

'Do you require a hand putting him in your van?' asked Hobbes. 'He may not go quietly.'

Mr Catt shook his head. 'He'll be fine as long as I keep his eyes covered.' He pulled a soft hood from his pocket, removed the towel, and blindfolded the bird before it could react.

In response, the bird vacated copiously down his leg.

'He's pooped on you, sir,' said Charlie with a gleeful

chuckle. 'The geese what I looked after for General Arthur would do the same given half a chance.'

With a rueful glance at his soiled trousers, Mr Catt handed back Hobbes's belt, looped a length of twine round the rhea's neck and led him through the cottage, out the front door and towards the van. We followed— all of us, including Cuthbert.

'The pig's escaped,' I said when I noticed him by my side.

'Don't you go worrying about Cuthbert,' said Charlie. 'He'll not run away—he hasn't had his supper yet, and he knows it.'

Indeed, Cuthbert proved as well behaved a pig as I'd ever met. He found a good place to watch and sat down while Mr Catt coaxed Dai into the back of the van, which was separated from the front by a sturdy, narrow-meshed grill. Dregs, alert and twitchy, kept well away, growling like a wasps' nest, and it was only after Mr Catt had removed the hood from Dai's head and had slammed the door shut, that he gave vent to his feelings. He barked ferociously as Dai glared at him through the rhea window.

'Thank you again for tracking him down,' said Mr Catt, and wiped his trouser leg with a silk handkerchief.

'Just doing my job, sir,' said Hobbes with a wolfish grin. 'I am delighted the public is no longer at risk.'

Mr Catt waved goodbye and got into the driver's seat.

'Rhea hunting is a most invigorating distraction,' said Hobbes as the van sped away, 'but I think it's now time to find out who killed young Timothy Rigg. DCI Kirten appears to be making a right dog's breakfast of the case. That last call came from Constable Poll—Kirten's arrested Mr Ching.'

'From Aye Ching's takeaway?' I asked.

Hobbes nodded.

'But I thought he was on holiday at the time.'

'He was,' said Hobbes with a sigh.

'What's a takeaway, sir?' asked Charlie. 'I never heard of such a thing.'

'It's a shop where you buy hot food to take home,' I said, wondering what sort of life Charlie led. Or was he joking? Hedbury, only a twenty-minute walk away, had both a fish and chip shop and a Chinese takeaway.

'Well, sirs, I'd better see to Cuthbert's dinner,' said Charlie. 'Drop in anytime.' He beckoned the pig and sauntered back to his cottage.

'Time to go,' said Hobbes. 'I smell rain coming, and you're not dressed for motorcycling in the wet.'

'I'm not dressed for motorcycling at all,' I said.

'Very true.' He chuckled. 'I hate to imagine what you are dressed for. Let's go.'

We hurried back to the motorbike. Dregs, tail wagging, bounded into the sidecar while I struggled to get my leg over the saddle—Charlie's overalls were exceedingly tight across my backside, and I feared they might split. Hobbes saw my difficulty, picked me up under my armpits as if I were a toddler, and plonked me into place. He leapt on, started the engine, and we sped away.

The road was dark. Too dark. I only worked out why when we overtook a white van. 'You've forgotten to turn the lights on!' I yelled, but the roar of the engine must have drowned out my voice because he didn't react.

I clung on, wishing I knew how fast we were going, though convinced it was too fast. Dregs had another opinion—the tongue-lolling, ear-flapping idiot was enjoying the ride. For a few moments there was light as

Hedbury passed in a blur and then we plunged back into darkness, tearing up the road to Sorenchester. If Hobbes's car driving hadn't toughened me up first, his motorbiking would have terrified me, but, of course, we reached Sorenchester intact.

He dropped me back home, said goodbye and pulled away. As I approached the front door, I reached into my pocket, only to find the pockets weren't where I expected them. And the ones I had were all empty, other than the balled-up, tattered remains of an old tissue.

My keys had been in my jacket pocket.

My jacket was with the rest of my dung encrusted clothes in the bin bag on Charlie's kitchen floor.

Other than a light in the porch, the house looked dark. I guessed Daphne had already turned in—not surprising as it had just gone midnight. Knowing she was a heavy sleeper, I pounded on the door. There was no response. No problem, I thought, and reached for my mobile—the beeps from our house phone could wake the dead. But my mobile was in my jacket, in the bag, on the floor in Charlie's kitchen. As was my wallet, now I came to think of it. In desperation, I pounded on the door again.

Rain came down, and it was not of the gentle rain that droppeth from heaven variety—it was a deluge, billowing up The Boulevard in horrible gusts. As I stood there wondering what to do, a waterfall started up from the broken bit of gutter and poured straight down my neck. I recoiled, but within seconds, Charlie's old overalls were drenched. I kept pounding for want of anything better to do, though horrible thoughts crossed my mind. Was she ill? Had she gone straight round to Grubbe's, accepted his offer and stayed on? The rational part of me knew I was being stupid—there was no reason to think she was not fit and well and, despite my insecurities and inadequacies, she was still in love with me, though why was a mystery.

Ten minutes of door thumping had no effect, except on my knuckles. My teeth were chattering, and hypothermia beckoned. I sat on the step, curled into a ball, and tried to think what to do. Should I head over to Blackdog Street and fling myself on Hobbes's mercy again? It would take me fifteen minutes to get there and he would have turned in, but I was already chilled and could think of nothing better.

Three shadowy figures were approaching under the cover of umbrellas.

A voice called out. 'Who are you? What do you want?'

It was Daphne, flanked by her beauteous friend Pinky and Pinky's vampire lover, Sid.

'Thank God!' I cried and stood up.

Daphne ran to me. 'Andy? Are you alright? What are you doing out here? Why are you dressed like that?'

'I had an accident ... '

'Are you hurt?'

'Not that kind of accident. I fell in some pig shit and had to borrow these things ... '

She threw her arms around me.

' ... and I put my dirty clothes in a bin bag which I forgot to pick up. My keys and everything are in it, so I couldn't get in and I couldn't wake you.'

'I wasn't asleep.'

'Oh, no ... of course not ... umm ... where were you?'

'You could talk outside in the rain and catch your death, or we could go inside,' said Pinky, giving me the kind but amused smile that always made me want to act like an over-eager puppy.

Daphne opened the door and let us in.

'Better strip those wet rags off him,' said Pinky, winking one of her big blue eyes at me.

A sudden blush warmed my face.

'A hot bath will take away the chills,' said Sid, a benevolent toothy grin creasing his plump face.

Daphne led me upstairs into the bathroom and ran the bath while I stripped off and shivered. When at last I stepped into the water, my chilled skin tingled with the blessed warmth. In no time, my teeth stopped chattering. I told Daphne of my evening and to give her credit, she only laughed twice. As I got up to dry myself, she left me to it. From below, I heard the rise and fall of voices, laughter, and finally a cheery 'goodnight' from Sid. The front door closed.

I made my way to the bedroom and snuggled into bed.

'I was so relieved when you came back,' I said, when Daphne joined me. 'Mind you, a few minutes earlier would have been better.'

'Sorry. If I'd expected such a tale of woe, I'd have been back earlier. I'd gone round to Sid and Pinky's to talk things through after what Mr Hobbes told me—she's a good listener and Sid's financial advice was helpful.'

'Why did you want financial advice at this time of night?'

'It wasn't this time of night when I went there. The thing is, I've decided to turn down Valentine's contract, though the money would have been useful. We're not too well off at the moment and the guttering needs fixing, and we could do with new windows.'

I nodded and yawned before what she'd said hit me. 'You've turned down the contract?'

She nodded. 'I couldn't square it with my conscience. Although I don't suppose Valentine means any harm, I feel I might expose some of our friends and other innocents to unwelcome scrutiny, and I'd never forgive myself if someone got hurt because of me. Mr Hobbes didn't seem worried about himself, but there are others.'

'But Grubbe would have paid you so much!' I said as the consequences struck. I had a horrible suspicion I'd been hoping she'd sign, so that I could signal my disapproval from the moral high ground, while being very glad of the money. One thing was clear, though—I couldn't afford to resign from the *Bugle*. I wasn't paid so well as a food critic and occasional reporter, but I was paid and my contribution to the household budget was still useful.

'Do you think I've made a mistake?' She asked, looking surprised. 'I thought you'd be pleased—I thought you didn't like Valentine.'

I shook my head. 'You've made the right moral decision. I was just thinking of the money.'

'We'll get by.'

'I suppose so. Did Sid have any suggestions?'

'He offered us a loan. Not from the bank, but from his own pocket. Interest free.'

'How much?' I asked.

'As much as we'd need. I turned it down, though. It's not good to borrow from friends, in case anything goes wrong.'

I bit my lip and nodded.

'We'll manage.'

'Yes.' I yawned again.

Daphne glanced at her watch. 'It's nearly one o'clock! We'd better get some sleep—I'm guiding a group of amateur archaeologists round the pre-Roman section first thing tomorrow.'

204

Daphne's gasp woke me.

'What's up?' I asked.

'Look at the time!' She leapt from bed.

It was eight-thirty.

'Why didn't the alarm work?' I began and stopped—the alarm was on my mobile, in my jacket pocket, in the bag on Charlie's kitchen floor.

She hurried to the bathroom.

I could so easily have dozed again, but I forced myself to roll out of bed, fearing Ralph's wrath if I wasn't on time. After dressing in record time, I scurried into the bathroom as Daphne ran out. A rudimentary set of morning ablutions followed, during which I spat toothpaste down my nice, clean shirt. A brisk scrub with a face flannel removed most of the mess and I rushed downstairs. Daphne was gulping down a glass of tap water.

'What would you like for breakfast?' I asked, opening a cupboard in hope.

She put down the glass. 'Sorry, there's no time. I'm off.' She dropped a quick kiss on my lips and was gone.

I dithered a moment, wondering whether to risk a quick bite before a mad rush to the office, but the clock showed eight forty-five, and my walk to work took fifteen minutes, if I was brisk and the traffic allowed me to cross roads without delay. Giving up on eating for the time being, I decided to head straight to work—hoping I'd find time for something later. I just wished I wasn't so hungry already! I ran and opened the front door.

The overnight downpour had washed the sky clean, and a watery sun glinted off damp streets. I blinked and was pulling the door behind me when I had a thought—my keys were at Charlie's. And so was my wallet, leaving me with nothing to buy a snack. I was in a quandary: should I leave the front door unlocked and risk burglars? Or should I not turn up at work? Basil's fate was in the forefront of my mind, but which was worse?

I dithered until my growling stomach made up my mind.

I went back inside, put the kettle on, shoved two slices of bread in the toaster and used the landline to call the office.

A posh female voice answered. '*Sorenchester and District Bugle*. Olivia speaking—how may I help you?'

'Umm ... what?' I said—I knew no Olivia. 'Who are you?'

'Olivia.'

'Yeah, but what are you doing there?'

'I am answering the telephone,' she said.

'But why?'

'Because it was ringing.'

I knew she'd just rolled her eyes.

Flummoxed, I changed my approach. 'Is Ralph in?'

'Yes, Mr Pildown is in.'

'Good. May I speak to him?'

'I'm afraid he's busy. Can I help?'

'Umm ... maybe. Could you give him a message?'

'I could.'

'Tell him I've lost my keys, mobile and wallet ... '

'I'm sorry to hear that,' said Olivia, 'but I'm afraid lost property is not newsworthy.'

'I know!'

'Then why bother calling a newspaper?'

The toaster made a muted ping.

'I'm not ringing in a story.'

'That's what I just said.'

'Look, I'm calling because I ... '

I sniffed the air—something was burning. Two plumes of smoke were rising from the toaster—the bread was wedged in. An unfortunate word escaped as I ran to the rescue.

'I'll thank you not to swear at me,' said Olivia.

'Sorry, but ... umm ...' The line went dead.

Several choice swear words, each worse than the last, burst forth as I jiggled the release, trying in vain to get my toast to pop out while there was still hope of salvaging something edible. An attempt at pinching a corner and pulling brought only pain—the slices were well and truly stuck. The smoke was thickening, and I wrestled with the blasted machine for several seconds before I thought to unplug it. After leaving it to cool for a few seconds, I prised out lumps of carbonised bread with a butter knife, though no amount of scraping would save them. Still, I'd learned to take adversity in my stride, so I made a pot of tea and tried again, keeping a close eye on the toaster to ensure nothing went wrong this time.

Nothing did go wrong, and I was left with two perfect slices of toast. Famished, I slavered butter and Mrs Goodfellow's marvellous marmalade on them, poured myself a mug of tea, and carried my breakfast to the table.

Only when I'd finished eating and had poured a second mug of tea did I call the office again. This time, I was prepared.

'*Sorenchester and District Bugle*. This is Olivia—how may I help you?'

'Good morning, Olivia,' I said, trying to exude confidence and authority. A rogue crumb caught my throat, and, despite my best efforts, my voice came out as a hoarse and strained whisper. 'My name is Andy

Caplet. Would you pass on a message?'

'Let me find a pencil,' said Olivia.

She put the phone down, but I heard her say, 'It's that weirdo again. What should I do? He claims he's called Randy Tablet or something.'

Another woman's voice said something too faint to hear, and Olivia got back to me. 'Now listen, creep! If you try this again, I'm calling the police. Get it?'

'But I need to tell ...'

The line went dead again.

18

It was only after my utter telephone failure that other options occurred to me, and I sent Ralph an email to explain. Two minutes later, a new mail pinged into my inbox. I opened it, expecting to have my face chewed off by a furious editor.

But it was Daphne. 'Hi, Andy, I've just remembered about your keys. Don't forget the set you hid under the sink.'

I'd put them there for safe-keeping, insisting that I wouldn't forget them. But, of course, I had.

Technically, there was now no reason for not going into work, but having already made my excuses, I felt free—a sneaky day off work is worth double a planned one. Hoping Hobbes might take me to pick up my stuff from Charlie's, I phoned Blackdog Street. Mrs Goodfellow said he'd already gone to the police station. I decided to go there too. After retrieving the spare keys, I headed out.

To reduce the possibility of being spotted by Ralph, I took the long way round, avoiding the end of The Shambles, scurrying furtively down the shadowy side of Vermin Street and sneaking down the alley to the police station. An altercation was going on inside. I looked through the open door to see what was happening.

DCI Kirten, either very brave or very stupid, was

yelling at Hobbes, who was facing him, stone-faced.

When Kirten broke off to breathe, Hobbes spoke. 'Use your brain. Mr Ching was not at home at the time of the killing. Therefore, it is clear he could not have fired the shot that killed Timmy.'

Kirten shook his head. 'He might claim he was away, but why should I believe him?'

'Because he can prove he was on a family holiday in Taiwan.'

Kirten sneered. 'You rustic coppers are so gullible! He could easily have fabricated this so-called proof.'

'No, he could not. There is compelling evidence that he and his family were exactly where he says he was. If I were you, I would put an end to this fiasco and put some effort into catching the real killer.'

'Don't tell me how to run my case, you bloody rural simpleton!' Kirten bellowed, his face red with rage. 'Back off, or I'll inform the chief constable of your gross insubordination. I will not be releasing Ching, but I will compile evidence against him.'

For a moment, I thought there'd be trouble. Hobbes, scowling, took a step forward, towering over Kirten like a guillotine blade over an exposed neck. Kirten retreated, stumbled over a paper bin, and fell back into a chair with an almighty thump. Hobbes turned around and stalked from the police station.

'Good morning,' he said on seeing me lurking. 'Did you hear all that?'

'Enough,' I said. 'Are you going to do anything about it?' I hoped he would—Aye Ching's was the best takeaway in town.

'Yes. First, I'm going to examine the crime scene,' said Hobbes.

'Can I come?' I asked.

When he nodded, I regretted my impulsiveness—the prospect of another bike ride gave me the heebie-jeebies. But Billy had put his little car back together, and it gleamed with fresh paint and polish in the police car park. Hobbes whistled and Dregs ran towards us, licking his lips and looking smug. Cake crumbs dusted his muzzle.

I took my usual inferior position in the back. Dregs got into the passenger seat and Hobbes started the engine. The speed at which we reversed from the parking space would have left me in the footwell had I not fitted my seatbelt. We set off. To distract myself from the driving, I watched Dregs, wondering how he seemed to anticipate the car's every swerve, lurch and brake, and wasn't thrown around like a rag doll. He leant into bends, braced himself as the car sped up or slowed, his tongue lolling and without an apparent care. Not that Hobbes braked much on that journey—his speed rarely dipped below eighty miles per hour through the narrow streets of central Sorenchester. We stopped on a quiet residential street. The large, Cotswold stone terraced houses showed we were in the Moorend part of town.

'This is Elvers End,' said Hobbes, unfolding himself and stepping into the street, with Dregs and me close behind. 'The boy's body was lying in Mr Ching's back garden. Follow me.'

His anger had dissipated, replaced by the quivering intensity that took him at crime scenes. He led us down a long side passage into a service road with extensive gardens backing onto it.

'Third gate on the right,' he said.

It was closed and decorated with police tape. He tried the catch, but the gate was bolted. That proved no obstacle—he vaulted it. A moment later, the bolt scraped back, and he let us into a large, overgrown garden with tall, unkempt, privet hedges along either side.

'You know the procedure,' said Hobbes.

Dregs and I stayed close to the gate as he began looking about.

'That is where they found Timmy's body.' He pointed to an area of flattened grass in front of the hedge on the right and crept towards it on all fours like a monstrous toad, examining the area from all angles, sniffing and poking. 'There's still a faint scent of blood, despite the rain and the trampling feet of the investigators.' He turned and frowned at the house. 'Kirten claims Mr Ching shot Timmy from the upstairs back window.'

'Does Mr Ching even have a gun?' I asked.

Hobbes shook his head. 'There is nothing to suggest that he does, and Kirten has located no weapon. Mr Ching denies ever having owned one, though he admits he knows how to shoot—he was in the army thirty years ago.'

I nodded. 'The whole thing makes no sense. Even if he had a gun, why would he shoot a child?'

'Because he's a psychopath, according to Kirten,' said Hobbes, crawling to examine a patch of grass that looked the same as all the others. 'But he refused to explain why he'd jumped to that ludicrous conclusion.'

'Umm ... there's another thing that bothers me,' I said. 'What was Timmy doing here? Did he know the Chings?'

Hobbes shook his head. 'Not really. Timmy's family ordered a takeaway now and then, but that's all that connects them—other than the body being here.'

'Kirten's case seems flimsy,' I said.

'It's not even as strong as that,' he said. 'Mr Ching has documentary proof he was in Taiwan at the time.'

'What … ?' I started.

He held up a hand, and I let the question slip.

'Hello 'ello 'ello, what's all this then?' He picked a small twig from the grass and turned towards the hedge.

'What is it?' I asked.

'Take a good look at this hedge. What do you observe?'

'Umm … leaves … twigs?'

'Near the top, Andy. Can't you see it?'

'No … umm … wait a moment.' A sudden thrill ran through me. 'Yes, I think so—there's a bit with lots of broken twigs. Umm … does that mean something?'

'It's food for thought,' said Hobbes. 'I think I should look next door. Come along.'

He loped out of the garden, with Dregs and me trotting behind. We returned to the road, and he knocked on a door. A plump, pretty, grey-haired woman opened up, gasped and recoiled, as if she intended to shut the door in his face, but he already had his police ID in his big hairy hand.

'I'm Inspector Hobbes,' he said. 'I'm investigating the murder of Timothy Rigg.'

'That poor boy,' said the woman, relaxing as she saw a police officer and not the monster she'd imagined. 'But we've already talked to a police inspector, though we didn't really know anything because we were away when it happened. If there's any way I can help … '

'All I need is to look in your garden,' said Hobbes. 'Do you mind?'

The woman looked surprised, but smiled. 'Not at all. I'm Penny Bright by the way. My husband, is at work.

Please come in.'

She led us through the house, a place of order and cleanliness, and opened the back door to the garden, which wasn't. It was similar in size and shape to Mr Ching's, but comprised a muddy lawn with a playhouse, footballs, bikes, a trampoline, and random toys scattered over it.

'Aha!' said Hobbes, rubbing his hands together.

'What's up?' I asked, but he was onto something and ignored me.

Dregs leapt onto the trampoline and bounced like the tail-wagging idiot he was, his tongue lolling, his expression one of unalloyed joy.

'He's just like our grandchildren,' said Penny, smiling at the loony antics. 'They love the trampoline too.'

Hobbes nodded. 'Do your grandchildren ever have friends round to play on it?' asked Hobbes.

It was a surprising question—he preferred to get straight down to business without any chitchat.

Penny nodded. 'Sometimes. Most kids seem to enjoy bouncing.'

'Was Timmy Rigg one of them?' asked Hobbes.

'Sort of,' said Penny. 'He was one of a bunch that came round here from time to time—I recognised his photograph in the *Bugle*. Now you come to mention it, I think he was always on it if he had the chance. Why do you ask?'

'I think I know what happened,' said Hobbes, examining the hedge.

I was groping at an idea, too, but it ran away before I could catch it.

'Do you mind if I try it?' asked Hobbes.

Penny looked him up and down. 'It's designed for children. Someone of your ... build might break it.'

'I'll try not to bounce,' said Hobbes. 'I just need to look.'

Penny shrugged. 'I don't understand why, but yes. Just take care.'

After persuading a reluctant Dregs to get down, Hobbes vaulted onto the trampoline, which pinged and sagged when he reached the middle. Penny looked nervous and was opening her mouth to speak when the telephone called. 'Excuse me,' she said, returning to the house.

Hobbes was still investigating the hedge. There was a little damage near the top, as if something had hit it. As soon as Penny was out of sight, he bounced high and looked over the hedge.

'You said you wouldn't do that,' I began as he bounced again.

As he landed this time, the distressed springs groaned and pinged, the jump mat split down the middle, and he plunged to the ground. 'Oops,' he said.

Penny, telephone to her ear, was staring from the back window, a look of horror on her face. She ran out. 'Oh god! Is he alright? Shall I call an ambulance?'

'I'm fine, Mrs Bright,' said Hobbes, brushing himself down and standing up. 'However, I've bust your trampoline. It did not die in vain, though—I've learned something important.'

'What?' she asked.

'Where the shot was fired from,' said Hobbes. 'Thank you for your help. I'll order a new trampoline at once.'

He took the mobile from his pocket and gave instructions to someone before turning to Penny with a smile. 'It will be here within the hour.'

'Thank you, Inspector.'

'No, Mrs Bright, thank you for your invaluable help.'

215

After leaving her, Hobbes ensured the crime scene was still secure and herded Dregs and me into the car.

I was bursting with curiosity as I fastened my seatbelt. 'What did you see?'

The car roared forward. 'I saw the landscape around Elvers End.'

'And?'

'I believe Timmy was shot from a distance.'

'But ... umm ... why?'

'By accident. The shooter probably intended the bullet for someone else.'

I scratched my head. 'You think Timmy was on the trampoline and bounced at the wrong time? But Mrs Bright said they weren't home—he couldn't have got into the garden.'

Hobbes gave me a grim smile. 'She also said Timmy was particularly keen on trampolining. I suspect he sneaked into the garden—the gate would be no obstacle to an active child. He was unlucky to be in the wrong place at the wrong time.'

I cottoned on at last. 'So, you reckon the impact of the bullet knocked him across the hedge?'

He nodded. 'There were traces of blood and fibres from clothes across the leaves and twigs at the top of the hedge. I'd be astonished if they hadn't come from the poor boy.'

'But ... umm ... shouldn't DCI Kirten have spotted all that?'

Hobbes shrugged. 'He should, but Kirten has a reputation for focusing on the immediate crime scene and getting confessions rather than checking further afield.'

'That's stupid,' I said.

'But that's his method, and it can get quick results,

which his bosses like because it saves time and resources. It's failed this time, though. He's floundering and panicking. That's why he's trying to pin it on poor Mr Ching.'

I nodded. 'All this gets you no closer to catching the murderer, though ….' Noticing an eighth of a smile twitch at the corner of his mouth, I added, 'Or does it?'

'Perhaps,' he said, threading the little car through the narrow streets.

Dregs gave me a smug look, letting me know that he'd already worked out what was going on, though there was no point asking him to explain. All I could do was sit and wait for the big reveal.

Two minutes later, we stopped on Wall Street, a residential dead end next to open ground, bounded on the far side by the remains of Sorenchester's Roman fortifications and the River Soren. Hobbes leapt out and led us down a path into the fields. When I caught up, he and Dregs were staring up a tree.

'Has he been chasing squirrels again?' I asked.

Hobbes shook his head. 'This, I suspect, is a crime scene.'

I looked up. It was just an old beech tree. 'You think the murderer shot from here?'

Hobbes nodded, dropped to all fours, and sniffed and rummaged through the leaf litter.

Dregs joined him, nose down, tail wagging, ears pricked. Knowing my place in the scheme of things, I kept well back and observed.

After a few moments, Hobbes grunted and stretched out an arm. I watched, fascinated as a sharp, yellow fingernail extended like a cat's claw to hook something pressed into the soil. Using his nails as tweezers, he held it up to the light. As his nails retracted, it dropped into his palm. He'd found a tiny, glittery red ring, smaller in diameter than a penny.

'What is it?' I asked.

'A small, red ring,' he said and sniffed. 'It's got a very faint smell ... antiseptic? It reminds me of something.'

'Is it relevant?'

He stood up. 'Perhaps—it's not been here very long, so it could have been dropped at the time of the shooting. I'm not sure what it is yet. Any ideas?'

I peered at it. It looked flimsy and had a split in the circumference. 'A little girl's toy ring?' I suggested.

A large man who'd been walking a tiny white dog on the other side of the field approached. It was 'Bruiser' Wainright. Adopting a fighting stance, and a fierce expression, he squared up to Hobbes, fists raised.

The little white dog wandered up to Dregs and yapped. Dregs ignored the pest.

I expected Bruiser was going to get flattened, but Hobbes chuckled and held out his hand.

Bruiser laughed and shook it. 'Hiya, coach—it's great to see you.'

'Coach?' It was a new nickname to me.

'Yes, Andy,' said Bruiser. 'Mr Hobbes taught me to box when I was a nipper, and I was being bullied.'

'I'm glad it worked out well for you,' said Hobbes.

Bruiser nodded. 'Thank you. What are you doing here?'

'Investigating a crime,' said Hobbes and showed him the ring. 'We were trying to work out what this is.'

'It's a hair ring,' said Bruiser. 'They are used for holding braids together and to add a bit of sparkle and colour to hair.'

'I've seen them,' I said. 'Not long ago.'

Hobbes grinned. 'If this proves significant, it'll be the

218

first time a red hair ring turns out to be a genuine clue.'

Bruiser glanced at his watch. 'Oops, I must be on my way—I've got a lady coming for a cut in twenty minutes. Great to see you, Coach. Andy.'

As Bruiser and his dog departed, Hobbes grabbed a low branch, swung himself into the beech tree like an ape, and began climbing. Now and then, he stopped to investigate something.

Seeing him go, Dregs barked, bounced and pawed the trunk, wanting to join in the fun. I'd seen him climb trees, and he wasn't bad—for a dog. However, the lower branches were just out of his reach. He gave me a hard stare, annoyed I wouldn't offer him a leg up.

Hobbes reached the higher parts of the tree and turned upside down, his boots hooked over a sturdy limb to enable him to sniff the top of the branch below. His eager expression suggested he was on the scent of something. 'That weird smell is up here, too. If only it hadn't rained.'

He unhooked himself, dropped, twisted, and landed feet first on the branch below. After gazing out over Sorenchester, he nodded.

'Found anything?' I asked.

He jumped down, landing between me and Dregs. 'The shooter fired from that branch—it overlooks the gardens at Elvers End and would have provided a stable platform.'

'The murderer must have been quite active,' I pointed out. 'I'd struggle to climb up there ... and they risked being seen—this is public land.'

Hobbes nodded. 'Your first point is valid, but I'm not so sure about the second. Yes, there would have been a risk of witnesses, but it's not busy round here. How many people can you see?'

'Umm ... none at the moment.'

'That's often the case. Dog walkers and the occasional rambler use this place. Children too—when they're not playing their electronic games. It would not be too difficult to stay out of sight.'

I shrugged. 'The shooter would still have to carry the rifle in public. Someone would have seen it—unless it was one of those rifles that can be taken apart and fitted back together—like a professional hitman would use.'

Hobbes grinned. 'That sort of thing is far more common in films than in real life, and assassins are rare in small Cotswold towns. I think it more likely that the shooter concealed the rifle in a bag, or even beneath baggy clothing.'

'But someone would have heard the shot,' I insisted.

'Very likely—but would anyone recognise it as a rifle shot? They'd think it was a car backfiring or a firework.'

He was right. Other than shotguns blasting away at the local pheasantry, gunfire was almost unheard of in Sorenchester.

I sighed, feeling a little peevish. 'This is all very interesting, but gets us no closer to the culprit.'

'I wouldn't say that,' said Hobbes.

'And another thing,' I said, 'if you're right about him shooting Timmy by accident, then he intended the bullet for somebody else. What if he tries again?'

'Good point,' said Hobbes.

'Thank you,' I said, flattered, though I suspected he'd thought of all this long ago and had been waiting for me to catch up.

Dregs, the canine clot, sniffed at a small brown feather. It stuck to his nose and made him sneeze. Hobbes picked it off and stared at it.

'What? It's just a feather,' I said.

'One that's come from the rhea,' said Hobbes, flicking it away. 'Now, where were we? Are, yes, the intended victim.'

'Do you know who it is?' I asked.

'Not yet, but I know where they live.'

'Umm ... how?' I asked.

'I lined up my position in the tree with Mrs Bright's garden and looked beyond. Only one house is in the right place, so that's where we're heading next.'

'Good. If you find the intended victim, you can stop another attack.'

'Precisely,' said Hobbes. 'And if this person knows of an enemy who is prepared to commit murder, then we have our shooter.'

He marched us back to the car.

19

A short but intense car ride took us to Moorend Road. Hobbes parked the car outside one of the imposing, red-brick Victorian houses that were common in that part of town.

'This is the place,' he said, getting out and looking back to where we'd come from.

Dregs and I followed as he stepped up to the front door and knocked.

No one answered.

'We're too late—the murderer has struck already!' I said, grim-faced.

'Or they are out at work,' said Hobbes.

'I suppose that is possible,' I conceded. 'You'll have to come back later.'

'Or I could ask a neighbour who keeps an eye on what's happening in this area. Come along.'

He took us a short walk up the road to the first in a row of impossibly cute alms-houses, the home of Augustus Godley, the oldest human in town. He rang the doorbell, and we waited. Dregs, getting bored, started worrying my shoe. The door opened at last, and a pickled-chestnut face enclosed by a fuzz of white whiskers and eyebrows looked out.

'Good day, Mr Godley,' said Hobbes.

Augustus peered at him. 'Why, it's Constable ... I

mean Sergeant ... no, Inspector Hobbes. What are you after?'

'Information,' said Hobbes, 'but first, I trust you are keeping well?'

'As well as can be expected,' said Augustus, 'but what with old-age and constipation, I've had to give up paintballing on Thursdays. Would you like to come in for a cup of tea? The kettle's on.'

'We'd love one,' said Hobbes. 'You remember Andy and Dregs?'

'The weird one and the hairy one? Of course. Come in.' Augustus chuckled.

'Weird?' I muttered, peeved, though conceding that the old man might have a point.

We followed him at a funeral march pace down a gloomy stone-paved corridor into a small room with three tatty old armchairs, a few other sticks of furniture and a blue budgerigar in a cage. 'Bugger off!' it said in an old woman's voice.

Augustus shook a gnarled finger at the bird. 'What have I told you about swearing?' He glanced at Hobbes. 'Sorry about Arthur's language. He's taken to mimicking Mrs Withers, my girlfriend—she's a lovely lady but, between you and me, she's a little common.'

He went into the kitchen, leaving Hobbes and me to sit. Dregs was eying an armchair, but Hobbes shook his head. 'That's Mr Godley's.'

The dog's tail dropped and he sat in front of me, fixing me with a mournful stare and trying to guilt me into giving up my seat. I was not to be intimidated and, with a near-human shrug, he sat on the mat. Remembering previous visits to Mr Godley's, I prepared for a wait.

Ten minutes later, he shuffled back, leaning on a

loaded trolley. He poured tea into three spotless white mugs and one white bowl. 'What do you wish to know?' he asked, and handed Hobbes a mug.

'Can you tell me who lives in the big house three doors down?' Hobbes asked.

'I can,' said the old man, passing a mug to me, and placing the bowl in front of Dregs. 'He's not been living there for long—only four or five years, I think.'

'So, who is it?' Hobbes sipped from his mug.

Dregs sniffed his tea and retreated. I took a sip of mine—it was scalding hot.

Augustus lowered himself into his armchair before speaking. 'The chap's name is Baker ... Trevor Baker. He runs his own engineering business.'

'I know him,' I said.

Hobbes raised his hairy eyebrows. 'Really?'

'Yes ... umm ... or rather, I know of him. He's the top SOD.'

'I'll have no more of that language in my house,' said Augustus, launching a tectonic frown at me. 'I don't want Arthur picking up any more off-colour words. Do you understand, young man?'

'Yes, but ... umm ... '

'What Andy is trying to mumble,' said Hobbes, 'is that Mr Baker is a leader of Sorenchester Opposes the Development—they use the acronym S.O.D.'

'In that case, I'll forgive him.' The old man smiled. 'I dislike the very thought of the development—it's criminal the way the countryside is being swallowed up these days. Young Toby Squire should know better, but he is a greedy, thoughtless man. It's shocking because his predecessors did so much good for the local people, particularly the previous owner, his uncle.'

'Hear, hear!' I said.

'To be honest,' he continued, 'I'm surprised young Toby has the right to do that. I seem to remember being told that old General Redvers Squire, who was a real gentleman, signed the ownership of the land to the Common People.'

'When was this?' I asked, and took another sip of tea, which had cooled sufficiently to be attempted by those without asbestos mouthparts. It was almost up to the old girl's standards.

'A long time ago, before I was born,' said Augustus. 'Though my memory's not what it was.'

'Never mind,' I said. 'I can't remember everything from my childhood, especially the school stuff—I never saw the point of it. I mean to say, who uses trigonometry in real life?'

'I do, young man,' said Augustus. 'It is a vital tool in navigation. I know there's all sorts of clever technology for helping pilots these days, but I like the trusted methods I learned in the Air Force best. Never underestimate the power of trigonometry!'

'Umm ... I won't,' I said, ashamed of my ignorance.

I sipped tea and shut up. Dregs finished his bowl in a series of slurps, which Arthur imitated while Hobbes and Augustus exchanged wartime anecdotes. After what he'd said earlier, the old man's language shocked me, until I worked out that a Focke was an aeroplane.

Hobbes put down his mug and rose to his feet. 'Thank you for the tea and the information, Mr Godley, but it's time we were on our way. Come along, Andy. And quickly! Dregs. We'll see ourselves out.'

I mumbled thanks, and Dregs wagged his tail as we left.

'Goodbye, and thank you for visiting,' said Augustus.

'SOD!' screeched Arthur, as I shut the door.

'Now what?' I asked when we were back in Moorend Road.

'We'll have a word with Mr Trevor Baker,' said Hobbes, striding back to the car.

'But he's out.'

'Which is why we'll try him at work.'

'But where is work?' I asked.

'It's on the industrial estate, off Collinson Road—I've seen the sign.'

'You know what I think?' I said, when we were back in the car.

'Very rarely,' said Hobbes as he started the engine.

'I think Trevor Baker was probably ... umm ... targeted because he opposes the development. Did you know Valentine Grubbe was in the army? I bet he can shoot. I reckon he's your culprit.'

'If I was a betting man,' said Hobbes, 'I'd take your bet.'

'Why? It all adds up as far as I can see. What do you think?'

'I think I'll wait for evidence,' said Hobbes. 'Hold on!'

He crushed the accelerator, and the car lunged forward, zigzagging through the traffic on Amour Lane until we reached the southern outskirts of Sorenchester, where there was a small, ugly, but vibrant industrial estate full of small and medium-sized businesses. We passed Collinson Road and stopped on a tarmac forecourt outside an unimaginative squat rectangular building of yellow bricks. A sign on the side declared it the home of *Baker Engineering*.

'Let's see what he has to say for himself,' said Hobbes, as we left the car.

Dregs relieved himself against a black Mercedes, and we approached the front door. Hobbes rang the bell and a smart young woman in a crisp, white blouse and neat, blue skirt answered.

'Hello?' she said and gasped when Hobbes smiled.

'Good day to you, miss,' said Hobbes. 'I'd like a word with Mr Baker. Is he in?'

'Who are you?' she asked, holding the door as if she longed to slam it.

'Inspector Hobbes of the Sorenchester and District Police.' Hobbes showed her his ID. 'These,' he indicated Dregs and me, 'are my esteemed colleagues, Dregs and Andy. Andy is the one on two legs.'

The woman smiled; her fears overcome by faith in an official document. 'Mr Baker is on the telephone at the moment, but I'm sure he won't be long. Please, come into reception and take a seat. I'll let him know you're here.'

We entered the reception, a small alcove with a desk, computer and various potted plants along one side and two leather-look chairs along the other. The woman left via a half-glazed door and two thirds of us took a seat. I stood and glared at Dregs, who did an almost believable impression of not noticing.

'Good day, Inspector!' Trevor Baker, dark-haired, good-looking, and an imposing figure, though no taller than me, entered the room and introduced himself. 'How may I help you?'

'I'd like to ask you a few questions about the murder of Timothy Rigg, sir,' said Hobbes, standing up and shaking hands with him.

'A terrible business. I'm not sure how I'll be able to help, but fire away, Inspector.'

'Were you at home on the evening of the shooting?'

Trevor thought for a moment. 'Yes, I believe I was.'

'Was anyone with you?'

Trevor shook his head and looked worried. 'No, I think I was alone. Why do you ask? You don't think I ... '

Hobbes held up his hand. 'No, sir. However, I suspect you were the intended victim.'

'What? Me? But why?'

'My investigations suggest the boy got in the way of a bullet aimed at you,' said Hobbes. 'Do you have any enemies?'

Trevor shrugged. 'I suppose I must have upset a few people over the years, but I can't believe anyone would want to kill me.'

Hobbes nodded and scribbled in his notebook. 'How would you describe your relationship with Colonel Squire?'

Trevor smiled. 'It wasn't great a few weeks ago when I opposed his development, but it's much better now.'

'Does that mean you are no longer opposing the development?' asked Hobbes.

'I am not. Over the last month, I've spoken to Toby Squire and Val Grubbe, and now recognise that the merits of their scheme far outweigh any minor inconveniences that may arise. The development will bring tremendous opportunities to the town and its people and all for the loss of a patch of useless wasteland.'

'But aren't you still the chairman of the SODs?' I asked.

'For the time being, yes,' said Trevor.

Hobbes scribbled again. 'Thank you, sir. That's very useful. Have you informed any of the SODs of your change of heart?'

'Not as yet,' said Trevor, 'though I will at the appropriate time.'

'Isn't that deceitful, sir?'

'I suppose it is a bit,' said Trevor. 'I hadn't thought about it very much since I changed my mind. I will disband the SODs.'

'Did you change your mind before the shooting?' asked Hobbes.

Trevor did a swift calculation on his fingers. 'Yes. Why?'

'Just gathering all the facts, sir.'

'Well, I ... umm ... think that's despicable,' I said, allowing my indignant rage to slip out. 'Anyone with any integrity would have stepped down at once and let the members elect a new chair.'

'Calm down, Andy,' said Hobbes. 'Sorry about that, sir.'

'He has a point,' said Trevor, looking contrite, 'but the thing is, I started the SODs, and no one else wanted to lead it. I have already mentioned my doubts to a few of the activists and pointed out how much the scheme will benefit them, despite a little disruption in the short term. I will resign, and I'll let them know when I've finished here for the day.'

'That would appear to be the honourable course in the circumstances,' said Hobbes with a nod.

'I suppose so, Inspector. I have no desire to let the SODs down—there are a lot of good people in the group, though I now believe they are on the wrong side. So many new jobs and opportunities will result from the plan, and no one can say those are bad things, can they?'

'No, sir. How many know you've changed your mind?' asked Hobbes.

'One or two probably suspect. You think that might have been the reason?'

'It is possible, sir.'

Trevor looked stunned, and then shook his head. 'No,

I can't accept that—they are good people.'

'All of them?' asked Hobbes.

'Yes … as far as I know. Some may be a little radical but they wouldn't hurt anyone.'

'I see,' said Hobbes. 'Thank you for your time.' He picked up one of Trevor's business cards. 'Goodbye, sir. I would advise vigilance. Call me if you feel threatened.'

The first rumblings of discontent arose from my hungry stomach.

'Come along,' said Hobbes, walking to the door and stopping.

Dregs rolled from the chair, stretched, and sauntered after him with me.

Hobbes looked back over his shoulder. 'As a matter of interest, Mr Baker, are you likely to profit from the development?'

The man flushed. 'Well, err, now you mention it, Colonel Squire has asked me to carry out a few minor jobs for him. I can't afford to turn down legitimate business.'

'Of course not,' said Hobbes. 'Thank you again, sir.' He opened the door and led us out into bright sunshine.

'It's coming up to lunch time,' I pointed out as we got back in the car, hoping to blag an invitation to Blackdog Street.

'Trust you to focus on what's important,' said Hobbes with a chuckle. 'I am aware of the time and I would invite you home if the old girl wasn't hosting lunch for her friends. There's no room for the likes of us … and particularly for you.' He pointed a banana-thick, hairy finger at the dog. 'I'm afraid Dregs disgraced himself with a tray of petite-fours the last time her friends came round.'

'What's the plan?' I asked.

'We'll find somewhere to eat.'

'Good idea. Do you have anywhere in mind?'

He thought for a moment. 'The Whippet in Sorington. It's not far away.'

'Great,' I said. I hadn't reviewed it for a year, and last time it had been well above average.

He stamped on the accelerator and we rocketed through the narrow streets and little country lanes until we reached the car park. All around were green fields and trees coming into leaf, while the old pub's Cotswold stone tiles glowed in the sun that came out to greet our arrival. The jaunty notes of a blackbird perched high on the mossy chimney welcomed us. Although only a ten-minute drive from the centre of Sorenchester (three minutes with Hobbes at the wheel) it felt like we'd entered a different world.

'Move yourself, Andy,' said Hobbes, who was already on his feet, with Dregs at his side. 'They might run out of food!'

Despite considering this outcome as unlikely, I was out in seconds.

We entered the pub through a stone porch, and immersed ourselves in the aromas of freshly cooked food, wood-smoke and beer. A cheerful log fire crackled, casting flickering shadows over the age-darkened beams above. Tables awaited customers, and a few already had occupants. Hobbes headed for the bar with its array of real ales, ciders and lagers. A rosy-cheeked barmaid welcomed us with a smile.

'Good afternoon, gentlemen.'

'Afternoon, ma'am,' said Hobbes, giving her an old-fashioned salute. 'We're here for some lunch.'

'There are menus on the tables, and the day's specials are on the chalkboard.' She gestured to one side. 'Can I get you a drink while you decide?'

'Yes, please,' said Hobbes. 'I'll have a quart of ginger beer. Dregs would like a pint of mild in a bowl, and I suspect Andy would like a lager?'

'Actually,' I said, trying to show how unpredictable I was, 'I'll try a pint of Garrulus Stout.' I pointed at the pump with a picture of a jay adorning the front.

The barmaid poured our drinks. It surprised me when she pulled a dog bowl from under the counter—I suspected they knew Dregs there.

I examined the chalkboard. 'Homity pie? What's that? I've never heard of it.'

'It's an open pie filled with potato, onion and leek and whatever vegetables are available all topped with melted cheese,' said Hobbes. 'It was common enough during the desperate days of the war, but is rarely seen these days.'

'That's right,' said the barmaid, placing our drinks on the counter. 'It's become quite popular here for some reason.'

'I'll have it,' I said, and sipped the top off my Garrulus Stout. It was cool with subtle hints of coffee and spice, and a smooth, almost creamy feel. 'Not bad,' I declared, more impressed than I cared to let on.

Hobbes ordered two steak and kidney puddings for himself and restricted Dregs to a lump of Porterhouse steak, cooked rare and without the trimmings. We sat at a table and I placed Dregs's mild before him. He sniffed, took a lick, rolled it around in his mouth like a connoisseur, wagged his tail and lapped it up in seconds.

'Do you think you'll catch Timmy's killer?' I asked Hobbes, who was taking a colossal swig from his enormous glass—how many pubs, I wondered, still served quarts?

He wiped his mouth with the back of his hand and nodded. 'Yes. I need to find somebody with a grudge against Mr Baker.'

'And someone with access to a rifle,' I said. 'That should narrow down the search—there can't be all that many people around here licensed to use them.'

A wry smile crossed his face. 'More than you might think, and that's assuming there are no illegal weapons. The forensic boys say the fatal bullet came from a point three-o-three calibre. There are a few in the district, but they have all been accounted for, according to Kirten.'

I nodded and swigged some more beer. A few minutes later, the kitchen doors opened and a smiling young woman, neat and pretty, brought us our meals.

'Thank you,' said Hobbes. He frowned, sniffed the air and, as she turned away, blocked her path with a tree-trunk arm.

'Is something the matter?' she asked, eyes wide.

'Not at all, miss and forgive me for stopping you in the course of your duties, but I have a question.'

'What's that?' she asked, still looking alarmed.

'What do you smell of?'

'I say!' His uncouth question had both shocked and embarrassed me. He had overstepped the bounds of decency, propriety and manners.

'I beg your pardon,' said the waitress, looking around for help.

'What scent are you wearing? It reminds me of something long ago.'

'It's none of your business.' She attempted to get away.

'It is my business,' said Hobbes and showed her his ID. 'I detected a similar scent at a crime scene earlier today.'

'I haven't done anything,' she said, looking scared.

'I'm sure you haven't,' said Hobbes with a smile and keeping his voice soft, 'but what is it?'

'It's patchouli oil.'

'Of course!' He slapped his forehead. 'That's why I remember it—the hippies were all using it at Monterey back in the sixties.'

'Do you mean the Monterey Festival?' asked the girl.

Hobbes nodded. 'I'm surprised you know such ancient history.'

'My grandmother was there—the stories she tells!' The girl looked at him and smiled. 'You don't look old enough.'

'But I'm afraid I am,' said Hobbes with a sad smile. 'Thank you for your help. It may prove vital.'

'Let's eat,' I said, as she left us.

20

We ate in silence. At least Hobbes and I did. Beneath the table, Dregs slobbered and growled over his steak.

After clearing his plate, Hobbes quaffed the remains of his ginger beer and relaxed with his eyes half-closed. I finished my homity pie, impressed and surprised that such humble ingredients could add up to such a satisfying and comforting meal—one for my column, I thought.

'How was the pie?' he asked.

'Much tastier than I expected.'

He nodded. 'At its best, it was good, but during the war, it was often an indigestible mess of soggy pastry with underdone potatoes and only a hint of cheese. It was, however, the only thing available sometimes.'

He mentioned some other atrocities on the wartime police menu, reserving special contempt for tinned snook fishcakes. I listened with interest, because it was rare for him to talk about his own history unless it had some bearing on a current case. On this occasion, however, I think it was his way of turning off his conscious brain and allowing his sub-conscious free rein.

'Fresh snook, however, is delicious,' he continued. 'I ate it many times in South Africa, just before the Boer War, when I was trying to quell the Third Tokoloshe

Uprising. Now, that was a tricky case, because the tokoloshes had holed up in the Drakensberg mountains and ... ' He stopped and clapped his hairy hands together, making me and other customers jump, to judge by the resulting grumbles.

'What's up?' I asked.

'I remember noticing the scent of patchouli during the attack on the SODs.'

'That doesn't surprise me,' I said. 'I remember reading how popular it was with hippies in days of yore, and a few of the older SODs look like they might have been hippies back in the day.'

He nodded and reached for his horrible, hairy wallet. 'Time to pay and get on the road.'

Once back in the car, Hobbes seemed thoughtful, and drove with such care and consideration that, if it were possible, it made me almost more nervous than usual. We were on the edge of town when a shiny, black Audi roared out of a side road, accelerated past and slammed on the brakes, forcing Hobbes to stop.

DCI Kirten burst from the Audi and marched towards us, scowling. 'What the hell do you think you're doing?' He was almost screaming. 'Back off or I'll have you disciplined!'

Hobbes sighed, opened the window, and smiled. I would have been terrified if he'd aimed that smile at me.

'I will, you know,' Kirten continued. 'It's my case and I will not have you messing it up with your antiquated, rustic methods. Back off!'

'Shan't,' said Hobbes. 'Have you released Mr Ching yet?'

'I do not release suspects!'

'He was on holiday at the time of the shooting,' said

236

Hobbes, shaking his head. 'Therefore, he cannot be regarded as a suspect. Besides, he has no access to a rifle and had no reason to kill the boy.'

'The body was in his garden,' said Kirten. 'He couldn't explain it!'

'Of course, he couldn't,' said Hobbes, 'because neither him, nor any of his family, knew anything about it—they were on holiday.'

'Ching cannot or will not explain the bullet wound.'

Hobbes sighed. 'Look, Kirten, there is no evidence against him, and you know it. Plus, it is clear Timmy was not the intended target—I know who that was, and I'm closing in on the shooter. I'd like to share my knowledge with you. You can take all the credit if you wish.'

'Don't make me laugh, Hobbes! Leave this case to the professionals and stick to arresting yokels.' Kirten appeared to notice me for the first time. 'What's he in for? Potato picking without a license?'

Hobbes shook his head, but kept smiling. 'Listen to me, if you wish to catch the killer.'

'No, you listen to me. Back off!' Kirten's face was twisted into a snarl and flecks of spittle decorated his lips. 'If you don't, I will inform the chief constable who's a friend of my father and he'll have you drummed out of the police for obstructing a murder investigation.'

'I have made significant progress toward solving the case, but feel free to do whatever you want,' said Hobbes.

'I will—just you wait and see.' Kirten turned around, stalked back to his car and drove away, screeching the tyres.

Hobbes laughed. 'He's rattled and must know he's messed up by now. He's looking for scapegoats.'

'Do you ... umm ... think his threat is serious?' I asked.

'Probably. His father does belong to the same golf club as the chief constable. However, although the chief constable and I have had our disagreements, he is no fool.'

'But Kirten is?'

'I did not say that,' said Hobbes.

'Though you might think it?' I suggested.

He grinned. 'Let's go.'

'Yeah … umm … where to?'

'To the *Bugle*.'

'Why?' I asked, wishing he'd said anywhere else—Ralph would be furious to see me gallivanting with Hobbes when I should have been in the office, cutting and pasting frivolous articles from social media.

'I wish to check something. Hang on!'

He floored the accelerator, inertia pushed me back in my seat, and the usual numb terror took over, though we'd reached the *Bugle's* offices before I reached the gibbering stage. The 'No Parking' signs at that end of The Shambles would have made most folk think twice. But not him—he stopped on the pavement, ignoring a warning shout from a passing traffic warden.

Hobbes and Dregs got out and strode up to the front door, while I dithered, reluctant and nervous.

'Are you coming?' asked Hobbes, his hand on the door handle.

I took a deep breath and followed them. He jogged up the echoing staircase toward the half-glass door at the top. When they entered the main office, I hung back.

Two expensively dressed young women with long blonde hair paused their chat to stare at Hobbes. One, slight and pale skinned, smiled at us. The other, tall and tanned, did not react.

'Good afternoon,' said Hobbes. 'Is your editor in?'

Dregs, tail wagging, loped towards them, hoping for a head scratch and let out a deep sigh when Hobbes called him back.

'Mr Pildown is out,' said the pale woman—her voice identifying her as Olivia. 'He won't be back until late.'

'Never mind,' said Hobbes. 'We only need to check your records.'

Olivia screwed up her face and looked flummoxed.

'Who do you think you are?' asked the tanned woman. 'You can't just waltz into the office and use our equipment.'

'I think I'm Inspector Hobbes,' said Hobbes, showing his ID, 'and I rarely waltz these days.'

'Oh, you're police.' Olivia frowned. 'But I don't know what to do. I'm new here and Arabella only started today. I don't think we can help you.'

'Never mind,' said Hobbes, reaching back and propelling me to the front. 'I'm sure Andy knows the ropes.'

'Andy Caplet?' asked Arabella. Her voice was a deeper version of Olivia's posh drawl.

'Umm ... yes,' I admitted.

Both women's eyes widened. They exchanged glances. Arabella giggled.

'What?' I asked.

'Mr Pildown told us that if you turned up, we were to let you know you're fired,' said Olivia. 'Arabella has taken over your job.'

'What? Why?' I stuttered and spluttered. At the back of my mind, I'd entertained an idea that, when the time was right, I would make a dramatic and impassioned resignation speech, and walk out, leaving Ralph aghast and bereft. The loss of such an opportunity hurt, though it was also a relief—I would not now need to build up that sort of courage.

Olivia shrugged.

'That doesn't matter for now,' said Hobbes, pushing Dregs away and ushering me toward Ralph's office. 'Take a seat, go into the news database and dig out photographs of the SODs.'

'Okay,' I said, sitting down in the editor's chair for the first time. It was new, with a soft-leather cover, far more comfortable than the tatty, utilitarian relics I was used to. According to Basil, getting the new chair had been Ralph's first action.

I logged in to Ralph's laptop. Or rather, I tried to. 'Umm ...'

'A problem?' asked Hobbes.

'It doesn't recognise my ID.'

'Because you no longer work here,' said Arabella, looking down her nose from the doorway.

I ignored her, and logged in using Ralph's password—I'd seen him use it, and it had stuck in my memory: Bugle*Editor.

I was about to minimise the email left open on the screen when a name caught my eye. Dumbstruck, I pointed at it. Dregs sighed and slumped into a corner.

Hi Ralph,

Well done for clearing out the dead wood at the Bugle, and I'm delighted it is on its way back into profit. I have reflected my thanks in your bonus—I've sent my man, Corbett, to hand it to you.

In addition, I have learned that your positive coverage of our development has converted a number of waverers and has helped bring a previously implacable enemy onto our side. Toby, of course, is delighted.

He is also grateful to you for employing Olivia—it's her first work experience, and he wants her to learn something about the world of work before she joins the family business.

Keep up the excellent work,

Val

Hobbes looked at the email and grunted. 'That reveals some interesting relationships. However, it's not what I need at the moment. Can you find the photographs?'

'Yes, of course,' I said, forcing ruffled feelings aside and poking at the keyboard. 'Here they are.' I showed him the index. 'They're in date order.' I opened the first one and stood up to allow him to take over.

Olivia and Arabella were muttering together.

Hobbes examined each picture as it came up.

Olivia had her mobile to her ear. 'Mr Pildown?' she said. 'I know you said not to disturb you, but there's a big policeman at your desk. He's using your account to look at photographs ... No, we didn't—Andy Caplet logged in for him ... Yes, I know you did, but he got in anyway. What could we do?'

'Aha!' said Hobbes.

'What?' I asked.

'The woman standing behind Trevor Baker.'

'Rosemary Crackers? What about her?'

'Her hair.' He pointed at it.

'Yeah, perhaps it is a little unusual for a woman of her

241

age to wear it in braids—or are they dreadlocks?'

'The style is unimportant, it's what's in her hair that may be significant.'

'What?' I leaned in for a better look.

He pointed. 'Those shiny little rings.'

'Just like the one you found,' I said, though it didn't strike me as particularly remarkable.

Hobbes nodded. 'It appears so.'

I laughed. 'It's not much use though—she doesn't look the sort who'd climb trees and shoot somebody. She may have poured mussels over Grubbe, but murder is hardly the same thing, is it? Anyway, if you're right about Trevor being the target, why? He was on her side at the time!'

Hobbes shrugged. 'Maybe she already knew he'd changed his mind.' He scrolled through more photos.

Arabella was on her mobile, too. 'How long will they be?' She bit her lip. 'Okay, we'll do our best.'

The two young women approached. 'Mr Pildown demands that you leave now,' said Arabella.

'My father says you have no right to be here, and you have no right to look at private computer files,' said Olivia.

'Your father is correct,' said Hobbes with a smile. 'However, I've found what I was looking for and it may well be an important clue to solve a murder case. When Mr Pildown returns, please give him my apologies … and thank him for his co-operation.'

Arabella shook a beringed finger at us. 'You should get out before you find yourself in deep trouble. My uncle is sending some men round.'

'Good,' said Hobbes. 'Perhaps, you would pass on our regards to them. We have what we need.' He turned to me. 'Alright, Andy?'

'Umm … yeah,' I said, though I wasn't. I'd lost my job! It wasn't that we'd starve—Daphne's wage would keep us going, but I hated being unable to contribute. Especially now she'd turned down Grubbe's easy money.

'Let's go,' said Hobbes.

Dregs sprang to his feet.

'Goodbye,' said Hobbes, saluting the two women. 'Sorry for the intrusion and for putting you into an uncomfortable position, but it was vital.'

We left the office. At the bottom of the stairs, Hobbes pushed Dregs and me into the shadowy stairwell, telling us to keep quiet as the front door burst open and three burly men charged in. They pounded up the stairs, and as soon as they were out of sight, Hobbes led us out into The Shambles.

A parking notice was stuck to the car's windscreen and the front wheel was clamped.

Hobbes squatted and grasped the clamp. The screech of twisting metal as it tore apart sounded like a pig in pain, and reminded me of Cuthbert and Charlie.

'Charlie said something funny, when you were out catching the rhea last night,' I said.

'Go on then,' said Hobbes. 'I could do with a laugh.'

'Umm … I meant funny as in peculiar.'

'Let's hear it,' he said, standing up with the broken sections of the clamp in his hands.

'He reckons Colonel Squire doesn't own Sorenchester Common.'

'How would he know?'

'General Squire told him over a cup of tea, or so he said.'

'Which General Squire?'

'Redvers Squire … no … not him … Arthur. Charlie

reckoned he was the General's pig man.'

Hobbes nodded. 'It's true. General Arthur Squire was a decent old fellow, if you ignore his being responsible for thousands of deaths during his campaigns. He lived to one hundred years old and looked good for a few more until he drowned.'

'Drowned?'

'He fell from a biplane when looping the loop and plunged into Church Lake. The story made quite a splash at the time ... as did he. But never mind that, Mr Brick's information is of interest.'

'He said General Redvers gave the land away,' I said. 'Do you think he might be right?'

'He might be. Mr Godley said much the same.'

'And are you going to do anything about it?' I asked.

'If time permits. Don't forget I have a killer to catch before Kirten messes up any more.'

'But you can't seriously believe Rosemary Crackers would do it? What about means, motive and opportunity? She's a tree hugger, and I'd bet she doesn't own a rifle, and she's busy with the SODs, so I reckon she's ruled out on all three counts.'

Hobbes grinned.

'Umm ... don't you agree?'

'I won't disagree until I find out, but let's see if we can have a chat with her first.'

'That would be sensible,' I said, 'if you knew where she is.'

'I'm good at finding people,' said Hobbes.

'So how are you going to do that?'

He scratched his head. 'I could use cunning, intelligence and diligence, though it may be quicker to try Google first.'

He poked at his mobile and shrugged. 'Low battery.

May I borrow your computer?'

'Yes, of course, but why not use your work one?'

He dropped the bits of wheel clamp into a bin. 'I think it might be diplomatic to keep a low profile while Kirten's still sulking.' He opened the car doors. 'Let's go.'

I let Hobbes and Dregs into our house and started up my laptop. Dregs disappeared for a moment, and returned with a pair of my dirty socks, before starting a game that involved tossing them across the room and springing onto them while growling like a wolf. After a failed attempt to retrieve them, I sat on the sofa and waited while Hobbes fiddled with the computer.

'I can find no mention of any likely person with the name Rosemary Crackers,' said Hobbes after a few minutes. 'There are, however, many recipes for cracker biscuits made using the herb rosemary. Are you sure you got her name right?'

'That's what Colonel Squire said.'

Hobbes looked sceptical.

'Why would he lie?'

'I doubt he was deliberately lying. On reflection, it sounds more like a jokey but disparaging nickname.'

'Because she's against his development—I get it,' I said. 'So, what's her real name? I bet Trevor Baker knows.'

'Just what I was thinking,' said Hobbes, taking out Trevor's card. 'Mind if I use your phone?'

Without waiting, he tapped in the number.

'Mr Baker? Inspector Hobbes here. I have a question. Do you know the name of the middle-aged woman with dreadlocks who's one of the SODs? ... And would you know where she lives? Thank you, sir.'

'Well?' I asked as he put the phone down.

'Very well, thanks,' said Hobbes. 'Her real name is Rosemary Cracknell, and she lives on Hairywart Close. Mr Baker said she's a not-very-talented artist but a passionate and committed environmentalist. I think we'd already guessed the latter.'

'A penny for your thoughts,' I said after Hobbes had stared into space for a few minutes.

'Somewhere in the back of my mind, I have an idea that Cracknell should ring a bell.'

'It's not an uncommon name,' I pointed out. 'There was that Olympic rower for one, and there must be loads of others.'

'I'm aware of that,' said Hobbes, 'and I recall once arresting a trick cyclist going by the name of "Crazy Cracknell" who'd burgled a garage for spare parts. However, he's been dead for years—he trick cycled over a cliff in Ireland. No, the person I'm thinking of had some official connection with the town. The trouble is, I suspect he was a law-abiding citizen, which means I would have had few dealings with him—it's a policeman's unhappy lot to know more about the baddies.'

'Are we going to see Rosemary now?' I asked.

'We could,' said Hobbes, looking thoughtful. 'But it might not be advisable since, as DCI Kirten pointed out, it is still his case, even if he's handling it badly.'

'But he'll keep on making mistakes,' I said. 'You can't let him keep Mr Ching in the cells any longer than necessary.'

'That is true,' said Hobbes. 'I believe it might be for the best if I apprise Kirten of what I have discovered so far. Do you mind if I use your computer to send him an email?'

'Not at all,' I said. 'I'll make a pot of tea.'

Hobbes nodded and started typing. Ten minutes later, as I brought him a mug of tea, he was still going, prodding at keys using his catlike nails. 'Thank you.'

I took my place on the sofa and tried to relax while Dregs glared at me—I'd forgotten to offer him a drink, which was rude of me. A saucer of tea made amends. He then returned to the sock game, which now involved using me as an obstacle to be growled at and bullied until I tossed them round the room.

'That's it,' said Hobbes at last. 'Kirten knows what I know. The rest is up to him.'

'What are you going to do now?' I asked, and chucked the slobbery socks into a corner. Dregs bounded after them with a resounding woof.

'I'm going to enjoy my cup of tea,' said Hobbes. After shaking a pile of sugar into the mug and stirring it in with his big, hairy index finger, he took a sip and looked surprised.

'Umm ... sorry,' I said, crestfallen. 'I did my best.'

'No need for apologies, Andy. That is a fine cup of tea. Well done.'

Amazed, I stammered out thanks and took a sip of mine. It was pretty good—careful and sustained watching of how Mrs G did it had improved my technique. I just hoped it wasn't a fluke.

21

'While I await DCI Kirten's next move,' said Hobbes, putting down his empty mug, 'I have time to think about the development. But before that, is there more tea?'

Proud to have passed the ultimate tea test, I poured him another and wondered where Dregs had got to— he'd grown bored with the sock game. I threw the soggy relics into the washing machine.

Hobbes continued. 'If Mr Brick's information proves correct, I believe it would mean the end of Colonel Squire's proposed development.'

'That's good,' I said, 'though I thought you weren't really bothered by it.'

'Although building developments are not normally matters for the police, I still have to be seen as impartial in my official capacity. I would prefer to keep the common as it is, and if I do find evidence of what Mr Brick claims, then I will ensure it goes to the right people.'

'What ... umm ... sort of proof?'

'Legal documentation.'

'And where will you find that? The Land Registry?'

'I'm sure the SODs have already checked there,' said Hobbes, 'but not all land is registered, and old records of ownership could be anywhere.'

'You could ... umm ... check Colonel Squire's family

records—these old families invariably keep them.'

'I doubt he would allow me access,' said Hobbes.

'You could break in—you've done it before,' I pointed out.

'I could, but where would I start looking in such a large house?'

Dregs returned bearing a new trophy, one of the socks I'd worn in the mountains. In retrospect, I wouldn't have missed that experience for anything, though I had one major regret—I should have been kinder to poor old Piers Twilly in his final hours.

Something stirred in the depths of my memory.

'You look unusually thoughtful,' Hobbes remarked.

'Yes ... I'm trying to think.'

'Careful not to strain anything!' He chuckled.

The memory surfaced. 'When I was in hospital after I'd hurt my leg, there was an old man called Mr Twilley in the bed next to me. I did something I shouldn't have, and he died.'

'Are you confessing to murder?' asked Hobbes, looking severe, though he was joking. Probably.

'No, I said something that upset him and he died.'

'You'll probably get off with a plea of manslaughter then.'

'He had a heart condition and could have gone anytime. But the thing is, before he died, he told me something.'

'It would be more remarkable if he'd told you after he'd died,' said Hobbes, 'but carry on.'

'Well ... umm ... the old man had been a mountaineer. He said he'd met Colonel Squire's uncle on an expedition.'

Hobbes nodded. 'That would have been Clarence Squire, who used to own the Squire estates. As I recall, he was a kindly, if somewhat eccentric man.'

'Yes, that was him,' I said, nodding. 'I'd heard Colonel Squire inherited everything from his uncle who died in a climbing accident, but Mr Twilley said he'd survived and was getting better before he was air-lifted home.'

'Very interesting,' said Hobbes. 'But what's your point?'

'What if Clarence is still alive? Might he have some information?'

'If he's alive,' said Hobbes with a nod. 'Of course, he might have died on the way home or since. If he is still alive, he'll be old now. Nevertheless, I agree, it might be worth pursuing. In the meantime, I intend to visit Mr Brick to see if he has any further information.'

'Good idea,' I said. 'I can't go with you—I said I'd make supper tonight, and I need to get to the shops first.'

'I never said you could come with me anyway,' said Hobbes, looking stern, though there was a twinkle in his eye.

'No ... umm ... of course not. But as you are going to Charlie's, would you mind bringing my stuff back? It's all in a bin bag. And could you take Charlie's things back with my thanks?'

Hobbes nodded. I fetched the freshly cleaned, dried, and ironed garments and handed them over.

I made a move for the shops as soon as Hobbes and Dregs left, but an idle thought crossed my mind as I reached for the door. Returning to my laptop, I searched for Sorenchester plus rifle plus Cracknell. After some time, a link looked promising. I clicked and brought up a forty-year-old story in *Sorenchester Life* about Major Lionel 'Crackshot' Cracknell, who was stationed at the Army camp just south of Sorington, and who had won a national all-comers sharp-shooting contest. The accompanying photograph showed the beaming major holding his rifle, and despite the poor resolution of the picture, it was clearly a younger version of the man who'd been with Rosemary at Le Sacré Bleu. My hands trembled with excitement as I searched for more details of the major and it wasn't long before I came across a reference to his family: wife, Lucinda; sons, Roderick and Victor; daughter, Rosemary.

Although I'd enjoyed the occasional scoop as a reporter, this struck me as massive—it might be the breakthrough in the murder case, and I wished Hobbes were there to see how clever I'd been. On reflection, though, my discovery proved nothing—a crack shot father didn't mean a daughter could shoot. After all, my father had been a dentist, and I never had any interest in that black art, despite the propaganda campaign he'd inflicted on me from the time I could speak. And yet, I knew many who'd taken after their parents. Perhaps I really was onto something.

I called Hobbes's mobile.

'Inspector Hobbes,' he answered.

'Hi, it's … umm … Andy,' I said. 'I've found something out.'

'So have I,' said Hobbes above the whine of his tortured engine. 'You go first.'

I told him.

'Very interesting,' he said, as I heard a key turn in the front door.

Daphne was home.

'You're early,' I said, covering the phone with my hand. 'Is everything okay?'

She frowned. 'It's my usual time.'

My few minutes of research had grown into two

hours, and I still hadn't done the shopping.

Remembering Hobbes was still on the line, I gestured at the phone and made a 'I've got a very important call' face. Daphne nodded and headed upstairs.

'What did you discover?' I asked Hobbes.

'Mr Brick offered me a lot more information on the development—he's still trying to create a good impression so I don't report his pig pollution. He was clearing all that up when I got there, and the stink around his cottage is thick enough to slice. Even Dregs found it hard going, never mind his poor neighbours. When I got there, an angry man was screaming abuse at Mr Brick. Only my intervention prevented a violent altercation.'

I remembered Charlie's neighbours—even though I'd only been an innocent passenger when Violet had crashed through their hedge, I'd feared I would be the one to get a taste of the owner's knuckle sandwich.

'What did Charlie say?' I asked.

'That Clarence Squire is still alive. He is now in his eighties, and lives in a secluded cottage at Edgecliff—he couldn't cope with normality after his accident. That's why he handed over the Squire estates to his nephew.'

'Are you going to talk to Clarence?' I asked.

'Yes, but not today, or I'll be late for my supper. I'll drop your things off tomorrow, if that's alright.'

I thanked him and he hung up.

Daphne came downstairs. 'I'm starving, I hope tea won't be too long.'

I gave her a guilty look. 'Sorry but ... umm ... I got distracted.'

She shrugged. 'I thought I couldn't smell anything. What are we going to do?'

'Fish and chips?' I suggested.

She smiled and nodded. I might have been a little paranoid, but was there a hint of relief in her expression? If so, it wasn't fair because my cooking was improving, and I hadn't killed anybody yet.

'I'll fetch it,' I said, attempting to make amends.

'Good idea,' she said and slumped, onto the sofa. 'I'll have plaice ... and a portion of mushy peas, please.'

I headed for the chippy, feeling unreasonably disgruntled that she hadn't offered to accompany me. Halfway there, my brain clicked into gear and reminded me that I was still without my wallet. I wished I'd thought to use that as my excuse for failing to cook as I hurried home. After borrowing Daphne's credit card, I set out again, and had reached Mosse Lane when a bellow made me glance towards The Feathers, a short way to my left. As I turned, its front door flew open, and a hefty man flew out backwards and landed on the pavement, his head in the gutter.

A larger, fatter, rougher-looking figure in a stained vest appeared in the doorway, scowling. Seeing me, he grinned and raised two fingers in salute. 'What are you staring at, Caplet?'

'Good evening, Featherlight,' I said. 'A bit of trouble tonight?'

The first man, groggy and dishevelled, turned over and tried to get back to his feet.

Featherlight stepped out, booted him up the backside and left him to groan in the road. 'No trouble, just an exercise in customer relations. This bastard was offensive to a young lady.'

'That's bad,' I said.

He glared at me. 'And you—where've you been? I haven't seen your ugly face in a while.'

'I was away and got injured and then I was busy and

then ... '

'Spare us the life story, Caplet. Are you going to come in or are you going to stand there looking gormless?'

'I'm going to get fish and chips,' I said.

'They'll keep. Come on in ... I'd like to catch up with the contents of your wallet.'

I hesitated. On the one hand, a nice cool glass of lager would go down well. On the other hand, the chances of getting one that was nice or cool were remote in The Feathers—I could never work out why I had such a perverse fondness for the place. On the third hand, Daphne was hungry after a hard day's work and I'd already cocked up the catering.

But a quick drink wouldn't hurt.

I walked towards The Feathers. Featherlight had already gone back inside, and a furious roar suggested he was playing the part of genial host with his usual finesse. The man in the gutter, his nose bloodied, pulled himself upright with the help of a lamppost, and spat out a tooth. It was a bicuspid—I had learned something from my father.

'Are you alright?' I asked.

'Do I bloody look alright? Piss off and leave me alone.' He staggered away, dripping blood.

Taking a tissue from my pocket, I retrieved the tooth—Mrs Goodfellow would welcome it to her collection, and might reward me with a treat from the oven.

Taking a deep breath, I entered The Feathers. It was quiet now, and Featherlight was out of sight. The disreputable faces of the locals glowered across pints of bad beer. Several nodded at me.

'Watcha, Andy,' said little Billy Shawcroft, still wearing the steel helmet he donned when trouble was in the air in the shape of flying glasses or customers.

'Evening, Billy. I'll have a pint of lager, please.'

'Right you are.'

'What was the trouble about?' I asked, as he filled a greasy glass.

'Some lout insulted a young lady.'

My eyes widened. 'There was a lady here?'

Billy grinned and nodded, but, though remarkable, it was not unheard of, and Featherlight always behaved impeccably towards women. It was his one redeeming feature. I took my pint and sipped with great trepidation, but it was drinkable, despite a faint tang of vinegar. I looked around. All the faces were male.

'Featherlight took her out back to comfort her,' said Billy.

'First time I've heard it called that, hur hur!' Monty 'Bloater' Black smirked from behind his Guinness. (I guessed it was Guinness because it looked black, though it might just have been a dirty glass.) The back door opened and a look of fear usurped the smirk as Featherlight entered with a young blonde-haired woman. Since Bloater remained in one piece, I assumed Featherlight had not heard his reckless remark.

The young woman was Olivia. The redness around her eyes suggested she'd been crying, and she was grasping Featherlight's hairy hand, looking more like a lost child than the monster who'd usurped my job.

'Bloater,' said Featherlight in a quiet voice, 'I have a job for you.'

'What?' asked Bloater, his eyes wide.

'You are to escort Miss Squire to her home.'

'Me?'

Featherlight nodded. 'You … and you'd better be on your best Sunday School behaviour, and no smutty

255

remarks. Or else … '

Bloater gulped and nodded. 'This way, miss,' he said.

'Mr Black will look after you,' said Featherlight gently.

Just before Bloater led her away, Olivia smiled and, much to my surprise, stretched up to plant a kiss on Featherlight's stubbly cheek. She didn't notice me.

I took another sip of lager and realised Billy was waiting—I hadn't paid yet. Without a thought, I reached for my wallet, which, of course, wasn't there. In a panic, I took out Daphne's card, but Billy shook his head— Featherlight had never invested in a card reader, which I knew full well.

'It's all I've got,' I said, feeling through my pockets in the futile hope of finding some loose change, 'but I'll have my wallet back tomorrow—I can pay for it then.'

'Oh, no you can't,' Featherlight thundered as he pointed to the scrawled notice above the bar: 'Don't ask for credit unless you want a punch in the gob.'

Amazingly fast for such a bulky man, he seized me by the seat of my trousers and the scruff of the neck.

'Don't trouble yourself,' I said, hoping to avoid pain. 'I can throw myself out.'

He must have been in one of his better moods, because he snorted with laughter and put me down. 'Go on then,' he said. 'But don't be too rough on yourself.'

I took myself by the collar, lugged myself through the pub and dived out onto the pavement, much to the astonishment of a passing cat.

'You're barred,' said Featherlight, looking out to make sure I'd done a good job. He grinned, which was not a pretty sight, and stomped back inside.

After picking myself up, I dusted myself down and felt grateful I'd got away with it, but beating up a customer often mellowed Featherlight for a time. Although I regretted the premature removal of lager, it was probably for the best—Daphne would not be impressed if I turned up later than expected, smelling of The Feathers. I hurried to The Fat Fryer.

There was an itch at the back of my mind, as if I'd missed something. But what?

I bought fish and chips and walked home.

'You took your time,' said Daphne as I walked in.

I blamed an imaginary queue and put the fish and chips onto plates. I'd just handed one to Daphne when I recalled that Featherlight had called Olivia 'Miss Squire'.

I swore under my breath.

'What's up?' asked Daphne, a chip halfway to her mouth.

'I've just thought of something.' I put my plate down, opened my laptop and did a quick search.

I found many photos of Miss Olivia Squire winning local gymkhanas. She was, indeed, Colonel Squire's daughter.

I told Daphne.

'So what?' she said. 'She probably wanted a job.' She speared a morsel of fried plaice and put it in her mouth.

'Yes, but why at the *Bugle*? And why wasn't the job advertised anywhere?'

Daphne finished chewing before replying. 'Ralph was doing the Colonel a favour—they probably know each other and talked at that soiree.'

'They did,' I said. 'And ... '

Daphne shook her head. 'I'm starving—let me eat first!'

It was a reasonable request.

I picked up my plate and joined her at the table. The

tang of fried fish and malt vinegar set my mouth to watering and I savoured every succulent mouthful, though my mind seethed.

After we'd finished, I indulged myself in a good, long rant, starting with Ralph firing me, and moving on to the evils of nepotism and 'jobs for the girls'. It was so unfair, I raged, that someone with the right connections could replace a hard-working, real reporter like me.

And then I laughed. Me, a hard-working, real reporter? Who was I kidding?

Yet, I was not the old Andy—I'd come a long way since those days of inept, lazy floundering, and had produced plenty of good, solid reporting, regularly filling my allotted pages. Admittedly, I should have reached this point years earlier, but I'd got there in the end and was still improving—at least I had been until Ralph fired me.

Daphne sympathised for a few minutes and then, as I returned to my rant, suggested that I should shut up and get things in perspective. Peeved, I sulked on the sofa. She sighed. 'Did you say there was another young woman in the office?'

'Yes ... umm ... Arabella.'

She nodded. 'I'm going to do a check on Colonel Squire's family.'

I sat and watched her.

'Aha!' she said after a few minutes. 'Arabella is his niece on his wife's side.'

'But why is Ralph doing favours for Squire?'

She shrugged. 'I'm not sure, but something smells rotten. Colonel Squire and Ralph may be too close for press impartiality.'

I nodded. 'It explains Ralph's support for Squire's development.'

Daphne was still tapping at her laptop. She gasped.

'What's up?' I asked.

'You said you didn't know who owns the *Bugle*?'

'Yes, it's just some faceless corporation.'

She smiled. 'Well, I've just put a face to it.'

'Whose face?'

She pointed at the screen where she'd pulled up a government website.

'Grubbe!' I yelled.

She nodded. 'Yes, Valentine is the new owner.'

'That stinks!' I said. 'It's corruption! It's cronyism! It's diabolical! It's ... not fair.'

'There's certainly a conflict of interest here,' said Daphne.

'I'll tell,' I said.

'Who?'

'Hobbes.'

22

I tossed and turned that night. It rankled that I'd lost my job to someone with no experience but the right connections.

I knew I would never drop off.

The doorbell rang.

'Someone's at the door,' I murmured.

Daphne did not respond.

I sat up, bleary and semi-conscious. She wasn't there.

Forcing myself from bed, I grabbed my dressing gown. It felt softer than usual. I headed downstairs, struggling to get my arms into the armholes.

It was too tight.

It was inside out.

And upside down.

And too pink.

The doorbell rang again. I tied the gown as securely as I could and hurried to the front door.

Hobbes chuckled as I opened it. 'Very fetching.'

Dregs stared at me in astonishment.

'It's Daphne's. I put it on by mistake and I don't know where she is.'

'Since it's approaching ten o'clock, I'd hazard a guess she's at work,' said Hobbes as he came inside. He was carrying a black bin bag.

Hurricane Dregs followed, bounding around me like a kangaroo on amphetamines as I shut the door.

Hobbes handed me the bin liner. 'From Mr Brick.'

'Thanks,' I said. 'It's been a real nuisance not having my things.'

'Glad to help,' said Hobbes, and gave Dregs a look that quelled his attempt to break into the fridge.

The reek of rotting pig dung overwhelmed me as I took a glance inside the bin bag. Dregs yelped and bolted upstairs.

'If I were you,' Hobbes suggested, 'I'd tip that lot straight into the washing machine.'

Knowing good advice when I heard it, I did as he said, and slammed the door to contain the pong. I put in a double scoop of detergent, and an extra helping of lavender-scented fabric conditioner and jabbed a finger towards the 'heavy soiling' button.

'You should take your valuables out before you do that,' Hobbes remarked.

Holding my breath, I rummaged through the shit-sodden clothes and retrieved my wallet, mobile and house keys. After wiping them down with disinfectant, I closed the door again, pressed the button, and left the machine to chug and slosh.

'Any news on the murder?' I asked, returning to the lounge, sliding my mobile into my pocket.

He grimaced. 'DCI Kirten has not yet opened my message, so I've passed my evidence to Superintendent Cooper. Much as I dislike undermining a fellow officer, I fear Kirten has made such a mess of the investigation that innocents are suffering and the guilty party will get away.'

I caught a hint of a gleam in his eye and wondered if, despite his words, he might be getting his own back for

Kirten's rudeness and arrogance.

I changed the subject. 'Did you get much out of Charlie Brick?'

Hobbes nodded. 'He confirmed what you said. If he's correct, Colonel Squire does not own the common.'

'But is he correct?'

'I would say that Mr Brick is a reliable witness and believes what he says.'

'Does that mean the development won't go ahead?' I asked.

'Unless Squire can persuade those who do own the land to sell it.'

'Which would put a dent in his profits,' I said, and smiled.

'And might make the entire project unviable,' said Hobbes.

Dregs thumped downstairs, ears standing to attention, my unchewed mountain boot in his mouth.

'Give it here!' I demanded, and tried to reclaim it.

He kept his grip, growling softly, his head on his front paws, his backside high, his tail wagging. A tug of war ensued, which was great fun for both of us and might have continued much longer had Hobbes not interrupted. 'I have arranged to meet Mr Clarence Squire this morning. Are you interested?'

'Of course,' I said, springing into action. 'I've got nothing better to do. Let's go.'

'Like that?'

I glanced at myself in a mirror. The fluffy pink dressing gown looked much better on Daphne. 'Give me ten minutes.'

'Make it five,' said Hobbes.

I started upstairs and stopped. 'Could you rescue my boot before it dissolves in dog drool?'

I ran the rest of the way, made a pit stop in the bathroom, and dressed. Although I doubted I'd been away for over four minutes, I galloped downstairs.

As I reached the last few steps, Dregs ran across my path in a bid to prove that a black dog crossing one's path could be even unluckier than a black cat.

Momentum too great to stop, I tried to hurdle him, but my leading foot struck his back. So did my following foot. We yelped in unison as he fell on his side and I flew toward the front door. I expected pain and injury, but Hobbes leapt forwards, caught my legs, spun me round and dropped me back onto my feet.

'Thank you,' I gasped. 'Is Dregs alright?'

He was, though he now believed we were enjoying a wonderful game of 'Flatten Andy,' and a bouncing takedown left me flat on my back, fighting off a pink, stinky tongue.

'Stop mucking about, you two,' said Hobbes, opening the front door.

Dregs bounded after him.

' … and quickly!' Hobbes demanded, as I got myself vertical.

There was no time to wash my dog-licked face.

I ran after them and pulled the door shut.

Twenty seconds later, still struggling to fasten my seatbelt, I was in the back seat of the car, racing through Sorenchester.

'Where does Clarence Squire live?' I asked when I'd mastered the belt and caught my breath.

'At Edgecliff,' said Hobbes, who was gripping the steering wheel like a bear hugs a careless hiker. 'That's about fifteen miles away.'

For anyone else, the journey along narrow, twisting country lanes would have taken at least fifteen minutes.

He did it in under ten, leaving me a nervous wreck, though I had enough experience to know terror was only transitory.

We pulled up on a gravel driveway outside a splendid three-storied country house with crenelations around the roof—not quite the quaint, secluded Cotswold cottage I'd envisaged. As we got out, a peacock strolled by to check we were legitimate visitors, and an early swallow swooped past on a warm breeze.

Hobbes marched to the door and rang the bell while I took a moment to admire the house, its lush green lawns and the massed ranks of spring flowers in the borders.

The polished oak door opened and the pink face of an elderly man with long white hair and old-fashioned round spectacles stared out and smiled.

Hobbes showed his ID and introduced Dregs and me.

'I'm Clarence Squire. I was expecting you. Come in.' The old man stepped aside to allow us in. He wore a white shirt down to his knees and baggy cream trousers.

'Hi!' I said.

'Not today, young man,' he said with a puzzling wink.

The hallway was decorated with vases and trinkets that reminded me of our time in the mountains. That short period, despite all the trials and tribulations, was already well on its way to becoming a romanticised memory. Given the chance, I would have gone back there in a shot.

The old man took us to a door at the far end, opened it and ushered us through.

'Wow!' I said.

Edgecliff was well named, for the ground fell almost vertically from the back of the house as the Cotswold escarpment dropped into the vale. Further off, a glinting ribbon of silver showed the course of the River Severn as it meandered through rich farmland and the occasional small town. Beyond that, I fancied I could make out the hazy shapes of the Blacker Mountains.

'Nice, isn't it?' said Clarence.

I nodded. Hobbes and I sat on a long, dusty, threadbare sofa, which blended in with the room's shabby decor. Dregs played at knowing his place and sat beside Hobbes, alert like the hero of a heroic dog film.

'I believe you have some questions,' said Clarence.

'Thank you, sir, I do,' said Hobbes. 'Have you heard about the intended development on Sorenchester Common?'

'No, I have not. The fact is, Inspector, that I rarely interact with the outside world and almost never hear any news.'

'Your nephew, Toby, has teamed up with a property developer,' said Hobbes.

Clarence's pink face turned a shade pinker. 'But it's not his to develop.'

Hobbes glanced at me. 'Surely, the land is part of the Squire Estate?'

'Not since my great-grandfather signed it over to people who'd done him a great service.'

'Which people?' asked Hobbes.

'The Common People, Inspector.'

'D'you mean the ordinary people of Sorenchester?' I asked.

'No,' said Clarence. 'I mean the people who live on the common—the Common People.'

'But no one lives there,' I said. 'There are no houses ... or roads ... or anything.'

'Not everyone lives as we do,' said Hobbes with a

frown that shut me up.

'Correct.' Clarence scratched his whiskers. 'These people are not, as I understand, like you and ... er ... me.'

The old man was looking at me, rather than Hobbes. An inkling of what he meant came into my mind. That masked face ...

'Please continue,' said Hobbes.

'How can I put it?' said Clarence. 'Some people are ... well, different. Such individuals and groups exist in many places around the world.' He darted a shrewd look at Hobbes. 'I suspect you know more about this than most, Inspector.'

Hobbes nodded.

Clarence continued. 'A small group has lived on the common since at least the fifteenth century. My family permitted them to stay, but had minimal contact with them. Then, one foggy winter's evening, my great-grandfather suffered a severe fall from his horse. The Common People found him unconscious in the snow, carried him to their encampment, if that's the right word, and cared for him. He would have died otherwise. When he was fit enough to go home, he signed over the common to them as a mark of his gratitude.'

'That's it then,' I said, clapping my hands. 'The development can't go ahead. That's one in the eye for the Colonel and Grubbe!'

'Would that be Valentine Grubbe?' asked Clarence.

'Yes, sir,' said Hobbes. 'I'm surprised a man who rarely hears news knows about him.'

Clarence smiled. 'He came here a few years ago asking questions when his wife went missing. I believe Toby thought I could help him find her.'

'So, Grubbe is married—I knew it! He denied it, you know?' I glanced at Hobbes, noted his expression, and shut up.

'Why would he think that?' asked Hobbes.

'Because back then, I still maintained intermittent contact with the Common People, and Grubbe suspected his wife had joined them. It turned out to be true—she'd become disillusioned with life with him and wanted no more dealings with "that supercilious bastard"—her words. As far as I know, she's still living there as an honorary Common Person.'

I compared my memory of the face on the common to ones I'd seen more recently. 'Are the Common People Yetis?'

'An interesting question and I understand why you might think so, but no, they are not Yetis. Not as such,' said Clarence, and a look of astonishment appeared on his face. 'What do you know about Yetis?'

'They looked after me ... umph.'

Hobbes's hand on my mouth cut me off. 'That's enough, Andy.'

'Don't worry,' said Clarence. 'I know that careless talk costs lives—the Yetis would be threatened if evidence of their existence and their whereabouts became known to the general public. I've never revealed my experiences with them, and I'm not going to now. The only reason I've told you about the Common People is to save their community.'

I broke free of Hobbes's gag and took a breath.

A dreamy look came into the old man's eyes. He sighed. 'Those were the days—I miss them. I had such great times in the mountains until my accident. I was in a bad way, until Piers, the leader of our expedition, contacted a wandering Yeti who treated me and saved my life. Piers must be long-dead by now.'

'You mean Piers Twilley?' I said. 'I met him when I

was in hospital—he was in the bed next to mine and we talked, but he died. It was his heart.'

'Poor old Piers. The other guys used to call him Holy Dick, though I never understood why—he wasn't religious.'

'It's because umf … ' Hobbes again cut me off mid-flow.

'Probably just an in-joke,' he said.

Clarence nodded. 'I heard from mountaineer friends that he'd stayed out there and I can't blame him—I'd have gone back if my leg was up to it. Still, it's not so bad here. I moved in because I'd grown bored with running the estates. I handed them over to young Toby and let him get on with it. It seemed the right thing to do—the boy had made a complete hash of his army career and needed some sort of income. It would all have gone to him eventually, in any case.'

A deep bell boomed from somewhere in the vicinity. Dregs, forgetting himself, sprang to his feet and barked a challenge. He glanced at Hobbes and sat back down, looking sheepish.

'What was that?' I asked.

'A reminder that my time to meditate is approaching,' said Clarence. 'Can I help you with anything else?'

'There is one thing,' said Hobbes. 'I don't suppose you still have any documentation that proves your great-grandfather gave the land away.'

'You suppose wrong,' said Clarence with a grin.

Hobbes smiled. 'Then you do have it?'

Clarence nodded. 'I believe so. I've kept the old family records—Toby never bothered about such things, and I feared he would throw them out. They're in a trunk in the attic. I'm prepared to let you have the relevant materials if you promise to bring them back when you've finished with them.'

'I promise,' said Hobbes.

'Wait here.' Clarence got to his feet and left us.

'That was a turn up for the books!' I said.

'If it's what Mr Squire claims, then I agree,' said Hobbes.

'It should mark the end of the development.' I said and laughed. 'Grubbe and Colonel Squire won't like it!'

'I expect not,' said Hobbes, standing up and staring out the window towards the Blacker Mountains where he'd lived long ago.

Enjoying the moment, I remained on the sofa, and had there been a bottle of vintage champagne on ice, I would have popped the cork and toasted Clarence Squire. Hobbes's mobile chirped.

He answered. 'How many armed officers?' His face became one huge frown. 'Why? ... Where? ... Yes, ma'am. I'm at Edgecliff at the moment, but I'll be there as soon as I can.' He ended the call.

'What's happened?' I asked, but he held up a hand and shook his head.

The bell resounded again as Clarence reappeared. He handed a manila folder to Hobbes. 'These are the relevant papers.'

'Thank you, sir,' said Hobbes after a glance inside.

'Is there anything else, Inspector? If not, you are welcome to join my meditation—if that's your thing.'

'I'd be delighted,' said Hobbes, 'but something has just come up and I need to make haste.'

He shook Clarence's hand, called Dregs and me to heel, and bustled us from the house and into the car.

I'd thought we'd reached Edgecliff at breakneck speed, but it was nothing to the return journey. The acceleration shoved me deep into my seat, holding me down as fear paralysed every muscle, including those in my eyelids. Fields, woods, cottages and cars passed in a frenzied blur, the engine screamed, the tyres rumbled and squealed as we snaked along stupidly narrow lanes. It was almost a relief to reach a broader road, even though it gave him a chance to crush the accelerator against the carpet.

'What's the rush?' I squeaked when I'd got my breathing under some control and the outskirts of Sorenchester were coming into view.

'Superintendent Cooper said Kirten has read my notes and has gone to talk with Ms Cracknell.'

'That sounds a reasonable thing to do,' I said. 'But you're driving like there's an emergency. Wah!'

I cowered in the back as a blind bend gave Hobbes an opportunity to hurtle past a tractor towing a long trailer. He looked at me over his shoulder as he did so. 'Apparently, Kirten has called in armed-response officers to back him up.'

'That seems excessive,' I said, and cringed as we overtook a speeding Porsche on the brow of a hill.

'Indeed,' said Hobbes, turning back to the road. 'Ms Cracknell may have access to firearms, but I don't consider her dangerous. What's wrong with knocking on the front door in a civilised fashion and asking a few questions?

'You might want to hold on here—there's going to be a few tricky manoeuvres.'

Instead of going the correct way through town, he took the shortest route, despite most of this being the wrong way up one-way streets or along pavements. His big, hairy hands blurred on the wheel, making the little car dance across the road. Circumstances made him brake now and again before gaps in the oncoming traffic allowed maximum acceleration. Despite my seat belt and clinging on for dear life, I bounced about like a dried pea in a jar. Dregs, to my frustration, swayed to the rhythm and looked cool. But we got there intact—I should have had his faith in Hobbes.

The action was developing in Hairywart Close, a nineteen-seventies development off Spittoon Way. It was lined with small semi-detached houses and the road was just wide enough for two vehicles to pass—or would have been had it not been half-clogged with parked cars. Hobbes drove onto someone's neatly striped front lawn and stopped.

'Everybody out,' he said. 'And quickly!'

The lawn's red-faced owner burst from the house. 'What the hell do you think … ' He saw Hobbes and retreated.

'Keep behind me,' said Hobbes, striding away, with Dregs at his side while I jogged to keep up. 'There are people with guns just ahead. Stay safe and don't make yourself a target.'

As we rounded a bend, two parked police cars and a police van, blue lights flashing, greeted us. In addition to three local officers, there were five others dressed in what looked like black commando suits, complete with matching body armour, helmets, and rifles. They looked tough and twitchy. Beyond them, squatting by a wall, I was amazed to see Ralph behind a camera with an impressive telephoto lens. He made himself comfortable and gave me a friendly wave, which surprised me until I realised it was for DCI Kirten on the other side. Kirten, cradling a megaphone, nodded as if at a signal and sauntered toward a large and much older house in the hollow next to Church Fields.

An officer in black approached us.

Hobbes held up his ID.

'Afternoon, sir. I'm Sergeant Armitage.'

'What's happening?' asked Hobbes.

'Well, sir, as you can see, DCI Kirten is making an approach to the suspect's house even though my team has only just arrived, has not been briefed and has had no time to assess the situation and deploy.'

The boom of Kirten's amplified voice made me jump and Dregs growl. 'This is the police, Miss Cracknell. Come out with your hands up ... and don't try any funny business.'

'This is not the way to handle these situations,' said Armitage. 'The DCI is rushing things and there's no need.'

'It looks like he wants to be the hero,' I said.

Armitage nodded. 'Yes, instead of asking that guy with the camera to clear the area, he waited for him to get in position before he made a move.'

'The camera guy is the editor of the *Bugle*,' I said. 'But how did he know to be here?'

Hobbes gave me a quizzical look.

'Alright,' I said, engaging my brain, 'I guess Kirten told him.'

Hobbes nodded.

'And who would you be, sir?' asked Armitage.

'I'm Andy Caplet. I'm a ... I was a reporter.'

'And why are you here?'

'He's with me as an observer,' said Hobbes, his tone leaving no room for argument.

I smiled—observer sounded so much better than bystander.

'Come out with your hands raised!' Kirten's metallic squawk echoed between the houses. He had adopted a heroically determined but casual pose. 'Come on, Miss Cracknell, you're only wasting your time and mine. I warn you that if you don't come out of your own volition, I will send armed men to drag you out and it will be the worst for you.'

'The damned fool,' said Armitage.

Hobbes shook his head. 'There's a time and a place for threats and this is not one of them.'

Kirten raised the megaphone again. 'I'm warning you …'

A shot made me dive over a garden wall, narrowly avoiding the nicely clipped roses. When I peeped back over the top, Kirten was flat on his back, the megaphone on the road behind him.

'She's brought the Kirten down,' said Hobbes with a grin.

Dregs wagged his tail.

Although I hadn't liked Kirten at all, their callous attitude was shocking.

23

Sergeant Armitage ran towards his men, shouting orders. Frantic activity took over.

I stared at Kirten's crumpled form from behind the wall. 'She's killed him!'

Hobbes sauntered towards me and laughed.

'Take cover!' I yelled, appalled by his disregard for his fallen colleague and his own safety.

'I don't think that's necessary,' he said.

'But you might be next!'

'I doubt it.'

As he spoke, Kirten scrambled to his feet and scuttled toward us like a lost soul pursued by the hounds of hell. 'She shot me. She bloody shot me! Somebody call me an ambulance.'

'Very well, sir. You're an ambulance,' said Hobbes, straight-faced.

Much to Dreg's amazement, Kirten dived over the wall and landed beside me, breathing hard.

'She tried to kill me and you're making lame jokes? I'll have you off the force!'

'Calm down. Shooting your megaphone does not constitute an attempt on your life ... sir,' said Hobbes.

'I'm bleeding!'

'It's a tiny scratch on your lip, so stop bellyaching.'

Indeed, DCI Kirten looked remarkably free of bullet

holes, though in fairness, a tiny bead of blood had bubbled up on his lower lip—I suspected he'd caught it on the rosebush he'd dived through.

'I think the bitch might have chipped my tooth,' he moaned, 'and I've only just had it fixed.'

'Get a grip, and find someone to clean you up,' said Hobbes.

Shaking like a wet kitten, Kirten crawled back to the police vans.

'Sir!' Sergeant Armitage pointed down the road. 'There's smoke coming from the suspect's house. What should I do?'

He'd directed the question at Hobbes, but Hobbes, hunched, his knuckles nearly grazing the ground, was already sprinting towards the house.

'Alert the fire brigade and an ambulance,' I said.

'Yes, sir, right away,' said Armitage, reaching for his radio.

I would have been astonished that an armed police officer had accepted my command, had I not been watching Hobbes. Despite his bulk, his heavy boots and his flapping raincoat, he was pounding down the road at a pace that would have put greyhounds to shame. Dregs was making a valiant attempt to keep up.

They were running straight for the house's front door.

I expected Hobbes would stop, but he accelerated, bursting through the door with a thud and the screech of tortured hinges. Black smoke billowed out and hid him.

Dregs knew when enough was enough, and sat down on the garden path, howling—he regarded fire as treacherous since a painful attempt to retrieve a dropped sausage on a barbecue. I ran towards him.

He whimpered when I put a reassuring hand on his back. 'What now?' I asked, as the first spears of flame penetrated the smoke.

He said nothing.

Intense heat seared my face, although we were still yards from the door. What next? Charge to Hobbes's rescue? But would that help or just make another casualty? Would I die? Would Daphne still love me if I got hideously burned?

A quick movement in Church Fields caught my eye.

A woman in an orange kaftan.

Her grey hair was in dreadlocks.

She had a rifle slung over her shoulder.

Rosemary was running away.

The ferocious heat drove us back as I bellowed at the top of my lungs, hoping Hobbes would still hear me above the crackle and roar of flame. 'She's out! She's getting away!'

For a moment, nothing happened.

I covered my face with my arm, fearing that even Hobbes could not survive such an inferno. Then an upstairs window shattered, and he dived through, raincoat blazing. He plummeted like a shooting star, bounced off a privet hedge and splashed down in a small ornamental fish pond. A moment later, he stood up, shook himself like a soggy dog, and strolled towards us, still steaming.

'Are you alright?' I asked.

'It was a trifle warm in there, but I'm fine—apart from my coat.' He glanced ruefully at the blackened holes in the fabric. 'Thank you for your shout—I couldn't find Ms Cracknell and feared she was a goner.'

'She's gone alright,' I said. 'She ran into Church Fields … and she's got a gun.'

'I'd better get after her before Kirten conjures up another hare-brained scheme.' Hobbes raised his voice. 'Sergeant Armitage, stay back, keep your lads out of sight, and don't even think of discharging your weapons.'

Dregs and I followed as Hobbes galloped into Church Fields. He was already out of sight when I reached the children's play area on the edge of the fields, but, half the field ahead, Dregs was bounding along. Assuming he was following Hobbes, I put on a spurt, determined not to fall too far behind. I had a strange feeling of being followed, but a glance over my shoulder revealed nothing but trees, flashing blue lights and smoke.

It wasn't long before a stitch in my side slowed me to a jog, and by the time I reached the footpath on the town side of Church Fields, I had to walk. I'd lost Dregs by then, but kept heading towards the place I'd last seen him. The footpath ran by the wall of the churchyard, passed a disgusting public toilet block, meandered between clumps of trees and shrubs, and crossed a brook that led into the Soren. It was only a five-minute stroll from the bustling centre of Sorenchester and was normally well used, but not another soul was in sight. Although I had a weird sense of loneliness, something made me look over my shoulder.

Although I was still alone, I shivered.

I could hear what sounded like feet splashing in the brook.

Which it was.

Rosemary, the rifle still slung across her back, her orange kaftan slimed with weed and mud, dripped as she emerged from under a bridge. She saw me and gasped.

'Hello,' I said, unsure how to react. 'Fancy meeting

you again ... umm ... '

She stared through red-rimmed eyes, apparently not recognising me until something seemed to click in her memory. She scowled. 'I know you—you're friends with that weasel Grubbe.' She swung the rifle into her hands, though I noticed she kept the dangerous end pointing at the ground.

I shook my head. 'I'm no friend of his—I could have cheered when you poured those mussels over him. I only wished I'd thought of it first.'

'That's all right then,' she said, as if we were having a normal conversation and my knees weren't knocking. The rifle looked huge in her delicate artist's hands, but she held it as if she knew what she was doing.

'What are you going to do?' I asked, wondering why she wasn't running away, which is what I'd expect of a killer on the run.

'I don't know,' she said. 'They're out to get me for some reason.'

'Because you shot Timmy Rigg,' I said.

'Oh that. I didn't think anyone would find out.' Her eyes teared up. 'It was awful, you know? I was aiming and just squeezing the trigger, when this horrible big bird made a booming noise. I jumped, and the gun went off, and the kid was in the way—he just popped up out of nowhere.'

'He was playing on a trampoline,' I said.

'Oh.' She wiped away a tear. 'I didn't want to kill anyone.'

'But you were trying to shoot Trevor Baker!'

She shook her head. 'I was only going to scare him. I was aiming at one of his plant pots. He'd taken Grubbe's thirty pieces of silver and betrayed the cause.'

I believed her and, though she was still holding the

rifle, felt I was in no danger.

'What do you think I should do?' she asked.

'Well,' I said, 'if I were you, I'd put the gun down and talk to Inspector Hobbes—he's already worked out that you did it and that it was an accident.'

She thought for a moment and nodded.

This was going well. I was keeping things calm and resolving a difficult situation without bloodshed.

'Armed police! Drop your weapon!'

As I turned, Kirten, armed with a police rifle, half-emerged from behind a tree. He was aiming at Rosemary.

'Drop the weapon,' he repeated.

Rosemary shook her head and raised her gun. Her finger was not on the trigger.

'No!' I said and stepped between them in an act of wilful recklessness that left me weak at the knees. What on earth was I thinking? Only that I didn't want to see her gunned down.

'Step away from the suspect,' Kirten called.

'Stay there,' said Rosemary. What I imagined to be a gun barrel prodded the middle of my back.

As I began to appreciate my position, I decided it wasn't a good one—I had a mad police officer aiming at my front and a mad hippy aiming at my back. 'Everybody calm down,' I said. 'I'm … umm … sure we can sort this out and be friends. There's no need for bloodshed.'

'She's already shed my blood,' said Kirten. 'I intend to eliminate the threat, so I would advise stepping away. You are obstructing a police officer in the execution of his duty, and I will not stand for it. Do you wish to be remembered as a child killer's accomplice?'

'I'm not obstructing you. I'm just standing in your

way.'

Kirten took aim.

I expected to die.

I did not expect the streak of hairy, black lightning.

And neither did he.

Dregs leapt, and Kirten went down as if someone had clubbed him. Dregs sat astride him, growling softly and wagging his tail.

'I'll take that,' said Hobbes, prising the rifle from Rosemary's grasp and tossing it into a bush. He said he was arresting her and began explaining her rights.

My legs gave way, but even on my way down, I felt the elation that I'd survived. The world was bright. In the distance, I could hear sirens—probably the fire brigade on its way to Rosemary's house.

My mobile rang.

I fished it from my pocket. 'Hello.'

'Hi,' said Daphne. 'I was wondering if you'd like to meet for lunch.'

'Umm ... I ... '

'Are you alright? You sound stressed.'

'Yes ... No ... I don't know.' I got to my feet.

Several young women came running onto the far side of Church Fields. One skimmed a frisbee to another, and Dregs gave in to temptation. In a clear case of dereliction of duty, he set off to join in the game.

Kirten, the light of madness in his eyes, spittle foaming on his bruised lip, rolled to one side, and grabbed his rifle. He rose, finger on the trigger, and something told me he wouldn't calm down until he'd killed somebody. Anybody would do—and I was first in line.

I didn't like it.

Nor did Hobbes.

Most of all, I didn't like what he did next.

Grabbing me by the shoulder and the seat of my trousers, he launched me at Kirten.

I howled like a banshee. (Hobbes later remarked that it was nothing like a banshee, but was reminiscent of the whine of a juvenile kelpie.) Then came the impact, the crack of the gun firing, and pain. I'd landed astride Kirten's face. Not that he complained—my groin had knocked him out for the count.

'Hold that pose! Lovely!' Ralph was approaching, camera clicking. 'That's great! This is going to make the *Bugle*—these pics will be fantastic. I can see the headline: "Hero Bugle reporter takes down mad cop with flying Kung Fu move".'

I clutched my tender parts, unable to speak, unable to remind him that he'd fired me.

'Sorry about that, Andy,' said Hobbes, running up. 'I thought he was going to kill you and had to act quickly.'

'Andy? Andy? What's happening?' My mobile was lying in the grass at my side.

Hobbes picked it up. 'Good day, Daphne,' he said. 'Andy's fine. There was an incident, but all is now under control ... Yes, you did hear a shot ... No, no one got hit, though the toilet block now has improved ventilation ... I wouldn't worry—in my experience, a little excitement gives him an appetite.'

Sergeant Armitage and his men appeared and took charge of Kirten, who was coming round, muttering curses and kicking out at anything within reach. Fortunately, he only made contact with a tree trunk. He yelped and calmed down.

As my groin pain diminished, I got to my feet. Rosemary was sitting on the path, clutching her knees and sobbing. Despite the terrible thing she'd done, I felt sorry for her. Hobbes handed me back the mobile.

'Hi Daphne,' I whispered. 'Hobbes just used me as a blunt instrument, but I'm alright. How about the Bear with a Sore Head? I heard they have a new menu.'

24

The great thing about my status as an amateur observer was that I could just walk away, leaving the professionals to deal with Rosemary and Kirten. Or, to be more accurate, I could hobble away with a slow, straddling gait. My whole body shook and my groin ached—it was not used to close encounters with a detective's face.

Daphne had already claimed a table by the time I limped into the Bear with a Sore Head.

She stood to kiss me. 'What were you up to? Who was shooting?'

She'd already bought me a pint of lager, so I took a soothing gulp before telling her of my starring role in ending the menace of Kirten, and the arrest of Timmy's killer. Her startled expression, the occasional gasp and the way she squeezed my hand were rewards for my tale of heroism and woe, especially as the pain was draining away by then.

I'd just finished my story when a young waitress approached.

Following a glance at the menu, I ordered shin of beef, slow-cooked in ale, while Daphne went for spinach and ricotta ravioli.

'How was your morning?' I asked her out of politeness.

'Strange,' she said, 'and not only because of the gunshot. That was terrifying—I don't know what Mr Hobbes was thinking, putting you in the way of trouble again.'

'It wasn't his fault. The truth is, I was only there because I wanted to be, and if there'd been a better way of taking down Kirten, then I'm sure he'd have used it ... I think. Anyway, apart from a bit of bruising down below, I'm alright. But you were telling me about something strange.'

'I had a visitor. You'll never guess who.'

I didn't. 'Tell me.'

'Valentine Grubbe's wife. His ex-wife, I should say.'

'What?' I said. 'Why? How?'

'You know I was working on cryptids?' she asked.

'I thought you'd stopped that.'

'I don't mean Valentine's job, but the research I was doing for Mr Hobbes. In all honesty, I didn't think I'd discovered much, but a couple of things I turned up pleased him.'

'What things?'

'I'm sorry—he asked me not to reveal what I discovered to anyone, not even to you. Besides, I didn't really understand much of it—there were some documents written in bad Latin, plus an artifact dating from the period of the Anarchy in the twelfth century. All I can say is that it was all linked to the area now known as Sorenchester Common. I think Mr Hobbes was looking for something that might help stop the development.'

That reminded me—so much had happened since that I'd forgotten to mention our visit to old Clarence Squire. I blurted it out.

She smiled. 'Great! That must mean the development

is finished.'

'I believe so,' I agreed, 'and I think Hobbes does, though he wouldn't say so.'

'Well, it sounds like good news,' said Daphne. 'Helen will be delighted.'

'Helen?'

'Valentine's ex-wife.'

'Why does this affect her?'

'She lives on the common ... with her friends.'

'Of course, she does! With the Not Yetis,' I said, remembering Clarence's story.

Daphne looked puzzled.

'The Common People,' I explained. 'I think they're Not Yetis.'

'Of course, they're not Yetis—what a weird thing to say.' She shook her head. 'Sometimes, Andy, I think I married a lunatic.'

'Only sometimes?' I asked.

She laughed.

'But I don't understand how the former Mrs Grubbe knew about you?' I said, getting back on to the subject.

Daphne shrugged. 'I suspect Mr Hobbes let her know what was going on.'

The waitress delivered our lunches. Hobbes was right—excitement did give me an appetite. My slow-cooked shin of beef was succulent and tasty, though the sauce was bland and salty. I gulped it down and was reaching for my notebook before remembering I was no longer the *Bugle*'s food critic.

'How's your ravioli?' I asked, struggling to overcome a sense of loss I hadn't expected.

'Not great,' she said. 'It could do with a lot more flavour and a lot less salt.'

'Oh no!' I gasped and clapped a hand to my forehead

She looked astonished by my reaction. 'It's not that bad!'

I shook my head. 'Not the food—I've just had a horrible thought. When we were leaving Clarence's, Hobbes put all the documents into his coat pocket.'

'So?' she asked through a spoonful of ravioli.

'Since then, his coat has caught fire and got dunked in a fish pond—the documents will be ruined!'

I grabbed my mobile and called him.

'Good afternoon, Andy. What do you want?'

'Are they alright?'

'Are what alright?'

'The ... umm ... papers from Clarence.'

'Yes, of course.'

'They didn't get burned or wet?'

'No.' He laughed. 'I see what you're getting at—you thought I'd left them in my coat pocket. However, I learned the hard way that it's best not to carry anything important into a situation where it might get lost or damaged. They were in the car.'

'That's a relief,' I said. 'How are you?'

'Fine thanks, apart from a bit of singeing here and there. I've had a quick chat with Rosemary—her story fits what we'd surmised already.'

'That's good,' I said, pleased by the 'we'. 'What about Clarence's documents?'

'I've handed them to Jane Mortimer ... '

'Who?'

'A solicitor, specialising in land law. She's been working pro bono for the SODs.'

'Umm ... Bono?'

'She's offered her services for free,' said Hobbes.

'I knew that,' I lied. 'Did she say anything about the documents?'

286

'She'll have to go through them all with a fine-tooth comb. However, she appeared relieved to receive them. Was there anything else?'

'Umm ... no.'

'Then I'll say goodbye for now. I'm off home for lunch.' He ended the call.

'Did you catch all that?' I asked.

Daphne nodded. 'Most of it. I must let Helen know—she feared her friends would lose their homes.'

'Of course,' I agreed. 'Did she leave an address or phone number?'

'No, I don't think she has such things. I'll have to pay a visit. It shouldn't be too difficult to find her.'

'It will be—the common is a vast area and there aren't any houses ... at least I didn't see any.'

'There must be,' said Daphne.

I shook my head. 'There are no roads either—just hidden paths. It's difficult to get to.'

She shrugged. 'But you've been there—you can take me.'

'Okay,' I said, hoping I wouldn't let her down. 'When?'

'After work. I'm finishing at five o'clock. Is that alright?'

'Why not? It's not as if I'll be working late at the *Bugle*?'

After our lunch, I walked her back to the museum.

'I'll see you here at five,' I said.

Alone and with no work to occupy me, I found myself at a loose end. I mooched around town for half an hour finding nothing to interest me, and was seriously considering going home and cleaning the kitchen when my mobile rang.

'Hi, Andy,' said Ralph. 'When are you coming in

today?'

'I'm not. It may have … umm … slipped your memory, but you fired me.'

'I never did, Andy, mate! Why would you think such a thing?'

'Because Olivia told me.'

'You shouldn't believe everything that silly girl says,' said Ralph with a nonchalant chuckle. 'Why would I fire a valued member of staff?'

'Are you sure you've got the right person?' I asked—he'd not had a problem dismissing Duncan and Basil.

He laughed. 'Positive. If you can come in now, you can help me with a story—it's going to be a big one!'

'Alright,' I said, 'though I've got to leave at five for an appointment.'

'Of course. When can you get here?'

'In ten minutes.'

'I'll see you then, buddy,' said Ralph, cheerful and affable like an old friend.

I didn't trust him at all, though I was intrigued, as well as feeling a glimmer of hope. Presumably, he wanted my account of the morning's action with Rosemary and Kirten and, with suitable modifications, I was prepared to give it. Plus, of course, I had the scoop about the development—how, I wondered, would he react to that? What positive spin could he apply to the story?

But did I really want to work for him? Did I really want to work for Grubbe's consortium? Then again, could I afford not to?

I dawdled down The Shambles, trotted up the stairs to the office and entered. My old desk was waiting for me, much as I'd left it, but tidy. Olivia and Arabella were sharing Basil's old desk in the corner. I greeted them with a cheery 'Good afternoon', but received only a glower from Arabella in response. Olivia nodded and smiled.

Beaming like a Cheshire cat, Ralph sallied from his office. 'Andy! Glad, you could make it. Come in here— I've got something to show you.' He led me into his office and sat me down in front of his computer screen. 'Look at these!'

There were pictures of the morning's action and, though I hated to admit it as I scrolled through, they looked sensational: Kirten, megaphone in hand, posing like a film star in front of Rosemary's house; Kirten sprawling in the road; Kirten crawling away; Kirten diving over the wall into a rose bush. Then came pictures of the fire—I looked heroic in front of the flames, but the most spectacular ones showed the fiery figure of Hobbes plunging from the window.

'They're great,' I said.

Ralph grinned. 'Wait until you see the next lot!'

These showed the incident in Church Fields—I guessed Ralph must have used his long lens. I saw myself talking calmly to Rosemary (tagged 'the armed assassin'), the arrival of Hobbes, and him disarming her with courtesy. The final scenes showed me flying through the air, bringing down Kirten, and knocking the rifle from his hands. It appeared Ralph had missed Hobbes hurling me.

'You see?' said Ralph, excited. 'This is going to be so big! It'll make the nationals ... even the telly news—I just wished I'd videoed it. You're going to be famous, Andy, my boy!'

Despite the apparent photographic evidence, I'd been no more than a convenient tool in Hobbes's hands, and I didn't want to be famous for being a tool. I grimaced.

'I've nearly finished the copy, too,' said Ralph, 'but I need a few more quotes from you. So far, I have you modestly saying, "I was in the right place at the right time".'

'I would never say that!'

Ralph smiled. 'You probably will some time.'

I shrugged. 'I suppose I might.'

'There you go!' said Ralph in triumph. 'You will say it, and time is relative.'

'Yeah, okay,' I admitted, and read out my next supposed quote: '"Anybody faced with a crazed man threatening people with a rifle would have done what I did". I never said that either.'

'You just did!' Ralph looked complacent. 'It's a fantastic photo story—it'll shift tons of copies.'

'But it's not true!'

'In essence it is,' said Ralph. 'Pictures don't lie, and all I've done is jazz up the story to make it more entertaining. It'll fill the front, second and third pages. Most of the rest of the paper is ready—the usual dog and pony show fluff, local clubs and such like, but we still need a good, solid story, if you wouldn't mind writing about five hundred words. Any ideas?'

I nodded. 'As it happens, I do have one.'

'Great! What about?'

'The end of the Sorenchester Common development.'

Ralph laughed. 'Very funny!'

'No, it's true—Colonel Squire doesn't own the land.'

'What do you mean?' asked Ralph, suddenly serious.

'One of the old General Squires signed it over to the Common People who'd saved his life. By the way, Valentine Grubbe's ex-wife lives with them.'

'What? On the common? Where did you pick up such

nonsense?' asked Ralph, attempting a condescending smile, but looking pale.

'It's not nonsense—I've seen the documents.'

'And where are they now?' asked Ralph, trying to sound casual and friendly, though I detected a sharp, angry edge to his voice that made me wary—perhaps I'd already said too much.

'In the hands of the authorities.'

'How did you get to see them?'

'I ... umm ... was in the right place at the right time.'

'Where and when?' Ralph's tone had become that of an interrogator, and I half feared he'd turn his desk lamp on me.

'This morning. I was ... out of town. I can't reveal any more—I have to protect my source.'

'Not from me,' said Ralph. 'You can trust me, can't you?'

'Of course, I can,' I said, smiling, though I didn't. At the back of my mind, my brain was forging seemingly random links of information into a chain.

'So, tell me,' said Ralph.

'Sorry, but I never reveal my sources. Not even to friends.' I'd spoken the truth in that no one had ever asked me before.

Ralph stared for a few uncomfortable seconds, shrugged, and smiled. 'Fair enough. I admire your integrity. Go and write the article.'

I returned to the main office, interrupting a conversation between Olivia and Arabella. They barely even spared me a glance between them. Under other circumstances, I might have felt affronted, but I was too busy wondering what Ralph was up to. His change of tone and manner had been too abrupt and, on the other side of the door, I could hear him making a phone call, though I couldn't hear what he was saying. Perhaps he was informing Colonel Squire of my news. If so, it was worrying, for Squire had a ruthless streak which I knew from painful, personal experience. Somehow, though, he'd always got away with it, keeping himself at a safe distance from any violence and criminality. Only his unfortunate henchmen ever got to feel the full force of the law. According to Hobbes, Squire maintained a barrier of plausible deniability—if things went wrong, he just blamed overzealous staff for misinterpreting his wishes.

I drafted my article anyway, but instead of emailing it to Ralph as normal, I sent it to my personal laptop and deleted the copy I'd been working on. I got up casually, told the ladies I was going to Cafe Nerd for a takeaway coffee, and asked if they wanted anything. Neither replied, so I sneaked away. I had no intention of visiting Cafe Nerd, but needed to think about the connections coming together in my head.

I'd just started walking when my mobile rang—it was Daphne.

'Hi, just reminding you we're going out soon.'

'Out?'

'To the common—you've forgotten, haven't you?'

'Me? Of course not. In fact, I'm on my way now. Thanks for the reminder, though. I'll see you ... ' I glanced at the time. ' ... in five minutes.'

25

I reached the museum just as the five o'clock bongs from the church tower were fading. Daphne emerged from the staff door and after a quick kiss, we set off for the common. I told her of my reinstatement at the *Bugle* and how Ralph had reacted to my news.

She frowned. 'It might have been better to have kept quiet, especially if he did phone Colonel Squire, as you suspect.'

'That's what I thought,' I admitted. 'I drafted the article for Ralph, but decided against sending it. The thing is, I suspect he might be ... '

She finished my sentence, ' ... working for Squire.'

I nodded. 'And also for Grubbe—he does own the *Bugle*.'

'Yes,' Daphne agreed. 'Which explains why it has become little more than their propaganda tool, favouring the development while ignoring or ridiculing the SODs. The days when it reported facts and let the readers make up their own minds are long gone.'

'I'm not sure it was ever quite as pure as that,' I said. 'Owners and editors have always had their own agendas, but Rex and Phil would at least report the truth as they understood it, and would always report opposing views. Thinking about it, I reckon that's why Ralph got rid of Duncan and Basil—they might have been cynical old hacks, but they would never write anything unless they believed it was substantially correct.'

Daphne smiled. 'He got rid of you, too.'

'And then he brought me back when he thought I might be useful to the paper.' Another of the links clinked into place in my brain. 'It explains why he's taken on Olivia and Arabella, too—they're both young and naive as well as being in the family—they'll do what Colonel Squire tells them to do.'

I walked on, shaking my head, appalled at the corruption, assuming our musings were right, and I had little doubt they were.

It was a warm, sunny evening with a gentle, cooling breeze. We reached the more modern housing on the edge of town, and I had a strange sensation that someone was behind us. When I looked back, no one was there. I tried to reason that I was just nervous because I'd felt the same way in the morning, and had been right then.

'I think we're being followed,' Daphne whispered.

I looked again, but there was no sign of anyone. Though I tried to reassure her, I wasn't quite convinced myself.

She fiddled with her mobile, and I kept a little closer to her.

Another fifteen minutes took us to the wooded edge of the common. We'd seen no one. I relaxed a little and led her along the paths Hobbes had used last winter, though they were now all but obscured by the spring growth, and there were far too many brambles, thistles, and nettles for my liking. Fortunately, I found a short stick and used it to beat a passage when all was too dense or prickly. The woods went on for longer than I remembered, and I was suspecting I'd made a mistake when the path opened out onto rough heathland. We'd found the common, now lush and alive with birdsong. Flowers and blossom perfumed the evening air.

'We're here,' I said. 'Now what?'

'We find Helen and tell her the news.'

'There's four square miles of this! The plants have grown over everything since I was last here, and I couldn't see any houses even then.'

Daphne nodded. 'Okay. Where did you see the face?'

'I'm not sure—everything looks so different now.' I gazed around. 'Maybe over there by that hawthorn.' I pointed—it could have been where I threw the frisbee for Dregs.'

There was a mass of spiky gorse bushes near the hawthorn, so I was almost sure I'd found the right place. There were no masked faces, though.

'We could try calling for her,' said Daphne.

But there was no need.

Frustrated, I whacked the bush with my stick.

The bush bellowed.

It wasn't all bush.

A figure, seven-foot tall and dressed in a loose green robe, burst from the gorse. I dropped the stick and gaped at the leaf-masked face, dumbfounded.

'Sorry about that,' said Daphne, smiling at the unexpected apparition, her voice soothing. 'Andy didn't see you. We are looking for Helen. Do you know her?'

'Helen?' the apparition said.

Its deep, rumbling voice reminded me of Yetis. He (I assumed it was he) beckoned, turned and loped away.

'I think he wants us to follow,' said Daphne.

We tagged along behind him, though I wondered if

we were being wise.

As we neared a huge thicket, the apparition whistled, and a barrier of briars and brambles moved aside. Before us was a compound of six large, low, round, thatched buildings.

Our guide led us inside, where a handful of masked figures, some even taller than him, appeared, staring at us as if we were the weird ones. Our guide spoke, though the only word I could distinguish was 'Helen'.

'I understand your Yeti reference now,' Daphne murmured, wrinkling her nose at the stink of unwashed bodies, decay and worse.

'Clarence Squire said they're Not Yetis.'

A pretty woman, a few years older than Daphne, emerged from the largest hut in the middle. She was much slighter than those around her and wore a robe similar to our guide's, but no mask.

She looked astonished and then smiled. 'Daphne, what a surprise! How did you find Dolmuk? He's one of our best at concealment.' Her words rolled out slowly and deliberately, as if she was groping for the right ones in the depth of memory.

'Andy accidentally hit him with a stick,' said Daphne, 'and ... Dolmuk ... kindly brought us here. I have some good news.'

'Yes?' said Helen.

'It appears that Colonel Squire doesn't own this land—one of his ancestors gave it to ... '

'So, this is where you've been hiding!' Valentine Grubbe, his hair sticking up, his usually immaculate clothes dishevelled, strode through the gap in the barrier, looking belligerent.

Helen grimaced. 'Hello, Val.'

'You gave up your life to live with these throwbacks!

Why?' Grubbe sneered at the Not Yetis, the ugly core beneath his charm in full view.

Helen shrugged. 'The company is so much better.'

Grubbe stopped as if she'd punched him. He burst into tears. 'We had plans.'

'No, darling,' said Helen, injecting total contempt into her words. 'You did. I don't remember being asked.'

'We were happy together!'

'No, we weren't,' said Helen, and the hesitancy in her speech had gone. 'You were always in a foul mood and we never went anywhere together and never did anything together, unless you were showing me off at some business do.'

Grubbe looked thunderstruck.

'I'd had a bellyful of being your trophy wife, as you so delicately described me to one of your bloated cronies.'

'Oh,' said Grubbe with a guilty start.

Helen, still looking cool, smiled.

'I'm delighted for this opportunity to remind you of all that, and I'm even more delighted to learn your latest money-grubbing scheme has hit the rocks.'

After wiping his eyes and blowing his nose on a large, white handkerchief, Grubbe scowled and set his jaw.

'That's it! I'm putting an end to this nonsense. You're coming back to the real world with me.' He lunged at her; his handsome features disfigured by fury.

It was time for me to act. As he rushed by, I gave him a shove, and he went down onto hands and knees.

Turning his head, he glared as if he hadn't noticed me until then.

'You bastard!' he roared as he got back to his feet. He charged, looking like a man intent on murder.

Daphne stuck out her leg.

As trips go, it was perfection.

Grubbe went down like a felled tree.

His chin smacked against my kneecap.

'Ow! Ow! Ow!' I hopped in a circle, trying to cradle my bruised knee as Grubbe attempted to get up.

He swayed to the left, lurched to the right, and collapsed.

As the Not Yetis crowded around, staring and murmuring in their strange, guttural language, a sound as if from a badly tuned donkey made me jump and Helen gasp.

'What was that?' asked Daphne.

'Umm … an alarm?' I suggested.

Three Not Yetis ran to close the barrier, but a mob of around thirty men wielding pick-axe handles as clubs swept them aside. The other Not Yetis fled.

My swift response came from years of experience. I grabbed Daphne's hand.

'Let's get out of here,' I said, dragging her towards the huts. The only thought in my head was to get us both away from harm.

'Who are they?' she asked as we ducked beneath a low wooden lintel into a gloomy, smoke-filled room.

'Squire's thugs? They look like the same ones who caused the trouble in town.'

A battle developed outside—the thugs' pick-axe handles battling nine or ten unarmed Not Yetis. It was clear that Squire's men must soon triumph. And then what? Perhaps hiding in a hut with only one door had been a foolish idea. Or was there somewhere to hide? Not really—I could make out little through the gloom. Smoke circulated from a wood fire in the middle, stinging my eyes. All I could see were a few cooking pots and utensils, several logs arranged like benches, and some bedding.

'What's happened to Helen?' asked Daphne before I could try breaking through the walls.

'Grubbe's got her!' I said, peeping out.

Before I could think of anything sensible to do, Daphne darted from the hut. Dodging and weaving, she slid through the melee.

'Shit!' I charged after her, my instinct for self-preservation nowhere near as powerful as my urge to keep her safe.

As reckless charges went, it wasn't my best.

In fact, I'd only just got outside when a blow to the head made pretty lights flicker before my eyes. Down I went. As I pushed myself onto my knees, trying to shake the confusion from my head, a huge, blubbery man in a white t-shirt fell on top of me—Colonel Squire's thugs weren't having it all their own way.

The bloated body crushed me flat against the hard ground, muffling the sounds of battle. Despite increasingly desperate wriggles, I couldn't free myself. I hoped Daphne was okay, because I wasn't—each breath was a struggle, and each breath made me wish the thug had showered more recently. Unable to shift him, I was helpless, and only convulsive jerks allowed me to catch even the slightest gasp. I was losing the battle.

The ground was so hard.

My only consolation was that all things must pass and my situation could not get any worse.

And then it did get worse.

The crushing weight doubled, and not even my most titanic efforts could inflate my lungs.

I despaired.

And then the pressure was gone and a gentle hand was

brushing my cheek.

I opened my eyes.

Daphne was kneeling at my side. There was blood on her face. 'Are you all right?' she asked.

'Yes, but you're bleeding!'

'It's just a nose bleed,' she said. 'You're bleeding too.'

I touched my head and saw she was right.

I sat up.

The sun was low and red, and all was peaceful as far as I could see. There was no battle, no thugs, no Not Yetis. I turned my head. Four neat rows of men were lying beneath a birch tree—Squire's thugs.

'What happened?' I asked. 'Where are Grubbe and Helen?'

Daphne applied a handful of tissues to my leaking head. 'I caught up with them and told him to let her go ...'

'Did he?'

'No, and he was hurting her. I tried to break his grip, and he hit me.'

'The swine!' If he'd been within kicking range, I would not have been responsible for my actions.

'So, I punched him like Mrs Goodfellow showed me and he went down like a ton of bricks and stayed down—I'd knocked him out cold.'

'Well done.' I was even more proud of my wife than normal. 'How's Helen?'

'Bruised, but nothing too bad.'

'And the Not Yetis?' I asked.

'Squire's bully boys were going crazy with their clubs and fists, and I feared someone would die, and then Mr Hobbes turned up.'

'How did he know to come here?'

'I texted him as soon as we thought we were being

followed. I was afraid something might happen. He would have got here sooner, but DCI Kirten had found his way onto the roof of the police station and was threatening to throw himself off, the poor man.'

I grimaced—that 'poor man' might have killed me a few hours ago. Still, Daphne's capacity for forgiveness had benefited me more often than I cared to remember, and I forgave her.

She continued. 'By the time he got here, Colonel Squire's thugs had more or less beaten down all resistance and there was nothing Helen or I could do.'

'And Hobbes?'

She smiled. 'He walked towards them and asked them to put their weapons down and go home.'

'Did they?'

'They did not,' said Daphne. 'Well, two local men he recognised did, to great jeers from their mates. The rest of them laughed and told him where to go in the foulest terms possible.'

'He wouldn't like that,' I said. 'What next?'

'He told them they were all under arrest and were to accompany him to the police station, which went down as well as you might expect. One lunged forward and swung his club at Mr Hobbes's head.'

'And then?'

'Everything happened rather fast. I don't know how he did it, but all of a sudden the club was in Mr Hobbes's hands and the guy was lying on the ground.'

'And then?'

'And then the rest of them charged in. There were so many, I couldn't even see him at first. They were all trying to club him, and I thought he was going to get badly beaten, if not killed. I tried to call the police, but couldn't get a signal. But there was no need to worry—

he just kept dodging and ducking, and I'm not sure any of them landed a blow. He just kept moving through them as if it was some sort of dance, and the strange thing is that I never saw him hit back—I think they ended up knocking each other out. How does he move so fast?'

'He's unhuman,' I said with a shrug. 'It's just what he does. He is weird—you've seen it before.'

She nodded. 'Yes, but it still amazes me ... and he's a friend of ours!'

'He is,' I admitted. 'Just as well—I wouldn't like to be his enemy.'

'Nor me.' She bit her lip. 'Can you imagine getting on his wrong side?'

I shivered. 'I'm afraid I can—he can get rather wild, and he's terrifying when he's angry. Fortunately, he's not like that very often, and he's determined to be one of the good guys—it's how he was brought up.'

I looked around. 'Where is he now?'

'He's gone to call for an ambulance. He took two of the more seriously injured men with him, balanced on his shoulders.'

'And Helen ... and the Not Yetis?'

'She's looking after her friends—none of them is as badly hurt as you might have expected.'

'Why didn't they put up more of a fight?' I asked. 'They're big and they look strong, and I can't believe the real Yetis in the mountains would have been so ... passive.'

'Helen said it was because most of the fit adults were away, hunting and gathering. The ones still here are too old, too young, or too sick. That's why she stayed here—she was a nurse before she married Grubbe.'

'Oh, yes, Grubbe! What about him?'

'He was back on his feet when Mr Hobbes turned up. He ran away.'

'What a coward!' I said and felt I had the right to say it. After all, I had once fought an unhuman who'd been as big as Hobbes, and who was attacking Daphne. I'd lost in the end, of course, but I'd kept her safe until Dregs turned up in fighting mood and saw him off.

'Are you up to walking home?' she asked.

I got up, tested my limbs, and nodded.

Something glinted in the grass. I picked it up—it was Grubbe's gold Rolex, but Rolex watches should not be rusty. I showed Daphne.

'Are you okay?' I asked—she looked troubled.

'Yes. It's just that I enjoyed punching Valentine. I didn't know I had a violent streak.'

'That's not what you are,' I said, giving her a hug, 'but everyone can fight if pushed too far. You were protecting Helen, and you succeeded. You should take pride in that.'

She thought for a moment and smiled. 'Home?'

'Home,' I agreed, taking her arm.

All in all, it had been an interesting day.

26

Over the next days, there was a great deal of legal palaver concerning the ownership of Sorenchester Common. Most of it went over my head, but in the end, Clarence's documents proved key to a ruling that the land still belonged to the Common People. The development was laid to rest with few mourners in the town. The afternoon of the verdict, Daphne and I set off to tell Helen the good news, but there was no sign of the path we'd used before. Furthermore, every potential route through the woods towards the common ended in a mass of dense thorn or holly bushes. We took the hint and left the Not Yetis alone.

The next day, I ran into Hobbes outside the church. He helped me back to my feet.

'Are you alright?' he asked. 'You appeared quite unaware of your surroundings.'

'Yeah—I was just thinking how to draft the latest episode of our mountain expedition.'

He nodded. 'The first two parts were most entertaining—and sometimes accurate.'

'Thank you.' I said, pleased. 'What have you been up to?'

'I've been dealing with Ms Cracknell, DCI Kirten, and twenty-three miscellaneous young hooligans. DCI Kirten is now on sick leave—he claims the stress of investigating Timmy Rigg's killing caused his breakdown and that he wasn't responsible for his actions.'

'Will he be charged with anything?'

Hobbes grimaced. 'I doubt it—he has connections. He'll probably recuperate for the politically correct time period and then return to work. However, I doubt he'll be allowed to work a case again—he'll get a dull desk job in London where he can do little harm and even some good.'

It didn't seem like justice, but perhaps it was—Kirten wasn't the first senior police officer to crack up after a dispute with Hobbes.

'I saw the pictures of you in the *Bugle*,' said Hobbes. 'You looked very brave.'

I blushed. 'That was nothing to do with me. I tried to explain what had happened, but Ralph insisted on presenting it that way. He said it would sell newspapers, and it did—sales increased by thousands.'

'I thought your article about the cancellation of the development, was fair and balanced, even the part about Mr Grubbe.'

'I'm glad you liked it. Olivia Squire helped with the research—it turns out that she really does want to be a newspaper reporter. She says she knew nothing about the shenanigans that got her the job in the first place— I wonder whether she has enough of an enquiring mind to be a top journalist.'

Hobbes shrugged. 'Perhaps not, but naivety and ignorance are not uncommon in people from privileged backgrounds. It rarely holds them back, though.'

His mobile buzzed. He held up his hand to silence me and answered. 'I'll be right there,' he said a minute later, and ended the call.

'What's up?'

'A suspected burglar is. He's got stuck upside down in a chimney. I'd better find a long stick to poke him out.' He loped away, paused, and looked over his shoulder. 'Would you and Daphne like to come to lunch on Sunday?'

I pretended to think about it. 'Yes, please!'

'I'll see you then.' He hurried up the road.

Later that week, the *Bugle* carried a statement from Colonel Squire in which he claimed to have been as surprised as anyone to learn that he didn't own the common. He hinted that he was secretly relieved the project had been stopped, and had only supported it to help out Valentine Grubbe, an old friend fallen on hard times. Squire expressed shock and outrage at the alleged dirty deeds, intimidation and violence, all of which had happened without his knowledge. Furthermore, he was puzzled and hurt by suggestions of nepotism at the *Bugle*—so far as he knew, his daughter and niece had been recruited purely because of their undoubted talents and potential. Learning that a consortium fronted by Grubbe owned the newspaper, had come as a great shock.

I was amazed and a little depressed by how many of the good townsfolk believed him.

On Sunday, Daphne and I headed for Blackdog Street. Hobbes opened the door for us, and the heavenly aroma of roasting beef greeted us, as did Dregs, who hurtled around me like a canine whirlwind before sidling up to Daphne for a head rub.

'Come in,' said Hobbes, as Dregs rushed back towards the kitchen, no doubt hoping for scraps.

We sat together on the old sofa while Hobbes took his seat in his armchair.

'I expect you'd like to hear what's been happening,' he said.

Daphne nodded. 'Have you any news about Grubbe yet?'

'Mr Grubbe appears to have vanished without a trace. He owes millions of pounds and, from what we have ascertained, much of the debt is to what you might call "informal" lenders who don't adhere to the normal rules, and who are reputed to employ massive debt collectors to retrieve massive debts.'

'But he gave the impression of wealth,' said Daphne. 'The flash cars, the Italian suits ... '

'All fake, or illusions bought on credit,' said Hobbes. 'Like his watch.'

'And Rosemary Crackers?' I asked.

'Ms Cracknell has been remanded in custody on suspicion of murdering Timothy Rigg. However, in my opinion, the charge will be reduced to manslaughter. She didn't mean to kill anyone.'

'Even so, firing off a gun like that was reckless at best,' said Daphne.

Hobbes nodded. 'Of course, it was, but the lack of intent to cause harm is a mitigating factor. Her father taught her to shoot, and believes she is an even better shot than he was at his peak.'

'Where did she get her rifle?' I asked.

'She stole it from his collection, intending to scare Mr Trevor Baker, who she considered had betrayed the cause.'

'With good reason!' said Daphne.

'Perhaps,' said Hobbes. 'However, a man is entitled to change his mind without being intimidated.'

'Even if he's done it for money?' I asked.

'Yes,' said Hobbes, 'unless it is regarded as a bribe in law.'

'It's still unethical,' I said virtuously. I'd been conflicted when Daphne turned down Grubbe's easy money, but now I supported her decision. Anyway, he probably wouldn't have paid her. Not that we needed it—the department had sent us, or rather Daphne, a generous cheque.

'Hello, dears,' said Mrs Goodfellow, poking her head round the door. 'Dinner will be in five minutes.'

'I'd better wash my hands,' said Hobbes, and padded upstairs. After all the years, it still amazed me how quietly he could move.

Dinner was a delight: sirloin of beef, perfectly cooked, butter-softened mixed greens, and the tastiest, crispiest roast potatoes I'd ever eaten since the last time she'd made them. We ate as ever in a rapturous silence, only broken by a pathetic whimper from Dregs who could never understand why he was not granted a place at the table. I knew why—it was his disgraceful table manners. I didn't worry about him, though. He'd do alright when we'd finished.

Then came the dessert, which the old girl had made for Daphne and me, since Hobbes was indifferent to sweet foods. It was a marmalade pudding, a wonderland of contrasting flavours and textures, made with her own marmalade and served with a cream custard. It was so amazingly tasty that even Hobbes went back for seconds. I would have done too, if I could have stretched my greedy stomach.

Afterwards, we returned to the sitting room.

'How are things at the *Bugle* now?' asked Hobbes, sipping a mug of tea.

'Umm ... peculiar,' I said. 'Ralph's still there, and he and I write most of the articles—Arabella walked out as soon as she learned the development was finished. When I say reporting, I mean we copy most of the stuff from other news sources and social media—it doesn't feel right, but at least I'm still getting paid. Olivia helps, though she's sometimes more of a hindrance—she's always asking awkward questions.'

'Ralph should get rid of her,' said Daphne.

I kept a straight face, but smiled on the inside. Had I detected a hint of jealousy there? Perhaps. Anyway, it made me feel good, though she had nothing to worry about.

'But who owns the paper now?' asked Hobbes.

I shrugged. 'I expect Grubbe still does. No one has said.'

The conversation turned towards the nasturtiums Hobbes was growing for the church fete.

A few days later, when I was plagiarising a story about an alleged sighting of a sea lion in the river at Glevchester, and Olivia was muttering as she drafted a regular feature about the bowls club's latest defeat, Ralph walked into the main office.

'What's the matter?' I asked, worried by his pale face and shocked eyes.

'To cut a long story short, we're in big trouble!' he said. 'I have just learned that Mr Grubbe's consortium does not actually own the *Bugle*.'

'So, who does?' asked Olivia.

'I don't know,' said Ralph. 'It turns out that Mr Grubbe embezzled the money put up by the consortium, fobbed off the original owner with excuses as to why payment kept getting delayed, and lied to his colleagues.'

'What does that mean?' I asked.

Ralph shook his head. 'I really don't know.'

'I expect that, since no money was paid over, the sale will be regarded as void,' said Olivia, sounding frighteningly knowledgeable for an eighteen-year-old. 'The *Bugle* will revert to its real owner.'

'Rex Witcherley,' I said.

Ralph nodded and staggered to his office. I almost felt sorry for him.

Just before lunchtime, heavy footsteps stamped up the stairs, and the office door burst open.

'Capstan,' bellowed Editorsaurus Rex Witcherley, as large as ever, but greyer than last time I'd seen him. 'I had the misfortune to dine at Papa's Piri-Piri Palace two days ago on the strength of your review and was as sick as a dog. Explain yourself!'

'Umm ... ' I stammered, caught unawares, browbeaten by Rex's overwhelming personality and annoyed he'd got my name wrong again.

'I doubt it was Andy's fault,' said Olivia, coming to my rescue. 'Ralph would've changed the article because the restaurant was owned by his mate, Valentine Grubbe.'

Rex asked my pardon—he'd never done that before.

He stomped into Ralph's office.

Ralph departed ten minutes later, carrying his personal effects in a black bin liner. 'Thanks for your hard work,' he told Olivia and me, and walked out of my life.

Rex beckoned me in. 'Come in, Capstan. The *Bugle* needs a new editor, so I thought I'd ask you ... '

My stomach clenched. Was it excitement or terror?

'Umm ... ' I began, but he hadn't finished.

' ... if you think Basil Dean would come back and take

the job?'

'Probably,' I said.

And Basil did take it.

Which came as a relief ... or was it a disappointment?
Anyway, it was all for the best.

Probably.

RAZOR by Wilkie Martin

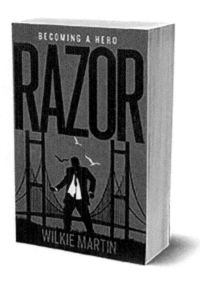

Becoming a hero

'It was ironic that having nothing left to lose except his life, his life had become interesting again.'

Read a sample now.
go.wilkiemartin.com/razor-book2look

Wilkie Martin

Wilkie Martin's novel, *Inspector Hobbes and the Blood*, was shortlisted for the Impress Prize for New Writers in 2012 under its original title: *Inspector Hobbes*. As well as novels, Wilkie writes short stories and silly poems, some available on YouTube. Like his characters, he relishes a good curry, which he enjoys cooking. In his spare time, he is a qualified scuba-diving instructor and a guitar twanger who should be stopped.

Born in Nottingham, he went to school in Sutton Coldfield, studied at the University of Leeds, worked in Cheltenham and now lives in the Cotswolds.

wilkiemartin.com

Get Wilkie's Newsletter and Join His Unhuman Readers

FREE ON SIGN UP

Sign up for Wilkie's Readers' List and get a free download copy of *Sorenchester Book Maps* and see where everything in the *unhuman* series takes place. You can also download a free copy of *Relative Disasters* – a little book of silly verse, and *Hobbes's Choice Recipes* by Wilkie, as his character A.C. Caplet.

Be among the first to hear about Wilkie's new books, publications and products, and for exclusive giveaways. Join here:

go.wilkiemartin.com/join-readers-list

Acknowledgements

Once again, I would like to thank the members of Catchword for their support, guidance and encouragement: Liz Carew, Meg Davies-Berry, Gill Garret, Derek Healy, Pam Keevil, Dr Rona Laycock, Pam Orr, Jan Petrie and Susannah White.

I would like to thank Kelly Owen of Ultimate Proof Ltd for copy-editing and proofreading, and Stuart Bache of Books Covered Ltd for the covers.

Finally, a huge thank you to my family, to Julia, and to The Witcherley Book Company.

Share Inspector Hobbes and the Common People

go.wilkiemartin.com/hobbes-commonpeople-book2look

315

Printed in Great Britain
by Amazon